V. Mahanenko

CONDEMNED

Lord Valevsky: Last of the Line

A Progression Fantasy Series

Book 8

Magic Dome Books

This book is entirely a work of fiction.
Any correlation with real people or events
is coincidental.

All Series
by Vasily Mahanenko:

The Way of the Shaman LitRPG Series

Dark Paladin LitRPG Series

Galactogon LitRPG Series

Invasion LitRPG Series

World of the Changed LitRPG Series

The Alchemist LitRPG Series

The Bear Clan LitRPG Series

Starting Point LitRPG Series

The Bard from Barliona LitRPG series
(with Eugenia Dmitrieva)

Condemned
(Lord Valevsky: Last of The Line)
a Progression Fantasy series

Law of the Jungle
A Wuxia Progression Fantasy Adventure Series

The Selected
A LitRPG Action Adventure Series
(with Yuri Vinokuroff)

Table of Contents:

Chapter 1

"MAX, WE HAVE a problem."

"That phrase has been uttered far too many times in my office as of late. I'll have to blacklist it. What is it this time?"

"Vyazemsky. He has managed to convince all the highest aristocracy not to do business with Hearth. Food, materials, resources, people — almost everything has been cut off. Trade caravans from the Shurgan and Kaliman empires have begun to bypass Hearth. The tax on trade with us has been raised so high that it was becoming too costly for merchants to bring goods here. This indicates that the Emperor has sided with Vyazemsky. Count Shub sent a letter threatening to break his agreement with us if we do not resolve the issue with the aristocrats. What kind of trade and production can there be if the city is isolated? General Khabensky reported that his army was leaving the territory of Hearth. They allegedly had more important things to do than protect those who work with the dark ones. Fanatics have started approaching the walls, there were several attacks. They were repelled, but I don't like the trend we're seeing. In just a week, they successfully isolated us from the entire Zarak Empire."

"How long will our resources last?"

"Hearth isn't facing any issues on that front for now. Provisions and materials flow in steadily from the dark ones. The only thing is that there is no one to finish building the city — we only have ten work teams left. That's a drop in the ocean. After the security system was activated, Hearth completely emptied. It turns out that not everyone likes having a symbol floating above their head. Even if it's exactly the same as those being sported by the servants of the Light."

"Can we find builders from the dark lands?"

"Maybe, but...Max, I've already checked, and converts are working among them. You know what they did to my family. I can tolerate the dark ones, but not these creatures. I will destroy them wherever I can. If you want to bring converts into Hearth, you'll have to do it without me."

"Why don't we ask the Kalimans for help? They have two rifts with metamorphs, let's draw up an agreement that I'll destroy the creatures and return their lands to them, and in exchange they will provide us with supplies. Both people and resources. Can we send a courier, or are they all being intercepted?"

"They are. Vyazemsky has connections with the Nocturnal Guild. They cannot penetrate our defenses, the security system would be triggered instantly, but outside the walls they are all-powerful. The only caravans they do not touch are those carrying representatives of the Church of the Light."

"Why isn't that an option? Let's use the Fortress."

"The High Priest has made an agreement with Vyazemsky to maintain neutrality. The Fortress will not reduce its activity in our area and will continue to travel between the capital and Hearth, but the churchmen will not protect us against guild assassins."

"So the Fortress refuses to cooperate with us?" I frowned. I hadn't expected that from Father Urg.

"No, they don't. But there are caveats. They will work with you and Alia. For them, the rest of Hearth does not exist. The Fortress is ready to hire you to close the rifts, destroy the Fog of Pharapho, and search for dark ones or converts among the high aristocracy or the church. But they won't shelter us under their wing or protect us from danger. The Fortress tries to distance itself from those who work openly with the darkness."

"And all this was organized by Count Vyazemsky?"

"Yes. I believe he has help — it is unlikely that Vyazemsky has enough resources to keep everyone in check. Remember when I said that several clans from remote regions of the Zarak Empire have started working with us?"

"I recall something of the sort," I said.

"Well, not anymore! We received a letter stating that they are cutting all ties with us. I believe that there was some outside interference here too. They've basically laid siege on us, Max. With particular damage done to our reputation — Hearth is now considered a dark spot on the lands of the Light. Vyazemsky or whoever is behind him has succeeded in their main goal — drawing everyone's attention to our city, forcing them to forget about their own problems. I have already told you the fanatics, but it seems that they won't be the last. I'm not even sure how to react."

"We need an army of high-level mages. At least thirty."

"The only question is, where will we find them? We need loyal people who will not betray us at the first opportunity. Because the pressure from outside will be simply colossal. People break. Right now you have ten people, including you and me, who can be trusted. The rest are dubious. How is Alia?"

"She's already getting better. Yesterday I took her out of her room for the first time. We walked along the corridor. I had to turn off the light, but there's clear progress being made. Although she still refuses to see anyone else."

"Yes, I wanted to go to her today, but she didn't want to see me. Is it that bad?"

All I could do was nod. Elor — I didn't even

want to call this bastard "Magister" — acted with confidence. If it weren't for the intervention of my now-deceased grandfather, Alia would have died. If not from the attack, then from the effects of the dark fire. More than ninety percent of her skin was disfigured by terrible scars it had left behind. They were completely impervious to all healing magic, transforming the once beautiful girl into a terrible monster. At least, that was what Alia said about herself. She had been delivered to Hearth five days ago, at precisely the same time that I gave Magister Meram over to the Temple of Skron. The dark ones assured me that the old man was in no danger, they just wanted to talk to him. The temple servant Four had personally guaranteed her safety, coming to negotiate. I had to agree, especially because there were twelve thousand destroyed human souls crying out for vengeance. This was the confirmed minimum number of the former runescribe's victims.

"Maybe you should still accept the Bartolomeo Clan's offer," Eleanore said. "Naira is a beautiful girl, what is your concern?"

"It's more that I have no concern whatsoever," I sighed. "Yes, Naira is smart, beautiful — gorgeous, but my heart doesn't belong to her. Not at all. Besides, this persistent desire of the Bartolomeo Clan to marry within our line is alarming. I don't understand how it benefits them. Instead of meeting me halfway and eliminating the consequences of the dark fire from both Alia and me, they started rolling out these conditions. Why do they need a child from me, Eleanore?"

"There is the opinion that your child might inherit some of your skills. Clans think long-term. Having a loyal conqueror of high-level rifts in your ranks does your rank and status a lot of good. They may even be willing to negotiate for such a thing."

"Status? This is all about stupid status?"

"The fact that you don't care about the opinions of others shouldn't mislead you into thinking that everyone else thinks the same way. For instance, status also plays an important role in my life. And in Alia's as well, as you can see. No one must see her weakness."

All I could do was grimace, admitting that she was right. Alia was extremely reluctant to meet even with me, and she simply sent everyone else away. It had gotten so bad that from the moment I returned, I'd had to personally deliver her food to the room where she had locked herself, since even the servants were forbidden to enter. The girl had been seriously shaken. Although for me, absolutely nothing had changed. Alia was still the center of my universe. Nevertheless, I made every effort to save her from her terrible wounds. The Temple of Skron immediately said that it did not have such technologies, since they did not need them, and the Bartolomeo Clan, supposedly an ally, demanded strange payment for the service: I must marry Naira.

What other notable events had occurred in the week since I had finished off Valdemar Valevsky, my grandfather? The Temple of Skron made an agreement with me to destroy all the sealed infected rifts throughout the dark lands. There were forty-two of these offworlder-made monstrosities, and thirty-five were on their territory — I would have to go eliminate them sooner rather than later. Two infected rifts were within the Zarak Empire, five in the Shurgan Empire, and only the Kaliman Empire turned out to be clean. They had already paid their dues — two metamorph rifts had wreaked havoc, reducing the habitable territory by nearly a third. At the same time, neither the Citadel nor the Fortress moved a finger to deal with the infected rifts, as if they knew something everyone else didn't, although they were also privy to the information that all the seals would expire in twenty-four days. In any case, this deal was profitable for me. The Temple of Skron helped me upgrade *Devour* to level three, providing the necessary stones, and all the resources and magic stones that I received while destroying the sealed rifts would be mine to keep. Because for the rest of the world, they didn't exist. In this matter of business, at least, everything was working out perfectly.

But this was the exception. As for the legacy of the first emperor's grandson and the knowledge he passed on...that was a complete failure — there was neither the knowledge nor the legacy. The key that my grandfather carelessly threw on the floor did not contain any mysteries. It turned out to be a simple piece of useless metal that dissolved into my belt, hiding it from prying eyes. I did not receive any global knowledge, revelations or other vital facts from possessing it. Killing my grandfather did not bring any bonuses — it just created one more corpse. Even the *Author* skill left much to be desired — I couldn't use it at all. It had been empirically established that symbolic magic operated with words and the meaning embedded in them. But to form these words, knowledge was required of what they consisted of and what they meant. I needed a dictionary, which Valdemar Valevsky had conveniently forgotten to pass on to me. Or had not wanted to, thinking that I would come to this knowledge on my own. My experiments didn't do any good — I lost three dark liquid stones without any result. If used incorrectly, symbolic magic ate away at your life force like crazy. I had to temporarily put the experiments on hold. Even the people who brought me Alia couldn't say anything — they had been hired a few weeks ago to look after the sick woman. That was it! The fact that I'd now become some kind of mysterious "keeper," as my grandfather had called me before his death, hadn't changed anything at all!

Although, no — there had been other changes. The Temple of Skron gave me back my mithril armor and, lo and behold, it recognized me as its master! With the pieces I already had, as well as a few others obtained through further manipulations of Pharapho's flesh, I now had a full set of armor, which allowed me to walk along the bottom of a river without worrying about breathing. I had already tested it myself. A full description of everything that my new armor was now capable of was, as expected, absent, but regardless, a feeling of general security remained. They made me new katars from vyrma, as well as a crossbow, and all of this was safely hidden under the armor. It camouflaged just as well as my previous set — to everyone else, I was dressed in the elegant everyday garb of a high-born aristocrat. Even the helmet that completely hid my head was invisible to others, and imperceptible to me. But as soon as I said the magic word *"Adapt,"* my skin and clothes turned into impenetrable armor. At least vyrma couldn't touch me from now on. The mithril armor did not make me immortal — it didn't work in the rifts or against dark attacks. Fardi would pierce right through it and swallow me whole like a raspberry tart. And I wouldn't risk going against a large crowd of mages, especially high-level ones. No matter how I saw it, mithril armor was a man-made item. What several people were able to create, just as many could destroy. During their experiments, the dark ones had somehow managed to destroy the chest plate and belt. That meant the mages of the Zarak Empire could do the same, especially when united by a common force. For example, their ire towards the dark ones and Hearth. Nevertheless, I was ready to face anyone from the light world one-on-one. Not taking into account the Citadel, as there wasn't a single ordinary human in the place.

"Okay, the Bartolomeo Clan left me no choice. I need a living and psychologically whole Alia, and not the husk she is gradually becoming. Eleanore, let the dark ones know that I agree to their demands. The wedding with Naira Jode will take place — tomorrow, even. We won't invite anyone from the lands of the Light anyway."

"And what of the city's defense?"

"Choose Viscount Kurpatsky and nine others, and we'll install stones in them. We cannot repeat the mistakes I made with you. At first the stones will be first level, and then in a week, once they've adapted, I will begin to gradually increase them. Pumping them straight up to level twenty is a recipe for trouble."

"I've practically adapted already. Of course, it's still hard to use my ability more than three times in a row, but I've got it up to three. Before, I couldn't even cast twice. Time, Max. Everything takes time."

"That's the thing, we don't have it. Listen, a hypothetical question — if Count Vyazemsky were to suddenly disappear, would that make things easier for us?"

"I don't think that would be the right decision," Eleanore answered after a pause. "Not only will you not be allowed to shoot him with a crossbow, but the entire Zarak Empire will finally turn against us. Many people doubt it now — we became the 'bad guys' too suddenly. However, if the main voice speaking out against us is suddenly silenced, the flames of indignation will engulf Hearth. We are not ready for that yet."

"Not great," I sighed. "So, is there nothing we

can do? What if we bribe someone? Or roll something out on the market that they can't find in the bright lands? And only those who trade with us will be able to obtain this something?"

"I have two people working on this problem right now." Eleanore found the strength to smile. "We are in constant consultations with representatives of both the Citadel and the Temple of Skron. For example, the vyrma armor that you brought. The Citadel has already placed an order for twenty sets. This is good advertising — all the cuirasses, in agreement with the church, will bear the brand of Hearth. I understand that this is a drop in the ocean, but we are actively working on it. Magic stones are also in good demand, but here the Fortress and the Magic Academy have the preferential right to purchase."

"Good thing you reminded me. Do you know Kimal Sarento's position?"

"The Magic Academy is keeping on the sidelines. Its job is to train mages without interfering in the affairs of the Empire or the Church. I don't think the chancellor can be won over, Max. We are alone in this confrontation. In fact, I'm surprised it took this long. In theory, Hearth should have been extinguished the moment the Emperor signed the decree establishing it as an autonomous city."

"Then they couldn't extinguish us, as you put it, because each of them believed that they would be able to profit off of us. Count Vyazemsky, Count Shub. Even Count Kuzminsky, supposedly a scholar, wanted in on the dark ones' secrets. Don't you remember how many spies we had? How many we sent away? What's happening now is a reaction to the new security system being installed and the stringent verification process everyone in the city must undergo. Since the other shareholders in the Zarak Empire cannot make a profit from an autonomous city in which there is an official portal to the dark lands, this city must be destroyed."

"Max, you know that I am against using force to resolve conflicts." Eleanore stroked her noticeably protruding belly. "However, my opinion is that we need to attack first. Let's start with Vyazemsky. We need a sabotage group. They will set fires, destroy infrastructure, poison animals, and sow chaos among peasants, industrialists, and the petty aristocracy. The more problems we create, the less time Vyazemsky will have for us."

"Eleanore!" I was surprised at her.

"Yes, that's been my name for the past forty years!" she replied tersely. "Understand, Max — if we just sit behind our walls, sooner or later we will be destroyed. History has seen many such examples. If you want peace, break your enemy's teeth. We have no other option to survive. Vyazemsky signed his own death warrant."

"Okay, let's say you're right. I still won't be able to run freely around the Zarak Empire without anyone knowing."

"And you won't need to. Your task is to attend receptions at the capital and show your face to everyone. The emperor has no right not to invite you. Show that you are loyal to the crown, that you are loyal to the Fortress. Demonstrate that you fully support the course of the Zarak Empire. Condemn what is happening. Demand the Inquisitor be summoned when unpleasant turns of fate begin to occur for Vyazemsky. Participate in duels — you will have many of them. Hundreds, I suppose. But do not even think of interfering in the activities of this sabotage group. You must not even come close to being privy to their plans. Because when the Inquisitor asks you who destroyed the latest sawmill or village, you must answer with absolute honesty that you have no idea exactly who did it. This is a cruel world, so let's play by its rules. As for who they will be...the Evil Engineer sent people. Four of them. Those he said could be trusted. I've already spoken to them. They will do what needs to be done."

Yes, the Evil Engineer and I had spoken about this. It was so long ago that I'd forgotten. But not him — he still sent his people. They need to be vetted via *Analyze*, but I had no doubt that everything would come up clean. If anyone could be trusted in this life, it was my former mentor.

"We have the necessary stones, but they need to be integrated. I can't even consider taking them on as pupils. If I did, I would know everything they do."

"Kimal Sarento," came her reply. "You will have to meet with the chancellor and buy his silence."

"Which will cost me Hearth and a half," I muttered. I had no desire to get involved with the chancellor. Right now, by all formal signs, we were neutral. No one owed anyone anything. But as soon as I used his academy to form a sabotage group, everything would change. I would become dependent on him again.

"The chancellor needs a *Thunderer* set. Give it to him," Eleanore suggested. "Even if he wants one of each set."

"Where is this group right now?"

"In the capital, at the Bronze Goose Inn. I planted them there three weeks ago. They will wait another month and a half, so you definitely have time. But, in my opinion, this issue needs to be taken care of as soon as possible. The longer we delay, the more time and resources Vyazemsky can spend on -us."

"I'm going to the capital today. I'll go alone. I wonder who will dare to attack me?"

"You must not move alone," Eleanore said, shaking her head. "You are not just Maximilian Valevsky, freelance rift conqueror. You are the Archduke of an autonomous city. At least two or three carriages, a dozen escorts and servants."

"In that case, we will become an excellent target for the Nocturnal Guild."

"You will. Both on the road and in Turb. I don't think that our estate will suddenly become secure. On the contrary, we won't have our security system. There will be invisibles in every nook and cranny. As well as assassins. Don't forget about the Faceless — Padishah Bayazid the Third certainly hasn't forgotten about you. If your source is to be believed, he's somehow tied to Vyazemsky. The Padishah will not work openly in the Zarak Empire, but he'll still be pulling strings. You need to be prepared for this too."

"And again we come up against the fact that we need more trusted people... Prepare a list of my escorts and the magic stones that we will insert into them all. Let's assume that in the worst case, they will have a four-by-four field. If we go to Kimal Sarento, there is no point in limiting ourselves to just a task force. We need to strengthen everyone. Including the servants. Every person who lives in Hearth must be able to stand up for themselves and their city."

"The escorts and carriages are already waiting for you," Eleanore smiled. "I knew where our conversation would lead, so I prepared in advance."

"It's nice to work with such a smart lady. Let's reiterate the main points: inform the Bartolomeo Clan about my decision regarding Naira Jode. The trip to Turb will take four to five days. Let's say a week. The wedding will take place in a week. I will have two weeks left to close all the rifts."

"Will you make it? There are forty-two of them, the passages into the rifts themselves only open at night. The risks are numerous. It's unlikely that the rifts are located next to each other."

"I'll make it if you help me. I need to make a schedule for closing the rifts and give it to the dark ones. For the Citadel too, Skron take them. I need to have a convert on duty near each rift. I'll use portals to move between the rifts and I'll be able to close five or six in one night. There aren't many high-level ones out there."

"Yes, that could work," Eleanore agreed. "Every night we'll start with the small ones that can be closed quickly, and closer to dawn, when the rift closes, you'll tackle the big ones. When you destroy them, the passage will open automatically. The question, of course, is when you'll sleep, but that's up to you. If you're sure you can handle it, I'll create a schedule and coordinate it with the Temple of Skron and the Citadel. While you're in Turb, I'll resolve this issue. Just like with Alia."

It didn't take much preparation. I went and said goodbye to Alia, wishing her a speedy recovery, and half an hour later a procession of two carriages left the central gates of Hearth. Eleanore had prepared everything, including the magic stones and the models for their installation. She worked without rest and, as it seemed to me, without sleep, protecting the city and turning it into an important trade center of the Light lands. Under her management, Hearth was turning into a force that the most powerful people of the Zarak Empire were suddenly forced to reckon with. So much so that they began to want to destroy us. Which, of course, we would not allow them to do. One small question was left undetermined: who was the true master of Hearth, me or Eleanore? Something told me that if I started thinking about it too hard, I would not like the answer.

Chapter 2

TURB WAS OPPRESSIVELY gloomy. I would never have thought so if I hadn't been spending all my time in Hearth, which was designed the way all human-oriented cities should be. Despite the endless construction, which, as I understood it, now may truly never end, my brainchild looked an order of magnitude nicer than the capital of the Zarak Empire. Here, there were narrow dirty streets, no decent storm drainage system, an ill-conceived layout of intersections, houses piled on top of each other and, most irritating of all, residential buildings pushed right up next to industrial workshops. I knew that it was easier this way — you live right next to where you work — but you're the only one who's pleased with that, while your neighbors, especially if you are a conventional blacksmith or alchemist, are not so thrilled.

Eleonore had designed Hearth much more effectively.

But what immediately caught my eye was the downcast faces. I was amazed by the looks they shot up at my carriages. Anger, irritation, sometimes even outright contempt — if it weren't for the servant of Light whom the Fortress had assigned to accompany me, they might have thrown mud at me. Fortunately for them, there was plenty of it everywhere. For some reason, people were embittered and saw Hearth as the embodiment of all their troubles. It was amazing how quickly Count Vyazemsky had managed to make enemies out of us! It seemed that the people had been in dire need of a scapegoat and had sunk their teeth into the first one they were given.

Several squads of guards were on duty around my estate. Here, the locals had been liberal with their mud-slinging — the gates and fence were filthy. The guards drove away the most zealous of the crowd, but they did it without much fanaticism. Just barely preventing them from crossing the line, where they might think about directly attacking the estate. They turned a blind eye to all else.

"Welcome home, Your Radiance." Despite the problems, the staff greeted me well. The servants left behind at the estate worked tirelessly. They could not go outside, so they tried to tidy up the house and the grounds. Fortunately, there was always work — the townspeople constantly created more.

"What about provisions? Water?" I was primarily concerned with the most pressing problems. Whether I liked it or not, my people were locked in the middle of a hostile city and might end up in a difficult situation.

"We've got enough to last a couple of months." My estate manager's response pleased me. "Two weeks ago, we had no problems with provisions, but then people went mad. We've never seen such open aggression towards us before."

"What's the total number of people here?"

"Twenty-two, Your Radiance!"

"Give the order to pack up, we're leaving for Hearth. We can't leave you here without protection. The further we go, the worse it gets. Gustav, will you organize two more carriages?"

"It will be done, Your Radiance!" Gustav replied. After Valdemar Valevsky's death, I'd spoken to Gustav about how he ended up as my mentor. The story proved quite interesting — Gustav was set to be the commander of the garrison, perhaps even commanding a whole section of the Wall, but a sudden and unexpected illness cut him down and he had to leave the Wall. The illness passed rather quickly, but the garrison commander position had already been filled. It was as if everyone had forgotten about Gustav, despite all his previous successes, even sending him into retirement for length of service, but then an unexpected offer from my father turned up. There was nothing left to do — Gustav had no family, so he happily took it on. Having no experience in training little ones, he approached me with the same requirements that he made for the most recent recruits to the Wall. That was why I turned out the way I did.

I had no doubt that Gustav would cope with the task. It was unlikely that there were any mages in the crowd that had gathered around my estate. Aristocrats had no business here. My first mentor could handle everyone else. As for the estate...today it would become a gift to the Fortress. The symbols I had installed were still working, so my connection with Eleanore persisted for the moment. We'd had time to discuss much in the two-day journey to Turb, including what to do with our estate in the capital. Keeping it for ourselves was not an option — sooner or later a crowd of angry townspeople would destroy it. Selling it was also not a good idea — that would be admitting defeat. Two equivalent options were considered: burn it to the ground or give it away. We agreed to give the estate to the High Priest. Judging by how the cleric accompanying us reacted to my question, he found the proposal extremely interesting. So much so that as soon as we arrived in the capital, the servant of Light ran to report to his superiors and informed them of my decision. Father Urg needed to discuss my gift with his entourage. Did the Fortress have the right to accept such a gift from a dark one who had officially become light, but at the same time still worked with the dark ones? Just from describing me, you could be sent to the stake.

No one attacked my carriage within the city

limits. Even the brainless crowd understood that the moment one of them decided to throw dirt or stones at me would be their last. The same went for anyone around them who allowed this to happen. And it would not be me who killed him, but the guards accompanying me. Turb approached the issue of my safety with the utmost responsibility.

"The chancellor is currently in class." Kimal Sarento's constant assistant ran the reception room as if it were her home. She had flowers, comfortable chairs, a shelf with books, and even lacy translucent curtains. For some reason, in all of the times I had visited him before, I had never found a minute to look around his reception room.

"Sit down, Your Radiance. I have already sent a messenger. Will you have some tea?"

"If it's not too much trouble," I nodded, barely restraining myself from scanning her with *Analyze*. It wouldn't cost me anything, but there was such a thing as keeping your word. Especially when you know that no one in this world can verify whether you keep it or not. It was a matter of principle. I wouldn't use *Analyze* on the chancellor, even knowing that I could break through his amulet, and I wouldn't use it on his strange assistant either. The one who seemed privy to all of her boss's affairs.

The tea in the lobby was on par with Kimal Sarento's wine — delicious, aromatic, and leaving behind a feeling of something homey and familiar. My mother used to make it for me when she was still alive. Need I explain why I began to feel genuine empathy for the chancellor's assistant? We even started a conversation about something inconsequential. For the first time in many months, I could talk about the weather without worrying about blurting out something unnecessary.

"Archduke Valevsky, what an unexpected but pleasant meeting," Kimal Sarento entered the reception room half an hour later. As always, he looked magnificent, as if he had just left the stylist's, where he had not only been dressed, but also beautified. Turning to his assistant, Kimal Sarento added:

"If anyone asks, I'm not here today. I'm away on business."

"I understand," the woman nodded. "Does Archduke Valevsky need to be verified?"

"I don't think so. Surely something in this world must be dependable? I hope our guest's ability to keep his word is one of those rare phenomena. Come in, Archduke. Make yourself at home. Although I wouldn't want my academy to be mistaken for your home. Lately, the estate seems to have run into some issues."

"Actually, that's precisely the reason why I came to you," I said, settling into the guest chair in Kimal Sarento's office.

"Of course, why else would a failed student come to the magic academy?" the chancellor did not miss the opportunity to tease me. "Not for the sake of knowledge and skills, right? Not for the sake of contributing to the development of the academy? They only recall that I exist when someone needs help."

"For which this very student is willing to pay well. Like no other student. You need a *Thunderer* set, right?"

"Not so much that I'm willing to go against the whole empire," he replied, becoming serious. "What Count Vyazemsky is doing now is an extremely interesting and, I dare say, productive way of destroying a reputation. I don't know where he gets his resources from, but there are leaflets and flyers calling for the people to rid the empire of the dark oppressors plastered on every wall in the city. After the well-known occurrence at the tournament, which became the Fog of Pharapho and the infected rift, there were too many outraged people in the Zarak Empire who had lost loved ones in the debacle. Count Vyazemsky managed to concentrate all the public's attention on you. Leaflets, heralds, supposedly 'random' passers-by and fellow travelers causing confusion. And the emperor doesn't spare a thought to stopping this — his popularity is growing every day. He is the personification of Light and purity. Hearth and, in particular, one zealous fellow named Valevsky are now synonymous with darkness in its purest form. What Count Vyazemsky managed to pull off in just two weeks is worthy of respect. Of course, a lot of things coincided, but the fact remains: this avalanche will be extremely difficult to stop. One might even suppose it is impossible. And there is no way I am going to expose my academy to this flow. Even for the sake of the *Thunderer*. Especially for the sake of this tempting and, I dare say, desirable set — everything that bears the brand of Hearth has now become extremely undesirable in the Zarak Empire."

"I don't need help in my battle with Count Vyazemsky. I can deal with him and his campaign myself. I need help with magic stones. I might have an idea of how to, if not stop, then significantly stall the current unrest."

I recounted my plan. Kimal was silent for a while, looking out the window, then he paced around the office. Finally, returning to his desk, he nodded:

"Let's just say that I agree to help you. Not specifically you, Archduke Valevsky, but a few random people who come to the magic academy to activate their field and install stones. How will I benefit? I will be the first to be asked for an explanation of why there are strange people with such rare magic stones operating in the empire. I will have to answer something. Invent. Prevaricate. Lie, again. I hate doing this. And what good would any of that do me, Maximilian?"

"A week ago I killed my own grandfather," I said, staring into the chancellor's face.

"Congratulations to you." Judging by his reaction, the news that one of my relatives had still been alive had come as a surprise. "I'm not certain of the relevance here?"

"My grandfather, Valdemar Valevsky, was Magister Meram's mentor."

Kimal Sarento frowned. The information I had revealed could not resonate with the knowledge the chancellor already had, for Magister Meram had last been a pupil over one hundred and fifty years ago.

"I still don't understand," Kimal Sarento conceded, boredom creeping across his face. "Maximilian, my friend, try to add more information to your sentences. And connections to the previous topic. The situation regarding the division of the Valevsky family inheritance interests me least of all."

"Yes, you are right. I need to provide more information. How about this fact: Magister Meram's teacher was the grandson of the first emperor of the Light lands."

Now the rector became serious. I'd only seen that expression on his face a few times. Since the office remained silent, I decided to give the finishing blow to the man who had spent most of his life collecting information about the first emperor:

"After killing my grandfather, I received the status of *'Keeper'* — though what exactly this means is still unclear — as well as a key. A key to a closed facility of the ancients, where even the one whom my ancestor called "the abominable Pharapho" has no access.

The chancellor leaned back in his chair and thought, not taking his eyes off me. I was compelled to continue:

"I am aware that you possess the notebook or personal notes of the first emperor. They were obtained from his tomb, following which no one has had any information about their whereabouts, or the whereabouts of the *Devour* stone that started all this. But the emperor's vault is with you. As is, I believe, his notebook. I need it, but this is a matter for later. First, we need to discuss what will happen to Hearth. If the lord chancellor helps my people wield magic stones, he will become the second member of the expedition party to the ancients' closed facility. The place where the first emperor gained his power."

"Yes, Maximilian, you know how to vex me. I thought I could see right through you, predict your every move, and then it turns out that, completely by chance, you happen to be the great-great-grandson of the first emperor. And this thought had occurred to me — your dark mirror is too similar to the ability of the nameless founder. I don't have his notebook. And I never did. Only a few notebooks that he filled out by hand. You are interested in the artifact, right? Where it is, no one knows. By the way, a question for your relatives. According to the information I have, the artifact was taken by the eldest son of the first emperor. Where to look for it is a big question."

I managed to keep quiet about the fact that his eldest son was dead, although the phrase practically flew out of my mouth. Kimal Sarento couldn't be told everything. I had already told him more than I had planned. In fact, I had not intended to tell him who I really was, but looking at the chancellor, I realized that he would refuse any offer I made. Kimal Sarento would not go against the Zarak Empire. Not now. But going *with* the heir of the first emperor was another matter. In that case, the cunning man might take a risk.

"What about the stones? They are already prepared. As is the layout for their installment. They have open mana at their disposal. All we need is integration. No one will know that it was Kimal Sarento who installed the stones. For the rest of the world, the stones appeared in Hearth."

"Which will make you the subject of the Citadel's rapt attention."

"I can't attract any more attention than I already have. The Church of the Light is carefully tracking my every move. Even while traveling to Turb, I was under the watchful eye of the servants of the Light."

"But they are not on academy territory." Kimal Sarento didn't even ask — he asserted.

"I made an offer to the Fortress, which my escort could not help but pass on."

"You gave them the estate?" The chancellor's foresight was enviable. "A wise decision. Gets rid of many problems. And removes the object of negativity from the capital. It will be harder to wind people up without a symbol in front of their eyes. Okay, Maximilian, I will install the stones for your people. I am waiting for them this evening at the academy. Without you."

All I could do was nod. The chancellor didn't say anything extra, but even without that it was clear that from now on I was in his debt. Again,

Skron take him.

"The notebooks," I reminded him. "I need to study them."

"I'm afraid this will prove quite problematic. I don't have them. They were stolen."

"Very funny. Someone stole something from Kimal Sarento and is still alive?"

"There are those who will exact serious consequences if you go against them. I do not have one hundred percent certainty, only a suspicion. However, I believe that the notebooks went to a famous collector. I will warn you right away, Maximilian, no names. Even walls sometimes have ears. Especially in the Magic Academy of the Zarak Empire."

"Understood. The glove that I made for Vyazemsky Jr. is with our mutual friend. So the notebooks could be there too."

"For the younger Count Vyazemsky," Kimal Sarento corrected me. "It is Eleanore who can be forgiven for being careless with titles. You, as an Archduke, cannot. Information has reached me that Alia has returned to Hearth. Do you already know who kidnapped her?"

"She was not kidnapped in the sense that is commonly believed. The Dark Orthodox Elor attacked her and burned her with dark fire. My grandfather intervened and prevented her from being killed. He took Alia back and managed to cure her."

"What about Elor?" He blurted the question out so quickly that it was clear the topic piqued his interest.

"You know who that is, right?"

"Stupid question. You know perfectly well that we are acquainted. Magister Elor is now Karina Fardi's teacher, and also a dark one who has accepted the orthodox views on the way this world should be developed and has declared war on everyone else."

"Not everyone — specifically the Light world, but you're basically correct. This is Karina Fardi's master. Do you know what she has become?"

"I don't have that information. Didn't she die at the stake?"

"She became a vessel of Skron. Literally. Before he died, my grandfather warned me about her. According to him, even he couldn't handle her. At the moment, Karina Fardi is the strongest human in the world. No — a being that was once human. If she gets to any of us, she'll finish us off. No exceptions."

"You didn't answer my question."

"Elor is alive, but he will be out of the game for some time. Why do you need him?"

"When we last met, he promised to kill me. So I'm asking purely out of my own practical interests. So, Elor is out of the game now. Do we know how long he'll be out of commission?"

"My grandfather made it so that Alia's kidnapping was connected to Elor. The Temple of Skron is hunting him to ask why the dark one decided to kill or kidnap my girl without their consent. There is no time frame, but there is a suspicion that we have a couple of months."

"Which by the standards of the current world is already an eternity," Kimal Sarento thought for a moment, then said: "One group will not be enough."

"I don't have any more people."

"Hire externally."

"The Nocturnal Guild is also eager to get a jab in at Hearth. I'm just not sure why."

"No one said anything about assassins," Kimal Sarento grinned. "Isn't there a reason you left our good friend alive? I suppose if you search hard enough, there are enough people in this world who have not lost interest in working with you or Hearth. That same Evil Engineer who, quite unexpectedly to the whole world, recently became gray. Do you know anything about this? Father Nor has already been recalled — grays cannot have personal servants. Here is a newly-minted gray wandering around my academy, not knowing what to do with himself. Because everything he did before no longer has meaning."

"I won't be able to coordinate several different groups."

"No one is asking you to. All that is required from your side is payment for their work. Gold, rift resources...There's a lot you can offer them. The only question is, will you do it?"

"The issue of supervising their activities remains."

"If you need names, although we agreed not to say them in this office, I will do it. Personally. I don't like what Count Vyazemsky is doing. Today it's you and Hearth, tomorrow it could be my academy. I spent too long building it to risk and hope for the favor of one individual. Your team will deal with Count Vyazemsky and his property, mine, or rather, I myself will deal with the provocateurs. Those who are actively promoting the idea of war with the autonomous city."

"How much will it cost me?"

"A lot, Maximilian, I won't lie to you. I need full information on what is currently in your inventory. The price will be determined based on this."

"Resources?" I was surprised beyond measure. "You need ordinary resources?"

"The information you have is too confidential even for me. At least until we go to that closed location you were talking about. For now, only resources."

For a while, I was frankly in shock — Kimal Sarento knew the phrase 'confidential.' And at his own expense! Scanning the contents of my inventory, I could hardly hold back a grin — almost all the resources that I had mined in the rifts had gone to the production of elixirs that increase the levels of magic stones. There was not much left — the minimum necessary to produce two *Thunderer* sets. Of course, there were still all sorts of "dark liquids" that I was not going to part with, but everything else was of no value to me. Even the essences, although I had found a use for them — feeding the Abyss and getting answers. Because after passing through the next forty-two rifts I would have so many essences that the Abyss would be mine, lock, stock and barrel, and I would find the location of the vault of the ancients.

So I had no problem compiling a list of everything that had been mined in the rifts and presenting it to Sarento. For me it was a trifle, but for the chancellor it was worth the entire capital, including himself. Judging by the way Kimal Sarento's eyebrows twitched, I was right — he had not expected such an impressive list.

But any further discussion was brazenly interrupted. Suddenly the office doors opened, and Kimal Sarento's assistant barely had time to shout:

"Sir Chancellor, you have a visitor!"

Considering the order he had given to clear his schedule, this guest must have broad powers. This proved true — suddenly an old acquaintance of mine burst into the office. Colonel of the Secret Chancellery of His Imperial Majesty Slovan Usminsky

"Are you here too?" The luxuriously mustachioed man measured me with a piercing gaze. I did not look away or avert my eyes. Right now I had nothing to share with this man. If there was one thing Hearth had not yet participated in, it was espionage. Not yet.

"That's even better, everything is falling into place. Sir Chancellor, Archduke Valevsky, you must come with me immediately. In thirty minutes there will be a meeting chaired by the Emperor."

"Is it so serious that they sent the colonel of the secret chancellery as a messenger?" Kimal Sarento raised an eyebrow eloquently, hiding the sheet with the description of my available resources in his pocket. This did not escape Slovan, but he barely showed it.

"It couldn't be more serious. The Wall in the northern region has been destroyed. Demolished. Devastated. An emergency council is being convened to determine how to stop the avalanche of monsters rushing into our lands. According to the report we received, this far outmatches even the Waves previously summoned by the dark ones. The monsters now swarming into the Zarak Empire are unlike any previously encountered by humankind."

Chapter 3

THE EMERGENCY MEETING was held in the emperor's office. The head honcho of the Zarak Empire had not changed at all. He was just as repulsive and unpleasant as ever. Those dumpling lips, sausage fingers, triple chin — his appearance was remarkable. Despite this, behind it was a sharp mind, able to make instant and surprisingly competent decisions based on a minimal set of input data. Twenty years as the head of the security service of the magic academy had affected both his character and his thinking.

Aside from Zurgan the First, there were several others in the office. I chuckled when I recognized Count Vyazemsky among them. The two-meter-tall giant, who resembled a slab of granite, did not even deign to glance at me, unaware that I could finish him off at any moment. Of course, I had been screened before visiting the palace, but could ordinary guards, even if there was a colonel of the secret chancellery among them, detect a full set of mithril armor? To the rest of the world, I was dressed in a traveling suit appropriate for my status. Count Shub and Count Kuzminsky nodded, and another old man was smoking a cigar with a businesslike air whom I was seeing for the first time. General Khabensky looked like a much-aged copy of his son, whose battalion had been stationed for some time near Hearth. The High Priest appeared immediately after us, also restraining himself to a short welcoming nod. I sat down on a chair not far from Kimal Sarento and prepared to enjoy the spectacle.

Why a spectacle, you ask? Because I had no intention of interfering in what was happening in any way.

"Bring everyone up to speed," the emperor ordered. An assistant standing nearby opened a folder and read:

"Report of the commander of the central section of the northern Wall. We received the first letter about a week ago. Text: 'Strange things have started happening to the Wall — it has lost all structural integrity. It seems as if all the stones have suddenly become unbound from one another. As if the mortar that held them together had disappeared, although visually everything was in its place. First, all the observation towers of the central span collapsed. Then the jagged masonry began to crumble. The Wall itself wobbles, like a heap of stones piled on top of each other without any bonds. The situation is getting out of control, urgent measures are needed to eliminate this peculiarity.'"

The assistant paused to allow those in the room to contemplate what they had heard.

"We received the second letter today. It was sent two days ago. Text: 'The Wall has fallen. Dark beasts unlike any we have ever seen have rushed in from the steppe. They are now demolishing the compromised Wall like a house of cards. The beasts are being buried under stones, flattened, but this does not stop them. Where one is snuffed out, ten more appear. Where ten are snuffed out, a hundred appear. This is not a Wave. This is something else. The creatures are squabbling among themselves like horibs. They have no obvious leader. However, this does not deter their onslaught. The Wall has been breached in at least two places. Enormous monsters, larger than a man, have moved into the empire. Soldiers, recruits, aristocrats and mages will defend the lands to the last and fulfill their duties. Additional forces are needed to hold back this attack."

Once again the assistant paused, allowing everyone to come to terms with the fact that the Zarak Empire was no longer protected from the north.

"Four drawings of monsters were attached. Whoever made them did not possess the creative gift, but was able to convey the main external features. A preliminary analysis of the archives did not yield any results — the Zarak Empire has not encountered such monsters before."

Four sheets were passed around the circle. They made their way over to me. Whoever had made these sketches truly did lack any semblance of artistic talent, because the monsters depicted looked as if a mountain of stones had suddenly acquired limbs, been given the spark of life and slouched into the Light lands. All four creatures resembled stone idols to one degree or another. I had never encountered anything like this in the rifts, the Abyss, among the offworlders, or in the fog of Pharapho. Had another force entered our world? By the looks of it, yes. The offworlders left, and their place was immediately occupied by...rocks? What to call these things in the sketches? And on the same topic, were they actually made out of stone, or was it some sort of intricate flesh? Or was it neither one nor the other, but simply the fantasy of a man scared out of his wits who drew his fears, and not what he actually saw?

The Emperor smacked his lips to attract attention and said:

"Gentlemen, I await a decision. I have no reason not to trust the messenger. A certain force has invaded the Zarak Empire. Where it is going remains unknown, but we can't count on the creatures to pass us by and invade the Kaliman Empire instead. General?"

"My army is ready to march today," General Khabensky's voice was dry and clear — a voice accustomed to giving orders. "It will take me five days to march to the northern region. We will meet the creatures at the Salmora Pass if they head towards the central region. In this place, we could destroy even Skron himself."

"In five days, the beasts have destroyed the entire northern region. They may have even seized the Northwestern Region as well," said Count Kuzminsky.

"Your proposal, Count?" The emperor turned his gaze to the old man.

"Use several squads of high-level mages. Let the army go at its own pace, the mages can reach the northern region in two days. Sir Chancellor, what say you to taking a stroll around the Zarak Empire?"

"I say that charging into an attack without gathering intel is tantamount to suicide." Kimal Sarento was not impressed by the old count's words. "We know nothing about these creatures. Judging by these masterpieces provided as a means of external description, the monsters are from three to five meters tall. It is not clear from the letter how they can be killed or whether any of them have yet been killed. The fact that they were buried under stones — is this a guarantee of victory? Or did they crawl out, shake themselves off and continue? In ten times greater numbers? There are many questions, and I see no point in rushing into a reckless attack."

"The magic academy maintains its usual stance!" snorted Count Vyazemsky. "I'm heading to the northern region directly after this meeting. If anyone should defend the empire from the dark ones, it is us, the highest aristocracy!"

During his fiery speech, the hulking mass of a man turned towards me. This did not escape the emperor. Zurgan the First also suddenly acknowledged my presence.

"Archduke Valevsky, what can you say about the invasion?"

"Nothing, Your Royal Highness. Absolutely nothing. Hearth fully supports the Zarak Empire's fight against the invading creatures and is morally on your side. We rely on the army and the highest aristocracy to protect the empire from this terrible danger."

"You are not going to take part in the defense against the monsters?" The emperor frowned.

"With my greatest regrets, I must inform you that I am unable to participate. There are urgent matters of global importance."

"If you're hinting at the fact that you're going to close all of the infected rifts because of the strange disappearance of rune magic, don't bother us with such stories," Father Urg said, which puzzled me greatly. Had he really taken a position against my city? Why? When had this change occurred? "After the seals disappear, the rifts will lose their 'infected' status."

"Is the High Priest one hundred percent certain of this?" Kimal Sarento said, taking my side. "Or will the situation with the tournament repeat itself? Is the Fortress ready to provide irrefutable evidence that the infected rifts scattered throughout the world will lose their power in twenty days, and will not destroy the already fragile peace? Do you have any precedents for this? What is the source of such confidence, Father Urg?"

I looked over at Father Urg and suddenly, it dawned on me! He knew what log was! The head of the Fortress knew what this material was and how to use it! He knew that the log had disappeared! I even got goosebumps from the full realization of the Fortress' lawlessness. Maybe not all the clerics were involved, but this particular man, who was now frowning at Kimal Sarento, not knowing what to say, was definitely privy to this information! It was on his orders that that infected rift that destroyed so many people was created near the tournament! Skron drag his soul down by the ankle! What sort of madness was happening in our world?!

"There are no precedents, but there is certainty," the High Priest nevertheless was able to respond.

"The same as during the tournament? Remind me, how many victims were there then, and how many more could have been, if not for the young man right over there? If my memory serves me right, he saved most of our lives. No, High Priest, I am against taking risks. If there is even the slightest possibility that you are wrong, then two infected rifts will suddenly appear in the Zarak Empire. And it will no longer be possible to seal them again. I suppose you are aware that the dark ones destroyed the rune magic? Everything that it supported is now toppling as well."

"Do you mean to say that the Wall was also fortified with runes?" There was a reason Count Kuzminsky was a scholar. He was quite adept at putting one and two together.

"Judging by the report," Kimal Sarento said with a nod towards the assistant, "that is the case. Rune magic left our world, the Wall began to quake and these strange beasts appeared. Considering the fact that they were not here before, even the dark ones have had issues with them and locked them up somewhere. It seems logical enough."

"So it seems the dark ones were unable to destroy these monsters?" Count Shub frowned. These words did not please Kimal Sarento.

"This is just an assumption." General Khabensky believed in only one thing — that his army was capable of countering any attack.

"With a completely reasonable basis." Old Count Kuzminsky was also inspired by Kimal Sarento's words. "Do not forget — information has arrived that the Wall has not encountered such creatures before. That they are aggressive towards each other, as if they are just beginning to fight for leadership. Somehow, it no longer seems like a good idea to go and destroy the creatures with a small detachment. We need an army."

"Everyone needs an army," the general grinned. "We will be there in five days and solve the problem."

"You'll just drive people away for no reason." Count Vyazemsky continued to push the image of his own exclusivity and strength. "In five days, there will be no trace left of the invasion. Count Kuzminsky, you also have your own task. We need to inspect the damage to the Wall and determine how it can be restored. If rune magic was used in the original construction, then we will not make such a mistake again. The Light lands do not need dark handouts or magic. We are one with the Light and only with the Light will we move forward!"

"Max, can you talk?" Eleanore's voice chimed in my head. My manager knew where I would be, so her sudden use of our connection was an unpleasant sign. I had to answer, drawing displeased glances from those around me.

"I can only listen. I'm in a meeting."

"That's perfect — I can tell you everything that has transpired. Representatives of the Temple of Skron arrived in Hearth. They need your help. After the rune magic was destroyed, the lithoids broke free. Creatures immune to both magic and physical damage. Many hundreds of years ago, they were contained by rune magic, but now that the offworlders have disappeared, the restraining force is gone too. According to the Temple of Skron, it is these creatures that have broken through the Wall's defenses and are mowing people down in the northern region. But those that have passed through to us are small fry compared to what follows. A real storm is coming, which no one can stop alone. The dark ones have offered to unite forces in order to have at least some chance of resisting the encroaching threat."

"I don't really understand what this has to do

with me," I couldn't resist saying, once again drawing the ire of those around me, who still had their attention focused on me. Evidently I was distracting the emergency council from their grandiose plans to save the Zarak Empire.

"The lithoids react negatively to the dark aura. The kronas that protected them from the offworlders have some influence on these creatures, but they cannot kill them. The Temple of Skron believes that you, as possessor of the dark mirror, will succeed. Time is running out. The Temple of Skron is ready to open a portal for you directly from the capital. They have converts and a connection with them. Contact me whenever you have the chance. The dark ones await your reply."

"Judging by the transformation that has taken place within Archduke Valevsky, the situation is even more complicated than we originally thought," Kimal Sarento said, showing considerable foresight in his assumptions of what my city manager might be telling me.

I looked at the group and shook my head. They had the wrath of Skron coming to them, not information about the lithoids. Let them figure it out themselves. Remembering the recent incident, I shamelessly lied:

"Another group of madmen has attacked Hearth in an attempt to destroy it. What can you do? Human stupidity is limitless. My people tried to reason with the poor fellows and suggested that they leave the city. But the fools did not listen to the voice of reason and were destroyed. They asked me whether to wait for my return or to destroy the bodies immediately."

"This haven of darkness should be burned to the ground!" Count Vyazemsky declared passionately, but then the High Priest took my side:

"Count Vyazemsky is walking on thin ice by daring to question the initiative of the highest hierarchs of the Church of the Light. The decision to create a trade center with the dark ones was made personally by the Pope. Information about what just happened will be sent to the Citadel today." Judging by how Vyazemsky blushed, he had something to say, but in a different situation and to different people. Even he could not openly go against the Church of the Light.

"In any case, what's happening in Hearth has nothing to do with the current issue," I continued, closing the topic. Complain and moan about being oppressed? Everyone present was well aware of this. No, I would not give anyone such pleasure. Overall, I would pretend to have everything under complete control. Let them bite their elbows and throw more of their men and money at me. We would see how they resolved the issue with the lithoids. And I needed to run around all of the sealed rifts. Those resources wouldn't collect themselves.

"In that case, Count Vyazemsky, I am relying on your speed and strength. General Khabensky — the army must be in the northern region in five days. We must act, gentlemen. We must return peace to the Zarak Empire. All the resources you need are at your disposal."

This emergency meeting chaired by the emperor clearly demonstrated who was in charge — General Khabensky with his huge army and Count Vyazemsky, who had subjugated almost the entire high aristocracy. Counts Shub and Kuzminsky, and even the High Priest, had, in fact, no authority in the Zarak Empire. Yes, they were rich and influential, but nothing more. When it came time to solve problems, they immediately gave way.

"Maximilian, can you spare a minute for an old man?" The High Priest intercepted me at the door.

"I was planning to visit you in the Fortress."

"I'm afraid that might be an issue. I will have to temporarily take my leave of Turb. Information has come in that you wish to donate your estate in the capital to the Church of the Light."

"That's right. That is, of course, if the Fortress has no qualms accepting such a gift."

"The Servants of the Light humbly accept any gifts that may strengthen the church. Be it a silver coin or an estate. We accept your donation, Archduke Valevsky. We will coordinate and sign all the necessary documents remotely. However, I want to warn you that this gift will not in any way affect our decision to return Mother Alia to the bosom of the Church of the Light. As soon as she gives birth to her child, your personal attendant will leave you."

"This is not required. Alia plans to fulfill her duty in full," I answered, barely containing my anger. I didn't know where it had come from, but

Alia's fanatical belief that she needed to leave me was oppressive. She didn't give a single justification or reason. She simply must go back to the Fortress, period. There was no other way.

"Do you need a ride?" Kimal Sarento was waiting for me at the main entrance. His carriage was parked nearby. You didn't need to be a genius to understand that the chancellor wanted to continue our suddenly interrupted conversation. I had to agree, as I still needed to get home somehow. Home, for now.

But instead of the estate, we went to the academy. Once again, Kimal Sarento warned his assistant that he definitely didn't have time for anyone else now, after which he poured two glasses of wine. Things were taking an interesting turn. The chancellor was not accustomed to breaking into his unique wine stores.

"What actually happened in Hearth? Let's move past the tall tales about fanatic attacks. I know Eleanore. She would never have contacted you over such a trifling matter. Especially since you warned her in my presence not to do so during the meeting."

"Will you tell me where Adeline is?" I answered his question with another.

"She was summoned to the clan five days ago. She says something happened, but she can't give details because of her obligations to the clan."

"Naira also left for her native estate four days ago. Do you see the connection?"

"Something is threatening the Bartolomeo

Clan, and they are consolidating their forces to counter this threat?"

"Not just the Bartolomeo Clan. All the dark ones. As well as the light ones. The creatures that broke the Wall are called lithoids. As for what they are and what to do with them, I have no idea. A delegation from the Temple of Skron has come to Hearth, wanting to involve me in destroying the monsters. According to the dark ones, these stones are immune to both physical and magical power. Only the dark aura has an effect. They will even give me a convert so that I can return to Hearth as soon as possible."

"Is what the High Priests said about the infected rifts true?"

"Absolutely. There are no more infected rifts left in this world. And the High Priest knows this very well. Why? The question is very topical, and I have an answer that may not be the most popular."

"Are you implying that our mutual friend might have something to do with the appearance of the infected rift at the tournament?"

"Something? He was directly involved! This rift was created either by him or by his direct order. I don't have 100% proof, but I don't need it. This is not the issue. I'm not going to stop Count Vyazemsky or General Khabensky's army. If the lithoids accidentally kill them, it won't cause me any grief. I have a different task. Until the dark ones find out that the infected rifts no longer exist, I want to appropriate all the rift resources. I still have to bargain with you."

"Your candidness bothers me. Before, I couldn't get a word out of you, but now you're spilling the beans yourself," Kimal Sarento noted. "Are you ill?"

"We're on the same side now, Sir Chancellor. And the more you know about what's going on, the more effectively you'll be able to make decisions. The meeting that just took place clearly showed the real balance of power. Khabensky and Vyazemsky. There is no third. If the pair of them is displeased in any way, whatever has started happening with Hearth will increase tenfold. So until the threat is eliminated, we are in the same boat. As far as I remember, Count Vyazemsky also has some dirt against you. If I suddenly disappear, all the efforts to find a scapegoat will turn toward the magic academy. So sabotage groups, troubles and constantly weeding out provocateurs is our future. And in this future, we need to have trust in each other. At the highest level. Since we are talking about trust, I have a question. Do you think the Zarak Empire would be terribly upset if the central palace of the Nocturnal Guild suddenly ceased to exist? Including all the inhabitants who currently reside there?"

"Do you have the power to do that?" The chancellor asked incredulously.

"I do. If anyone thinks they can attack my messengers, they are sadly mistaken. I will easily overlook any disregard for treaty obligations. I will simply no longer work with these people. I will ignore attempts to isolate my city or unleash fanatics upon us. It is stupid and senseless and speaks only of one man's meager imagination. But I will not forgive the murder of my people. So I plan to enter the central house of the assassins' guild and destroy everyone there. By the way — I am not asking permission, the matter has already been decided. I am interested in the consequences of my actions. For I have no plans to keep silent about who committed this act and why. The Zarak Empire must understand what will happen if the people of Hearth start dying."

"There are several dozen captives in the palace of the Nocturnal Guild, as you called it. Some of them have quite tangible value. Miralda Lertan, for example. I made a mistake by letting her go free. The emperor felt this chance for power and began to neglect his previous agreements. If you manage to pull the true heir of the Zarak Empire out of captivity and hide her in Hearth, my gratitude will know no bounds. This is dangerous — the assassins guaranteed the emperor that his niece was dead, but kept her alive for better times. Everyone in this world wants to control each other. Both the emperor and the assassins will do everything to ensure that Miralda does not live to be twenty-one, when she will be able to declare her right to the throne. But if you are ready to take the risk, the princess can be made a symbol of Hearth. A cover. Use Count Vyazemsky's own weapon against him — rumors and distorted information."

"Make Hearth not a haven for the dark ones,

but a place to save the true heir to the throne?" The idea Sarento was advancing seemed like an insane risk, but I liked it. However, I had no plans to blindly agree. First, I'd talk to Eleanore. I'd had enough of talking to the Duke of Turb, a madman eager to return to his former power. There were plenty of people like him, and they could become a force I could rely on in my confrontation with Count Vyazemsky. But would all this serve me? As soon as Miralda sensed her power, she would turn into a complete fool. We'd been there before. Hearth was already under enough pressure without a crazy princess running amok. Basically, I needed time to think.

Nevertheless, Kimal Sarento's idea made me think that I should take a more productive approach with the Nocturnal Guild. Not simply slashing through people left and right, but doing it for the benefit of Hearth. Resources, gold, jewelry. The killers must have all of this in huge quantities, so why should I leave it all to them? They had chosen their own fate.

"Should I give you the address?" Kimal Sarento grinned when I rose from my chair.

"I'll sniff it out. I really hope that I won't find any of your men there, Sir Chancellor. Because I intend to show no mercy. The assassin's guild accepted the wrong contract. And today is the day I let them know it."

Chapter 4

THE HUGE BUILDING was located not far from the central square of Turb. The Nocturnal Guild had grown so comfortable that they had lost all fear and didn't even bother to hide. Every time anyone came out against the assassins, their attack quickly piddled out, for one reason or another. Either they died, or they changed their mind, as their relatives had suddenly fallen into the clutches of the ruthless creatures. It had reached the point that the guild actually carried weight in the political world. Others began to heed their opinion. The assassins were ruled by a council of three rotating leaders. They were constantly shifting, so at one time or another, every member of the top brass had held this position. It was believed that this was an extremely effective means against any aggression — it is useless to pull out the teeth of a snake if it is strangling you. Of course, there were still some rumors about a leader who actually oversaw the process of changing power in the guild, but there was no confirmation of this to be found. And, as it seemed to me, there never would be. The assassins kept their information close to their chest.

But I couldn't care less about all the intricacies of the inner workings of the Nocturnal Guild. I wasn't going to destroy it completely. Let it live. It was hard to admit, but the invisible spies were an extremely pleasant tool for control and obtaining information. Or eliminating someone entirely, if it came down to that. However, I was going to ask for the six couriers who were killed by this brother- and sisterhood. And I wouldn't ask them with a one-to-one ratio of fighters. All of them against all of my people. Because for me, each of my people was more than worth their weight in gold — they were priceless!

"Can I help you with something?" I was greeted at the entrance by a sweet and friendly girl. She seemed like a ray of Light in this kingdom of dark- ness and horror. Smiling, beautiful, with a perfect figure. Not a girl — a dream! But *Analyze* showed that in front of me was not just an extremely dan- gerous person, but a seasoned killer! It was un- likely that a simple administrative worker who greeted guests would be given a level thirty *Phan- tom*. This particular woman could hide in the shadows from almost anyone!

"Of course you can," I said, smiling in response. "I want you to make a note of something. I am Archduke Valevsky. I have come here to kill everyone in this building. Including such a sweet and charming girl as you. But I do not want to do that until this information is recorded and passed on to higher authorities."

"How sweet," the girl's face didn't even twitch. "What a sophisticated way to commit suicide, Your Highness. Do you want us to inform your relatives? Or have you already written a will?"

"My dear girl, have you sent a note informing the others of my arrival?" It was stupid to react to her sarcasm. "You have thirty seconds before…"

The attack was swift but ineffective. The girl's silhouette dissolved into thin air and appeared a few steps away from me. Sparks flashed, and my would-be killer flew into the opposite wall. Having managed to get her bearings, the girl turned around in the air and, crashing into the wall with both feet, immediately pushed off, rushing back in my direction. This time, she was not holding blades in her hands, but something made of glass. Probably some nasty deadly poison that could penetrate any defense. Which made sense. *Golden Dome of Protection* did not protect against liquids.

But the master of the Nocturnal Guild's reception lobby failed to take two things into account. First, I wasn't a suicidal man who would break into a den of killers with only magic armor. Second, I was no less fast than she was. Taking a step forward, I allowed the poison to be smeared over my defenses and, thrusting my hand into her chest, ignoring several types of defense, including a lethal damage amulet, I pulled out a whole bunch of magic stones. The girl's face was frozen in genuine bewilderment. She still had no idea what had killed her. Brushing off the blood, I put the stones I had extracted in my pocket. When I'd learned about this feature of the mithril armor, I wanted to jump for joy — from now on I had a built-in backpack for storing small items, inaccessible to all other people. Magic stones, elixirs, gold, jewelry — anything smaller than my head could easily fit. It was experimentally established that the backpack's volume was unlimited, but the mass of objects, unlike in my inventory, was not reduced. That is, if I found three tons of gold and put it all in my pocket, I would likely be pinned to the spot.

Nevertheless, I'd already made certain advances in this regard. After the passion of murdering my grandfather had died down within me and it became possible to deal with the mithril armor that the Temple of Skron had given me, I went to the altar of development. Magister Meram was right when he said that the basis of any symbol work was strengthening one's own body. I strengthened myself to the maximum, spending two hundred development points on it at once. The only thing that stopped me was the message in front of my eyes, notifying me that in the next twelve months, the gallo crystals would become useless to me. I had oversaturated the field.

Of course, the assassin hadn't passed along

any message. I had to correct her mistake and add myself to the visitors' log. The assassins' guild kept a strict record of everyone who entered their lair. Checking the table for anything valuable and finding nothing, I moved on.

I went from office to office, destroying every living thing that crossed my path. I never even had to turn on my mirror — there was no point, they came running to me themselves, not even trying to hide. Although some did hide in the shadows, attacking me at what they thought was the most convenient moment. But thanks to the bracelet I knew there were invisibles in the room, and my pumped-up perception allowed me to determine where exactly they were. I didn't even need to look at them. *Dash* to the side from which the danger and offworld presence wafted, and, thanks to *Insidious Strike*, the invisible ones returned to their normal state. The mithril glove was activated, and more magic stones appeared in my hands.

The first time I had to turn on the dark aura was in a spacious hall about fifteen minutes after I started my campaign. The members of the Nocturnal Guild had realized that something out of the ordinary was happening and decided to combine their forces to fight back against the madman. I was attacked by ten people at once. Their tactics were competent and, I admit, their technique was perfect in some ways. The speed and power of the blows were such that my protective dome was swept away in a matter of seconds! Considering the level of magical support stones surrounding

Golden Dome of Protection, these ten were clearly among the best fighters here. But they were unable to achieve any result — I didn't even try to turn my dome back on, limiting myself to just my mithril armor. The assassins did not have a weapon capable of penetrating it. No matter how they jumped around me, trying to find a joint or weak point in my armor, it was all in vain. Even the blows did not particularly affect me — the armor managed to absorb most of the energy, keeping me on my feet. After using *Dash* several times in the hopes of stopping the lightning-fast assassins, I was forced to admit that it was useless. The nimble creatures managed to get out of my attack before I got close.

So, the level twenty-five ousel. I was not petty — I wasn't going to pity or give any of the Nocturnal Guild the chance to survive. There were no twitches, no groans. Ten twisted dead bodies fell to the floor — their insides had exploded. The delicate souls could not withstand the darkness of the rift. It made no difference to me where I got them — from the living or the dead. The latter was even easier. Less blood and the amulets remained intact. The perfect solution for what I had in mind.

My journey through the Nocturnal Guild lair could not be considered hasty. I was in no hurry. I carefully examined each room I entered for anything interesting. My new backpack gradually began to fill up — gems, gold, various decorations and even several beautiful statues gradually increased my weight. I understood perfectly well that all the most interesting things were below — I got something that looked like a map from one of the people I'd killed. The man kept reports of his visits to certain rooms, giving the overall structure of the lair. I suppose if someone from management saw this, this poor guy would die. Or he was a spy who had infiltrated the organization and the figures listed here were not the number of visits to rooms, but the number of killers who had access there. I had certain overall questions about the records, but at least it had a structure of the building drawn on it, albeit incomplete. According to this impartial map, the killers' lair had three underground floors. And, as logic suggested, the most interesting thing was located directly below me.

I still made sure to clear the entire first level. And there were dark beasts here as well — phantoms who hung from the ceiling and attacked me. Moreover, at some point I realized that some of the attacks were coming from the rooms I had already passed through — additional forces were being pulled into the lair. Apparently, several quick-footed assassins had managed to jump out into the street through the windows and rushed to where they could get help. It was unlikely that all the capital's killers were in one place. Many were resting at home, in taverns, or were on the job. But this turn of events only made me more pleased — the more I managed to kill now, the more effective the idea that I was going to convey to the killers would be. I knew that the guild would take revenge. They would do everything to finish off either me or my loved ones, but it was already difficult to do. Any invisibles in Hearth instantly lost their main advantage — invisibility. And no one except me planned to leave the autonomous city in the near future.

I decided not to go to the second floor. The dark aura that was constantly emanating from me should break through the partitions, so that not a single living person remained there. Of course, I could go up there to get the stones, but I was literally weighed down by all I was carrying now. Again, a habit associated with the rifts. The most interesting things are always below.

According to the diagram, there were three staircases leading down. Plus, there were probably some secret passages that the spy simply didn't know about. I decided to play it safe and not let the killers manage to escape. The vyrma blades helped me tear down the walls and throw huge beams and stones across two passages. Now, someone would have to really work up a sweat to get through these stairs. And I'd be able to hear them coming.

I missed the second attack. When I reached the third passage, fireballs, lightning and stone spikes suddenly flew in my direction. I can't explain how I was able to get out of the line of attack. Apparently, my new body enhancements had worked, turning me into a superhuman. I *Dashed* to the side and with another *Dash*, instantly reached the mages. At this point, the attack died out — the bodies of the attackers had exploded from the inside. But this made me frown. I had sincerely believed that there wasn't a single person left on the first underground level, but it turned out that a whole group of them had not only survived, but had also launched an attack.

New information made me take a different look at the second floor. What if there are people alive there too? Could that be possible? It was. So that meant I definitely had to check it out. But to do that, I needed to block the third passage down. I'd take it apart later. I couldn't let the killers escape from my punishing hand. I wasn't letting anyone off easy today.

It didn't take long to block the passage. When I got up, I didn't find a single body. Everyone who was here had fled. My vaunted aura couldn't pierce through floors, which meant that...I bent down and made a cut with my vyrma blade. Yes, the night guild had taken a thorough approach when constructing their lair. The floors between levels were made of thick steel beams layered on top of each other. One of the best defenses against mages — even if they came to this lair and wanted to destroy it, all they would achieve was to break their teeth and lose their mana. Because no fireball could penetrate such protection. My dark aura couldn't either.

All that was left was to walk around the level, looking for something valuable. After fighting off several attacks, I realized the key element — the majority of the night guild members, who were on the second floor, had escaped through the open windows. I walked around the rooms and found several open safes. People were walking away not only with their lives, but also their valuables. Which was bad.

I had to go back. Some screams were heard from the street, but no one dared to enter the huge house. Most likely, the guards had come running, but, realizing where they had been called, they froze in indecision. Without the secret chancellery of his imperial majesty, no one would come here, and they would be hard to convince. They also stood to benefit from having fewer murderers in the capital.

The barricade I had set up flew out of the stairwell like a cork from a bottle. Not by itself — it was pushed through by a fairly powerful fireball. In any case, the sheer size of the hole it made inspired respect. Activating *Golden Dome of Protection*, I rushed forward. The third group was rising from below. They looked much more formidable than the previous groups. They were dressed in a full set of plated armor, had shields, moved in formation and were ready for almost anything. Just not the twenty-fifth level of the rift! That said, this was the first group of Nocturnal Guild assassins who didn't explode instantly. The steel armor was able to extinguish some of the dark aura, so they simply rolled down the stairs. I had to catch up with them and extract the stones through the steel armor. I wondered what those who came here to clean up the aftermath of my appearance would think. Where did the holes in the steel cuirass that looked as if they had been made by a ballista spear come from?

The third squad yielded significantly more loot than the previous ones. They not only had excellent level ten stones, but also a whole smattering of defensive and offensive amulets, several dozen vials of green poison, and some unknown elixirs, which I also snatched up. Flask would figure out what they were and how to use them. One attacker made me especially happy — he had level fifteen stones, and on his hand I found a signet ring. Anyone who possessed this ring was one of the Council of Three. This meant that the Nocturnal Guild only had two leaders left.

The first underground floor brought many interesting discoveries. Mostly safes, which I found and opened in almost every room. I completely ignored the gold, and took out everything I had scooped up so far. I could easily carry off about two hundred kilograms of the yellow metal, no more. Then I would become slow and clumsy. Any slightly faster-than-average lackey would be able to catch up to me, so it wasn't worth it. I couldn't give my opponents a chance to hit against my armor with their weapons. But the best part of my bottomless backpack was the jewelry that the killers' safes were bursting with. The jewelry weighed significantly less and cost several orders of magnitude more. Rings, earrings, pendants, chains, bracelets...A whole heaping pile of jewelry suddenly became mine, and there was no way I would give it up now. Especially one of the full sets — two rings, earrings, and a necklace. It looked so attractive that I could easily imagine it on my Alia. She would definitely love something like this.

The assassins gathered in groups to fight me twice more, but each time it ended in complete failure. It was enough for me to close the distance with *Dash,* and any resistance ended. They tried to talk to me several times. There were even especially gifted people who threatened both me and my family. I did not pay any attention to this — I pushed forward, destroying everything in my path. In my mithril armor, especially in such a tight space, I was invulnerable.

The second underground level offered nothing new — the same rooms, the same safes, the same people. Not exactly the same, but similar enough that it didn't change the essence. I started to come across some documents. They also went into my backpack — even if they turned out to be complete nonsense, they could be used to kindle the fireplaces. I also took away books — I had the idea of creating my own library in Hearth. And not from the trivial little books lining the walls of any bookshop. I was interested in ancient works. Such as those kept in the Nocturnal Guild. There were connoisseurs here, as well.

Another massive door appeared in front of me. Like all the previous ones, this one was locked. Apparently, those who the entire empire feared were hiding behind it too. Of course — bogeymen who knew how to hide in the shadows. But once you backed these people into a corner and stood in front of them, blasting a dark aura, where did all their cool power go? Did it really hide itself behind a huge set of doors in the hope that I would pass by, unable to break through?

The vyrma blade sunk into the door with ease. I made a huge circle, cutting a passageway. I had no interest in fiddling with locks. Several crossbows clicked, sparks appeared across my shield, and the acrid green fog began to seep out once again. Persistently, time after time, the assassins tried to poison me. Apparently, it never occurred to them that there was such a hermetic shield of armor that I could walk along the bottom of a river for quite a while before needing to take a breath. But for the whole rest of the world, I was completely without armor! I didn't shape the mithril into a beautiful piece of iron. Why, if it worked regardless of how it looked?

The piece of the door fell inward. I followed it through and saw two men. I knew one of them — we had met before. The rings that adorned the fingers of each man immediately caught my eye. Two of three. Or rather, two of two. The last living leaders of the Nocturnal Guild.

"Gentlemen." I nodded theatrically to them as equals. Again, two crossbow bolts slammed into my shield and, creating a beautiful fountain of sparks, flew off to the side. Judging by the elongated faces, the bolts were not ordinary ones. Vyrma? Most likely. The weapon, which had never failed them before, had now malfunctioned. And my ordinary protective dome handled it with no problem.

"The situation is as follows: I do not intend to kill all members of the Nocturnal Guild. One of you will remain alive and will calmly leave this building. I suggest you decide amongst yourselves who will be the lucky one."

"Why are you doing this? Do you even understand the consequences of your actions? Your entire city will be destroyed!" Judging by their question, they recognized me. That was a good start.

"The Nocturnal Guild did something very foolish — they accepted a contract to kill my people. The couriers you intercepted served me. You killed them. You tried to kill my other people. I wasn't too happy with that, so I'm here on a return visit. So that you understand who you can act out against and who it's better to leave alone. You threaten to destroy my city? Go ahead and try. I'll be happy to finish what I started. Only I won't limit myself to just your central lair anymore, I'll go through all the major cities. Every foolish act must be paid for, gentlemen. I believe that the Nocturnal Guild has almost paid its debt."

"Almost?" one of them said, baring his teeth. It was the one I hadn't met yet.

"One of you is still alive. And I haven't been to the third floor yet. I want to see what's there. Maybe there's one of your guests that might interest me? Time's up, gentlemen. Or do you want me to make the choice?"

"I have another proposal," the leader continued to growl. "Die!"

At the same time as he spoke, he pressed a

lever, and steel rods as thick as my thumb grew out of the floor in front of me! From the rustling sound I heard, similar rods had jumped up behind me. They rested against the ceiling, forming a secure trap. The distance between them was so small that not even a hand could pass through them. But the matter was not limited to just the rods — sharp stakes appeared from the ceiling and slowly began to descend. Contented laughter sounded out — apparently, they were enjoying the spectacle.

The spikes descended slowly. The victim, caught in such a simple trap, should have realized the unenviable nature of his situation. Smiling, I activated vyrma blades and struck the bars. A metallic ringing sound was heard, and my weapon flew to the side. It was not steel. The Nocturnal Guild had created a cage of pure vyrma! The laughter grew even more unpleasant. These men were clearly enjoying themselves. Turning towards the descending spikes, I struck them as well. The result was the same — vyrma could do nothing against vyrma. I struck the floor, and this proved to be made of the same valuable metal! I specially checked it, testing its strength. I couldn't even imagine where the assassins had found so much vyrma. There were at least fifty kilograms here!

What a lucky find! Not a single gram would go to waste. Unlike the jewelry, even processed vyrma would fit in my inventory with no problems. All that remained was a small matter — escaping from this current trap. And for this I had one extremely valuable tool, which the uproariously laughing leaders knew nothing about. My mithril gloves!

It took only two blows to create a hole wide enough to break free. Mithril pierced through vyrma with the same ease with which it crushed steel. I did not throw away the pieces that I tore off, but stuck them in my inventory. I was in no rush — the exit was blocked by a descending plate. Turning around, I assessed how accurately the spikes entered special grooves in the floor, where custom holes had been made to house them. The plate descended completely and just as slowly began to rise. Judging by the weights that pulled this press, the victim should have been turned into a pancake regardless of what armor they were wearing. This is where I began to worry — if the plate now returned to the ceiling, the spikes would disappear too. How would I then extract them? I had to forget about the leaders, who had turned into two snow-white statues, and concentrate all my attention on the rods. I managed to appropriate more than half of it before the mechanism finally worked. The cage, or rather what was left of it, disappeared. The last thing I managed to do was to drive my hand into the floor and, standing next to it, lift the vyrma plate with a single jerk. It was thin, but even that had been enough to block my blades. I urgently needed sellar. A material mined from the ninetieth level of the rift and capable of cutting everything possible. Except perhaps mithril and high level essences.

"Have you made up your mind?" I asked the

leaders as if nothing had happened when the plate had also slipped into my inventory. "Which one of you dies now, and which one runs to tell the whole world what happened here? Hurry up, please. I have several more things planned for today. And they're all much more difficult than destroying your overhyped lair. I wonder why no one has even tried before me. So?"

Chapter 5

"STAND ASIDE, PLEASE." I noticed something that looked like a safe behind the leader of the Nocturnal Guild and decided to see what it held.

"What are you doing?" The sole surviving council member of the Nocturnal Guild nearly stumbled over his own feet to protect his property.

"I'm collecting my spoils," I replied, sincerely confused as to why he was asking. "The fact that I spared your life doesn't mean that I'm not going to thoroughly ransack this lair. By the way, you can leave. There are no claims against you specifically right now. I have some advice: don't take orders against Hearth. Next time, I don't intend to leave anyone alive. Although I must admit that you acted wisely."

He had done the right thing. When it became clear that the trap hadn't worked on me, he pulled out a knife and deftly sent his partner to his eternal sleep. The series of treacherous blows to the back were so swift and powerful that the other man hadn't had a single chance of salvation. Even the fatal damage blocking amulets didn't help. I was thorough, bending down to pierce through his chest, taking the magic stones and the remaining amulets. It must have looked creepy. I grinned, imagining how the remaining leader would speak of me. A man in a set of beautiful garments came to visit and broke through the strongest metal in this world with his bare hands. I was even glad that I decided to spare this man's life. When no one truly understands what's going on, it gives rise to a mountain of rumors. The more rumors there are, the more cautious people will be about Hearth. The fewer people there will be who want to destroy my city. Although there certainly will be those willing and ready to attack.

"You are a reasonable man, Archduke Valevsky." A respect suddenly awoke within him. "You shouldn't commit an act for which you definitely won't be forgiven. It's one thing to avenge your people, and another thing entirely to steal the very shirts off of your enemy's back. I'm sure you've already taken a thorough walk through the upper floors."

"I have," I said, gazing intently at the safe. My desire to open it intensified. This guy was just trying to distract me in order to save his most valuable stuff. "But what I found there still isn't adequate compensation for the damage done to my city. I believe that right here, in this safe, is something that will make me the happiest man on the planet."

"It will make you a dead man," he said. The leader of the Nocturnal Guild was actually trying to threaten me right now. What brazenness! This forced me to approach the safe even closer, when suddenly I heard an unprecedented offer: "The Nocturnal Guild will pay you one hundred thousand gold if you do not open this safe!"

I stared at the man in surprise, taken aback by this proposal. He realized that he had said something stupid and corrected himself:

"Did I say a hundred thousand? Great Light, what an unforgivable mistake! Five hundred thousand gold! The Nocturnal Guild offers Hearth five hundred thousand gold to leave the contents of this safe in place."

Five hundred thousand was already a decent sum, comparable to the price of closing two or three high-level rifts, if the resources extracted from them were all sold. The only problem was that in the Zarak Empire, and even among the dark ones, there were not many people and organizations willing to part with such a sum. Hearth could really use five hundred thousand right now. Incidentally, maybe I should start healing people again. What if they stop fearing us so much after that? I needed to speak to Eleanore about this.

However, I was not going to agree to such a proposal right away. I needed the money, of course, but I still had to actually get my hands on it somehow. Even if the last of the three council members of the Nocturnal Guild wrote me a check right now, where would I cash it? Five hundred thousand gold was several tons of round coins. I couldn't just stick them in my pocket.

"I see you have some doubts?" He managed to correctly interpret my confusion. "Apparently, I have just failed to guess the right amount? Of course, what is five hundred thousand for the only Archduke, not only in the Zarak Empire, but the entire lands of the Light? A million! The Nocturnal Guild will provide Archduke Valevsky with a million gold, refuse all contracts related to Hearth or the elimination of the people associated with the Archduke. Moreover, we will independently deliver the specified amount to the autonomous city as payment for the inconvenience. Let's say, in two weeks. Is this a sufficient incentive not to open this safe?"

I looked back at the safe. Could it be that the name of the mysterious man who appoints the council members of the Nocturnal Guild was in there? But the mayor in me kicked in. Even if I appropriated everything in this lair, it wouldn't amount to a million gold. This amount was too huge to simply ignore. The longer Hearth existed in isolation, the more money it needed to maintain its usual standard of living without halting construction. And I was not keen to do the latter.

"And how can I be sure that the Nocturnal Guild will fulfill its obligations?" I asked.

"My word is enough," he assured me. "The

Nocturnal Guild has never backed down from a decision, once made. If we promise something, we will fulfill it, even to our own detriment. So what do you say, Archduke Valevsky? One million gold pieces to forget about the existence of this safe!"

"I assume your proposal doesn't apply to your prisoners?" I asked just in case.

"I'd be happy to accompany you and give you a tour of our estate. There are rumors about us, like the fact that thousands and thousands of innocent citizens are languishing in the depths of our home, so you'll be surprised to see what's really there. We only have two guests, and if you're so eager to give them freedom, we'll help transport them to Hearth. All done at our expense."

I looked at the safe again. The man was winning me over. His words seemed so captivating and persuasive. The whole thing was so enticing, so convincing, that the greedy Archduke in me almost managed to win at some point. If it weren't for the pile of contracts with various families, which were now worth no more than toilet paper for me, I could easily agree to such madness. I could believe the leader of the Nocturnal Guild, agree to a million gold, maybe even receive it. But I wasn't here for that. Not everything in this world could be bought off with gold. If anyone thought otherwise, I had unpleasant news for them. For they are not much different than a common lady of the night who prefers to call herself a courtesan.

"No!" When I struck the safe and tore off one side, the man tried to dash in my direction, but ran into my protective dome and flew to the side. Peering inside, I chuckled — the safe turned out to contain a surprise. If I had broken through the front door, the vials of flammable liquid inside would have turned everything in the safe to ash. Whoever designed it clearly did not think that someone would have enough brains to break it open from the side. After all, the device, as became clear, was made of vyrma. Where had the Nocturnal Guild obtained so much? Along with the trap, this already represented a formidable mass of metal that would normally be inaccessible to ordinary mortals. I had a long conversation ahead of me with the man who was now struggling to get to his feet. I needed answers. Trying not to touch the vials of red liquid, I carefully pulled out something from the safe that looked like a registration log. Names, dates, terms. And the first entry went back four hundred years. I started leafing through the record book and stopped almost immediately. A phrase that stood out from the orderly row caught my eye:

Coordinator №1 has resigned. Coordinator №2 has assumed his post.

The note had been written in a different hand. The next few lines of text, right up to the note that Coordinator №3 was assuming the post, were all written in the same hand. Once again, I looked at the inscriptions and realized that I had my hands on a record of the Nocturnal Guild's shifting Council of Three. It contained all changes in leadership, and the longest period I could find in the same handwriting was one and a half years. That was how long a certain Lorgan Brysch had been in power two hundred years ago. The council member got to his feet, but made no new attempts to attack me. At the same time, he was not going to run away — he just stood and sullenly followed my movements. I got to the last entry about Coordinator №14 taking up the post, and my heart started pounding. The change had occurred about twenty years ago. All the entries after that date had been made by the same hand. Having reached the last line, I put the log on the table and sat down, wondering what this world had come to. I knew this handwriting. I had seen it many times. And now, having realized who was actually behind the Nocturnal Guild, I didn't know what to do. Because everything that this man had told me up to this point now had to be taken as an outright and unconditional lie. His words hadn't coincided with his actions at all. Although this did clear up a lot of things. A whole lot.

There was nothing else in the safe. Just the record book and a pile of vials designed to destroy it. I slid the loot toward the surviving council member. He grabbed the magazine and hugged it like a child.

"We must make sure that the Coordinator does not learn that I have seen this record book," I said. "This is in your own interests."

"We can pretend that I left the base before you reached this office," he suggested. "Realizing that there was danger, I took the book and left the base with it. Only in this case, I will not be able to accompany you to the third floor. I must not be seen with you."

"You mustn't," I agreed. "There remains one last, no less important issue to be resolved. Where is your treasury?"

He flinched, as if he had been hit with a whip.

"You understand that I can't let you go without receiving this information? I'm afraid I'll have to beat it out of you, get it through brute strength. If you think that the poison embedded in your body will help you, I'm sorry to disappoint — it won't kill you. I won't allow it. So you'll save us both a lot of time and pain if you tell me where I should go. So that the suspicion wouldn't fall on you. The rest of the world will think that this unpleasant man with a scar across his face gave me information about the treasury. By the time I entered this room, you were no longer at the base."

"Who are you?" the leader whispered in shock, continuing to clutch the book to his chest.

"A man who you have offended slightly. And who came to avenge the hit to his nerves. Just in case you think I'm bluffing, this isn't even ten percent of the wrath I'll rain down on you. Not even close."

With these words, I activated the fifth-level ousel. The way the leader wheezed indicated that he had never been in a rift before in his life. I held it for only ten seconds. I didn't want to completely destroy the man. However, in his stupid naivety, he activated one of the built-in capsules. His eyes rolled back and foam came out of his mouth. I had to pull the poor wretch back from the brink of death. You should have seen his eyes when he opened them and realized that he was still alive and lying next to me. There was so much horror and fear in them that I began to grow concerned for his psyche. Just in case, I used *Heal* a few more times to block even the slightest possibility that the man's heart would give out.

His heart held out. Standing up, the leader of the Nocturnal Guild once again hugged the book like a child.

"I repeat: that was just a taste. The lowest level of what you'll be exposed to if I don't get the information I need. And, as you know, you can't be the hero here. I won't allow it. Where is the treasury and how do I get inside? What is the security system and how do I bypass it? I'm all ears."

There were no more questions or hesitation, and soon I was descending to the third level of the Nocturnal Guild's lair. The situation here was strikingly different from the previous floors. It turned out to be an open space strewn with cages. Not cells, as mages could damage the stones they were made of, but steel cages that blocked any magic. The leader, who remained somewhere on the floors above, hadn't deceived me — despite its large size, the floor was empty, with the exception of two cells located on opposite sides. I approached the first prisoner. He was an exceedingly unkempt man. His appearance prevented me from estimating his age — his hair, which had remained uncut for a long time, hung in huge tangles, and the smell emanating from him almost made me gag. His emaciated body looked like mine after a particularly heroic campaign through the rifts. However, despite his terrible appearance, the man stood firmly on his feet, and his gaze was clear and distinct. His eyes were not glassy or clouded, and contained no hint of madness. This man had managed to keep his mind, even while locked in a cage and in that state. Before I saved anyone, I wanted to find out who I was dealing with.

"My name is Archduke Valevsky. I am currently cleansing this building of the Nocturnal Guild. Who are you and why are you in this cage?"

"There is darkness in you," he replied in a low voice.

"I am a dark human recognized by the Citadel. You didn't answer my question."

"I have no business with dark ones who come to tempt my soul."

"Okay, so if that's the case..." I was curious about who this person was, so I put up *Golden Dome of Protection.* So he could check people for darkness, even through a steel cage? Quite a rare gift. "Is there still darkness in me?"

"No," he said after a pause. "I don't understand."

"And you don't need to. Who are you?"

"There is no darkness within you. But there was before. This isn't possible. A person cannot change their predisposition at will. Only the gods have the right to do this."

"I'm going to pay a visit to the second prisoner now, after which I'll return to you. If you won't answer my question, I'll leave you here. I think the Nocturnal Guild would be pleased with this parting gift to them."

"Wait!" the prisoner cried. "There is no darkness in you. I do not know my name now, twenty years ago I was the High Priest of the Zarak Empire, a monitor of darkness named Father Locke. After my defrocking, I was not given a new name. For the last twenty years, I have been called Nameless."

"For a prisoner who has been sitting in a cage for twenty years, your mind is too well preserved."

"Turn around. It wasn't always so empty here. Faith and the unfortunate people who were locked in cages next to me helped me survive. I supported them and taught them, helped them find faith. It supported me too. Stopped me from breaking. The Light tests everyone according to their strength."

"I don't like the name Nameless. I'll call you Father Locke. So, Father Locke, do you wish to escape this place that the Light has forsaken? Or do you wish to continue to sit in this cage and instruct the poor wretches who come through?"

"Since when has the hereditary title of Duke been recognized in the Zarak Empire?" Again, the man refused to answer my questions.

"Since I became the head of an autonomous city. Home to a trade portal with the dark ones, approved by the Citadel and the Fortress. The world has changed in the twenty years you've been sitting in that cage, Father Locke. That's why I'm asking, do you want to go back? The dark ones aren't as dark as they used to be. They're starting to cooperate. Not with everyone, of course, only with those who've become gray, but that doesn't change the fact that things are different now."

"They are," he said. "Those who are gray have taken the first step away from Skron. They have come closer to the Light. Yes, Archduke Valevsky, I would like to gain my freedom."

My vyrma blades flashed and the lock on the doors was rendered useless. Opening the doors, I stepped aside, ready to block an attack. Who knew what could happen to a man over the course of twenty years? However, Father Locke left the cage without offering any surprises. He only shuddered as he looked around. In twenty years he had become accustomed to a closed cage, and now the cage in which he found himself was much larger.

"Keep up," I said and walked over to the second prisoner. It really was Miralda Lertan. But this girl was a distant shadow of the girl I once knew. She seemed to have shrunk by half. And only two months had passed since I last saw her! But the saddest thing was her eyes. It was hard to find any glint of reason in them. The layout of the Nocturnal Guild's "human warehouse" meant that almost anything you did was visible to all, including going to the toilet. Or rather, squatting over the small hole in the center of the cage. Apparently, Miralda could not handle the idea of two pairs of eyes on her, because at the moment, she smelled like a pile of manure. The girl sat on the floor and quietly howled, rocking back and forth. I suddenly had a wild desire to go back and finish off the third council member. Because it simply wasn't right to bring another human to the state that Miralda was in now. It would have been more humane to simply kill her.

"Come on out," I ordered, breaking down the door. The princess didn't hear me — she had withdrawn into herself, and for her, the entire world was housed inside this cage. In just two months! Where was that self-confident and impudent young lady who had infuriated most of the magic academy?

"She has little Light left in her eyes," said Father Locke. "She has practically given up, but there is still a chance to bring her back. Who is she?"

"Miralda Lertan, daughter of Emperor Devalon the Sixth. The slain emperor. Her uncle, Zurgan the First, currently holds the throne, and he ordered the Nocturnal Guild to kill anyone who might become a problem in the future. For some reason, the assassins didn't comply, instead turning Miralda into this..."

"I saw her broken. Tortured. Defiled. Starved. Doused with slop and cold water. Not allowed to sleep. No human could endure that. Neither could she. But there is still hope. There is still Light in her eyes."

"She needs to be brought back into human form. We can't drag the princess out here like this.

Will you take care of her, Father Locke? There's water by that wall, if I understand correctly."

"You're leaving us?" The former High Priest frowned. Although, as practice had shown, no one ever really left the church.

"Not for long. I want to pass through this floor and make sure nothing else is hidden here. I must ensure that anyone capable of doing this to another human isn't left alive."

"May the Light go with you," said Father Locke, after which, without any disgust, he entered Miralda's cage and carried her out in his arms. In this regard, I was grateful to the man. I didn't want to have to touch the creature that the girl had become. After making sure that no one else was left in the room, I moved on. According to the story the remaining council member had told me, the treasury was on the fourth basement level. Yes, there was a fourth level here, which only a few knew about. The entrance to it was in the torture chamber, not the most popular place. And in the torture chamber itself lived five creatures that had long since lost their human appearance. No, they still looked like people, but their brains had long since devolved into that of a beast. Insatiable, soulless, revelling in the suffering of others.

I didn't want to stoop to their level. I should have done the same to them that they did to their victims, but I didn't even want to sully myself by touching them. I suppose even the rift beasts were more human than these things. So I entered the torture chamber with a level twenty-five dark aura, allowing the executioners to simply explode. I was so disgusted that I didn't even use *Analyze* on them, let alone take their magic stones or amulets. There are some things you shouldn't touch.

If I hadn't been told exactly where to search for the door, I never would have found it. It was hidden very well. And so, after tearing out several pieces of wall paneling and cutting through several blocks, I reached a smooth, wide descending passage. The Nocturnal Guild dragged a lot of all sorts of things to their lair, and they were paid well, so the passage to the treasury had to be well hidden. There were no guards or additional traps here. The fourth basement level, which was not even supposed to exist, was not a place where thieves could move freely. So I boldly went down and cut through the last door, opening access to the most covert and consecrated room in the lair. I hadn't been told how to turn on the light, so I had to use a light crystal. When the space lit up, I involuntarily swallowed. The assassin's treasury was huge. Much larger than the one in Hearth. And almost all the space was occupied by shelves packed to the brim. Gold, gold and more gold. There were so many coins that I was even taken aback — it could not have been hauled out by one person alone. If I were to take a million gold pieces, as the council member had suggested, the treasury wouldn't even notice the loss. I walked between the rows, amazed at the thriftiness of these killers. Perhaps even the imperial bank could not boast of having such a huge sum of money. However, the treasury was not limited to gold alone. I looked at a pile of gray, unremarkable metal that was neatly stacked on one of the shelves. Fifty kilograms of vyrma. As the leader told me, the metal from which the trap was made was obtained several centuries ago from one of the curators. Since then, the assassins had been hoarding every gram they could get of this material. As well as many other resources extracted from the rift. Everything was neatly stacked in boxes, and even labeled. Vyrma, tram, dorim. Resources from high-level rifts indicated that the trade relationship with the dark ones had been established in the distant past — it had just been carefully hidden.

On the wall furthest from the entrance, there was an incredible alcove. It was quite spacious, there was even a chair so that someone could come and enjoy the unprecedented spectacle. Several artifacts were hanging on the wall. Five blue, three gold and one red. The artifacts were unidentified — the guild had gotten their hands on them, but still couldn't determine exactly what it was they had. I couldn't spend the time to figure it out right now either. Throwing the artifacts into my armor's special storage space, I went to the wall and stared at a small piece of paper that was placed in a protective frame and lay on a velvet pillow. For some reason, my heart began to beat wildly. I knew this map. My childhood had been spent here. These rivers, forests, the border with the ocean. Everything was familiar to me. Except for the strange cross that was located where the forests had always been. A map of the Zarak Empire appeared before my eyes. One map was superimposed on another — there were three fourth-level rifts located around this cross. Moreover, the rifts formed a perfect triangle, with the cross in the very center.

Evidently, I'd have to pay a visit to my homelands very soon. Because the realization dawned on me of what might be hidden behind the cross, which at first glance seemed so inconspicuous. It was no accident that the Valevskys had settled on these lands. Far from it.

Chapter 6

"ARCHDUKE VALEVSKY?"

The convert who came to the Nocturnal Guild's lair was vaguely familiar to me. We had crossed paths at some reception before I had learned to identify these dark creatures. A baron or something. It didn't matter anymore. This man had chosen his path, and it was not for me to dissuade him. When we met again, I would try to hit him with a dark aura, so that he was never reborn again. However, even now I couldn't resist commenting when the newcomer began to unbutton his jacket.

"Aren't you sorry to give everything up, just like that?"

"Here, I am an ordinary, lowly baron, of no interest to anyone. There I was promised eternal life, and Skron will also raise me one step higher if I complete his task now. I will have a chance to escape to the dark lands. To touch greatness! Here, among the light ones, there is no freedom. The Church of the Light cuts short any ambition. Any deviation. In the dark lands, there is none of that. Everyone is equal there.

"A controversial statement, but I'm not going to dissuade you. Open the portal."

"The man's a convert! Kill him!" Father Locke appeared in the doorway. After the princess' bath, she had lost consciousness, so the convert's murmuring song had not affected her. Nor on the former High Priest. Monitors of darkness were inert to such things.

"This is our way out of the capital," I replied, watching the former baron rip open his belly and take out his entrails. A few moments later, a shimmering arch appeared, and a minotaur entered the lair.

"The Temple of Skron awaits you, Archduke Valevsky," the horned monster boomed. I looked at Father Locke, who had turned white.

"There are two paths. Either you come with me and gain your freedom, or you stay here and meet the man who locked you up here for twenty years. I suppose he'd be interested in seeing you in a different setting. You've crossed paths with him before, haven't you? He came to see you, more than once. He couldn't help himself. Not this man."

Father Locke's eyes flashed, but he said nothing.

"I have not seen your handwriting, Father

Locke, but somehow I do not doubt that if I ask you to write even a single line, it will become clear that you are the one who twenty years ago was called not only Father Locke, but also Coordinator №13. The one who appointed three council members over the course of ten years, until you were overthrown by a more agile competitor. Will you answer the question? Since when did the Nocturnal Guild become a branch of the Fortress?"

"Since its founding," Father Locke answered after a long pause. "The assassins were originally all members of the Church of the Light."

Of course they were! You didn't just find *Phantom*-level stones lying around in this world. Even if you had a lot of money. Considering that there are only two mechanisms for integrating stones, in the Academy and the Fortress, there were few options as to who the killers could call "Master." I could have guessed it myself without using the hints in the form of the High Priest's handwriting. Father Locke nodded at the portal and asked:

"Is it safe?"

"For now, yes. The Temple of Skron is interested in collaborating with me and my city."

"There's one issue yet to be decided, Archduke Valevsky. Why did you break me out? No, it wasn't even that intentional, you pulled me out before you knew who I was. Why do you need me now?"

"The answer is simple — the Fortress treasury. Who knows it better than the High Priest? Even a former one. Now that I have finally understood what the Fortress is, I have an insatiable need to get inside. There is not even a hint of light in the Fortress. That is what I need you for. After you tell me about the treasury, you will be free to do as you will. We will be even."

"The Fortress will never forgive you for breaking into its treasury. This is not the Nocturnal Guild we're speaking of — the church has real power behind it."

"And I have the truth behind me. In any case, this isn't an issue that will be resolved in the next couple of days. Not even the next couple of weeks or months. Now I just need information so that I can use it at a convenient time. So will you help me? Or are we going to go our separate ways? My plans don't include getting on the bad side of another High Priest. I'd still like to sort things out with Father Urg."

"Alright, Archduke. I'll tell you everything I know about the Fortress' treasury. Let's get out of this place. I'm even willing to step into a dark portal, for the sake of revenge."

"A portal to Hearth?" I asked the minotaur just in case. Receiving an affirmative nod, I pointed to the shimmering veil to Father Locke. "Go ahead through and don't worry about the pillar of light that will appear above your head. In my city, this is a normal phenomenon."

A few moments later, I found myself two days' journey from the capital city. Nothing had changed during my absence, except that a misty servant of the Temple of Skron had appeared near the portal. Father Locke, shining with a huge column of light, stood not far from the dark one, and undisguised hatred slid into the former High Priest's gaze. I was sure that if it were not for Miralda, whom the man was still holding in his arms, he would not have been able to resist and would have thrown himself bare-handed at the servant for both the Fortress and the Nocturnal Guild.

"Archduke Valevsky, we have little time. The portal is ready. We need to leave immediately." I didn't recognize his voice. He was probably from the B team.

"I'll be ready in thirty minutes," I replied. Adding Miralda and Father Locke to the city's guest list, I nodded my head to indicate that they should go with the guards.

"Feed them and get them into human condition. They are guests of the city. Eleanore, I need you in the treasury. Preferably as quickly as possible."

I had neither the moral nor the legal right to go and fight the lithoids with a full inventory and backpack. Life is an unpredictable thing, you never know what might happen to you or where you might end up. You should always have space for loot.

"Max!" I heard a joyful cry when I had almost finished unloading the backpack. Turning around, I couldn't help but smile. Alia was standing in the doorway. Alive, healthy and, what was extremely important for the girl, with not a single burn mark remaining from the dark fire. Eleanore had nevertheless made an agreement with the Bartolomeo

Clan, and they had purified Alia before I took Naira as my wife. So the dark ones were trying to win my favor? They were apparently chomping at the bit to seal the deal before I had the chance to back out.

"Get over here," I said and the girl jumped into my arms. I felt a pleasant warmth wash over me. Now it finally felt like I was home. The place where I was loved.

"The Bartolomeo Clan has accepted your proposal," Eleanore came up next. She was tactful, giving us a few minutes alone. "The wedding will take place right after you complete the Temple of Skron's request. What did you want?"

"Two guests arrived with me. Miralda Lertan and Father Locke."

"The princess lives?" Eleanore said, surprised. "She has already been officially buried."

"She needs to be rehabilitated. I fear she's gone mad. I patched up her body, but it took professionals two months to break her."

"Understood — it will be done. I know a skillful shrink. What about the cleric?"

"The former High Priest," Alia answered for me. "But he died a long time ago, Max!"

"I think you should talk to this man. You in particular. But a quick debrief: the Nocturnal Guild base in the capital has been destroyed. The assassins will be seeking revenge, so prepare for their arrival. The three leaders have a coordinator who appoints them to their positions every nine months. I left one of the leaders alive. Father

Locke, who I dragged over here, is not only the former High Priest, but also the former Assassin Coordinator. Thirteenth on the list in the entire existence of the Nocturnal Guild."

"Do you mean to say…" began Eleanore, but she fell silent and looked at Alia. I, however, had no intention of keeping my mouth shut.

"That's right, Father Urg is the fourteenth. I'm not going to hide the truth from Alia. She needs to know who she's so eager to return to. Talk to Father Locke, my love. I'm sure you'll learn a lot of interesting new things. Damn it! I wanted to give you gifts, but now I don't even know if there's any point."

"What kind of gifts?" asked Eleanore, closing the sensitive topic. "We girls love gifts. They help distract us from all this nonsense. Show us!"

"Here," I said, pulling out the three sets of jewelry that I had prepared in advance from my backpack.

"Great Light! They're gorgeous!" Eleanore said in amazement. Judging by the way Alia perked up, she liked the jewelry too.

"May I?" I approached my personal attendant. After a moment's hesitation, she finally extended her hand. The ring was a little too big, but that was okay — there was a jeweler in Hearth who could fix it. Unlike artifacts, ordinary items did not adjust to a person's size. I had to tinker with the earrings — the fastening mechanism was unfamiliar to me, but the necklace took its place perfectly inside the enticing hollow of her neck. I did the same with Eleanore, except with a different set. Alia received cold and delicate diamonds, while Eleanore got the fiery red rubies.

"Is that one for Naira?" Eleanore asked, nodding at the third set. Also made of diamonds, but a little simpler than the one my girl was wearing. I could only nod. Whether I liked it or not, the dark one was my betrothed. And wives need gifts.

"That's proper, we shouldn't forget her either," Eleanore said, rubbing her protruding belly. "Have you already taken stock of everything you dragged in? Or should I set the fleet of guards on it? Just from what I've seen already, I'm sure the Nocturnal Guild will have its revenge, and in a big way. I would certainly be offended if such a huge mountain of valuables was taken away from me. By the way, who among them is left to experience this offense?"

"I left one of the Council of Three alive. I needed witnesses. Oh, and here's another thing! Eleanore, Gustav and the servants are still in Turb. The estate is being transferred to the Fortress's control, We need to get all of our people out of there."

"Done."

"Alia, you're in charge of Miralda Lertan. Try to bring her to her senses. If anyone can do it, it's you."

"Not to pose a silly question, but why do we need her?" asked Eleanore. "A princess that everyone thinks is dead is not the most useful acquisition for a disgraced city."

"We will make her a symbol. We will turn Hearth from a haven for the dark ones into a place where traditions are kept. Where the true ruler of the Zarak Empire resides."

"I will remind you of this lofty message you want to send when the army is marching toward our walls. They won't even have to enter the city — they will throw stones from afar and raze Hearth to the ground. We are powerless against such an attack."

"In five days there will be no such army in the Zarak Empire. They're on their way to meet the lithoids."

"General Khabensky has two armies, if you didn't know. He controls the first one himself, and his son is in charge of the second one. The second one, by the way, stood under our walls for some time. It's a well-coordinated mechanism, Max. You can't treat it so recklessly. Even if the lithoids destroy one army, there will always be another one. And we won't be able to do anything against it. So I'll repeat my thought — turning Hearth into the antithesis of Turb, especially when we're close to the capital, is not the best idea. Not now, when we haven't even finished building the wall yet. Heed my words."

"Miralda will live," I insisted. "I'm not thrilled that she's a guest in my city, but she's the ticket out of the situation we've been forced into. We can't do it on our own, no matter how hard we try. As for the army...First, you'll restore Miralda's mind. Turn her back into a human. Then we'll talk some more."

"And what shall be done with Father Locke? This is another figure whose presence in the Hearth could have a detrimental effect on us. Even if the Emperor does nothing, the High Priest will not rest as long as there is a living witness to who Father Urg really is. I would not be surprised if the order to kill this accomplice of the dark ones goes to Alia. Alternatively, they will declare us completely mired in darkness, and even the protection of the Citadel will not save us from the wrath of the human mobs. If I'm right, the current Coordinator of the Night Guild will do everything to destroy the previous one. And his resources are much greater than those of the Emperor. Are you ready to confront two forces at once?"

I looked at Eleanore in silence, unsure how to respond. She was right, her arguments were reasonable, her reasons were impeccable. She cared about the city, about our child, about the fact that Hearth was meant to stand proud for several millennia, not a few months. We had to send the right message. But I didn't want to slide into the bestial behavior running rampant across the Zarak Empire. Just close your eyes, renounce humanity, don't look in their direction, let the powerful do whatever they want, and don't interfere. Become convenient, and then your life will be spared. Most people lived by such rules. Most, but not all. There were others. Those who, despite everything, continued to retain their humanity. Ready to challenge the strongest and rightfully take their place, bringing their philosophy into this world. Did I want to leave my children in a world where people looked at each other like animals? Where people behaved in a way that even animals were incapable of? Six months ago, when I first became a doomed soldier, I had been ready to adapt to everyone in order to survive. Now that I had gained strength, I had the opportunity and the right to declare how I wanted to live.

"I understand," Eleanore nodded. Apparently, she had read my thoughts in my eyes. "I need a week to finish the main part of the wall. During this time, we will restore Miralda and Father Locke, after which we will reveal them to the world."

All I could do was nod. The Temple of Skron hadn't gone anywhere — the servant was waiting for me near the portal. Except that my appearance now shocked him. And of course it did — I looked as if I was ready to go to a fancy dinner party. A formal suit, a white shirt, patent leather shoes. Not a rift conqueror, but a real nobleman! Which I was, in fact. The dark servant even asked:

"Would you like to change into more comfortable clothes?"

"Why, do I look bad?" I looked down at myself theatrically, as if trying to find a flaw. But there was none. "First impressions are the most important, as the Temple of Skron knows. I haven't had the pleasure of encountering the lithoids before, so I must look impeccable for our first meeting."

"But you're not going there to negotiate with them!" the dark one flatly refused to accept my appearance.

"Who said such nonsense? It is always nice to have a little chat with a sentient creature, as long as that creature can speak. Are we going to argue about my appearance or are we going to go deal with the big stone monsters?"

The servant only shook his head and ordered the minotaurs around a bit, but this gave me a clever idea. Why was it necessary to destroy the stone giants? As my experience with the offworlders had shown, establishing a trade relationship was quite possible. I just needed to find out what they needed. *Tainted Blood* still haunts me. The weapon was too strong. Too tempting. It was a shame that I had only been able to use it for a few hours. Returning to the stone giants — since they moved from one point to another, it meant they had some intelligence. This meant that I could negotiate with them. Maybe even trade. What if they were crazy about Pharapho fog-spawn? I'd set them on the Black Mountain, and that would be the end of it! Let the two forces stamp each other out. Although I did want to hold on to Pharapho for as long as possible. There was too much tied up in him. My mithril armor, for example. No, let the fog monster live. He certainly wasn't bothering me.

The space blurred for a moment and turned into an endless steppe. Completely bare, not a single tree visible on the horizon. And there were no hills, no elevated terrain, no valleys. Just a flat steppe with short grass that was just starting to dry out. Autumn was already in full swing, and soon a harsh winter would descend upon our world. I'd need to find out what winter looked like in Hearth. At the Valevsky estate, for instance, which was located much further south, it still got exceedingly cold.

Upon closer inspection, however, the steppe was not so bare. Sure, there wasn't much to write home about as far as the landscape, but not so about the local lifeforms. At a considerable distance from us there was a stone river, flowing from north to south. The space was filled with the roar of crushed stones. Now that I saw the creatures with my own eyes, I realized that the artist from the Wall had been quite adept. He had managed to convey the appearance of the creatures, which consisted of separate blocks, almost perfectly. The distance did not allow me to see the details, but the general picture was clear. I stood on my toes, trying to see the beginning or end of this stone river. There was none! The advance detachment had already reached the horizon, while the rearguard had not even appeared yet.

But while the sketches had depicted four types of creatures, there was, in fact, significantly more variety. The largest ones stood out in particular, two or three times taller than all their fellows and spaced a considerable distance from one other. They looked like huge commanders watching over their army. They rolled from place to place like mountains, trampling their gaping fellows under themselves. But without killing them! Before my eyes, a monster ran into a smaller group and crushed it into a pancake, but after the mountain moved on, the seemingly shattered stones came back together! Physical damage meant little to them, as I had been warned earlier.

"How did you manage to seal them away?" I asked, dumbfounded.

"The Temple of Skron does not have this information," came the answer. Standing next to me was Four. "Karina Fardi was able to stop this wave for a short time. Skron's vessel is still weak and can only give its body over to the god for fifteen minutes. However, even this was enough to significantly slow the advance of the stone monsters. We do not understand what drives them. We do not understand the mechanics behind their functioning. We do not know how these creatures were locked up earlier. But we need to stop them."

"Have you tried to get answers from the Fog Stalker? You have the key. From what I know, the second one has already been activated."

"The key was used for other purposes. If you have another, the Temple of Skron is prepared to buy it."

"My city needs construction crews that don't have any converts. It needs resources. It needs protection from sieges. Can the Temple of Skron provide all of this? Help rebuild and protect Hearth and you'll get the key to the Fog Arena. Are these conditions acceptable? Great, discuss it amongst yourselves, but for now let's decide what you need from me. Do you want me to launch a deadly attack, knowing only that stone monsters have a weakness to the dark aura? Or do you need something else?"

"What you see is a side branch of the main army moving toward Kerux. The smallest branch. The lithoids are moving slowly, but tomorrow they will be near Zudar, the central city of the Valdez Clan. They will destroy everything in their path, leaving not a single being alive. They even kill the birds and other animals, not to mention the humans. We are under a protective dome — they cannot see us. As soon as these creatures find out that there are living beings here, they will instantly change their path and rush to destroy us. That is why we chose this place. So that you can see with your own eyes what is happening. So that you can test your strength."

"But how are there so many? Where are they coming from?"

"We lack this information as well. It was believed that the lithoids were a very closed-off race with a limited amount of manpower. The Temple of Skron will not pay you to destroy or attempt to destroy the creatures. If this avalanche is not stopped now, it will descend on the Light lands. This is a disaster for the entire world, not just the Kerux metropolitan area. Time is running out, Archduke Valevsky. Use the dark mirror and stop this stream. In two hours we will be back to assess the results of your work."

Be back?? I turned sharply towards the Four, but he was no longer there. He had vanished, just like the other dark humans who had dragged me to this Skron-forsaken place. Even the minotaurs were gone! The portal collapsed before my eyes and the remains of the converts that formed it fell to the ground. Suddenly, the stone rumbling stopped, only to increase in intensity a moment later. Turning towards the lithoids, I cursed foully. The Temple of Skron had exposed me to an attack! The camouflage field had also disappeared along with the portal, which is why the lithoids had now turned their attention to me.

When I got back to Hearth, which I would do at any cost, these misty freaks would pay for treating me this way! But for now, putting my hand on my thigh, I said:

"Alia, I'm going dark for a while. I'm going to the Abyss — I need advice on how to fight the creatures."

"Got it. Thanks for warning me! Love you!"

"Love you too. Warn Eleanore. I'll try not to be long."

As I spoke, a mysterious triangle appeared in my other hand, offered to me by one of the great powers of this world. Placing it on the ground, I kept my cool and without looking up at the river of stone rushing towards me, carefully laid out ten krona essences around it. A spark appeared, and all the essences were sucked into the triangle. It flared brightly, painting the world with white light for a moment, and when the bright flash disappeared, I found myself in front of the white seraph. The Abyss had accepted my offering.

"The Abyss welcomes you once again, human. You have questions, I have answers. After all, you are interested in how to defeat the lithoids, are you not? Is this the knowledge you are here for?"

"I see there is no longer a fifty-year time lag. Information from the world above has suddenly started arriving instantaneously?"

"Your world is still as closed to me as it was before. However, I could not help but feel that a powerful force has dwindled. The offworlders are gone, and with them all their runic magic. Many centuries ago, one man managed to seal the progenitor of the lithoids although he failed to destroy it. He did not know how to do this, so he took the path of least resistance. Runic seals were used. Now that the offworlders are gone, so are the seals. The lithoids have broken free. The Abyss does not need to know what is happening in the world right now. The Abyss can reason for itself. In the past, this man was unable to defeat the lithoids, even using the flesh of Pharapho and runic magic. However, it is quite possible to defeat them. Now, all that's left is to decide: what are you willing to give for this knowledge? I warn you, the price for such knowledge will be immense."

Chapter 7

I FELT DISGUSTED. I was being used again. Both by the dark ones, who had left me to fend for myself against a huge crowd of lithoids, and by the Abyss. Not now — earlier, when it threw out the bait that the offworlders could be defeated. It even told me how to do it, as long as I didn't lose my desire to wipe them all out. Damn it! How infuriating it was just to get access to information! Looking at the white seraph again, I couldn't help but say:

"So the Abyss knew that expelling the offworlders would lead to the appearance of the lithoids, but did not warn me about it?"

"You did not ask the right question, human. The Abyss has always been honest with you. You received the information you desired. You did not ask about the consequences."

"Still, the Abyss knew what was coming. It

knew that I would come to it again for answers, and it was prepared to bargain, correct?"

"Correct. Knowledge is the basis of my existence. As is trading in it. Last time you said that you had the essence of a Riftmaster. The Abyss is prepared to tell you how to destroy the lithoids in exchange for such an essence."

"Will the destruction of the lithoids have any other effect on our world?"

"The Abyss does not answer questions for free, human. There is always a price. Those are the rules."

"You determine the rules," I said, disagreeing with the Abyss' way of framing the situation. "And you can change them. I have information that Skron's vessel managed to stop the avalanche of lithoids for fifteen minutes. Destroying invulnerable monsters like cockroaches. If the Abyss' reply about how to destroy the lithoids is on the order of simply 'mirror the level twenty-five riftbeast,' then this advice is worth a dime. I know this myself. Why should I pay for it?"

"The darkness from the rift that you use is capable of stopping the lithoids, but not defeating them," the Abyss answered after a pause. "Once immersed in the darkness, the soul that gives life to the stone monsters returns to the progenitor, from whence it begins its journey again. That is all I can say for free, human. From here on, only essences."

I sat down on the floor in front of the white seraph and laid out ten essences in front of me.

They were once infected, but the disappearance of the offworlders had changed my inventory as well. It had been jumbled again, and the orbs that had the status of "infected" had returned to their original state.

"Can the progenitor be destroyed or banished from our world?" I began my interrogation, in no hurry to part with the Riftmaster essence.

"These are two names for the same thing." The two essences in front of me disappeared. "By destroying the source of power, you expel it from this world, freeing up space for the forces that remain on the planet. Making them stronger. The last force that remains on the planet will be omnipotent."

"So it is the goal of the Abyss to become the strongest and take over this world? To subjugate Skron and the Light?"

"My goal is to regain control over the rifts. Ideally, to destroy Pharapho and its fog. To become equal to the forces of the first order. The Abyss is not interested in small fry like offworlders, lithoids or mechanoids."

This answer cost five more essences. The Abyss did not stand on ceremony, evaluating its answers on a scale known only to it. I added another ten essences to the row. I had plenty, and besides, I needed to clear space up before my grand race through forty-two rifts that I'd be doing in the next two weeks. There was no way I'd refuse the work. I only needed to figure out how to knock the lithoids out at the same time.

"Can the lithoids be reasoned with? Bargained with?"

"No. The progenitor is not sentient in a way that humans would recognize. It is a rational being, but its intelligence is beyond your understanding. As are its desires. You will not be able to satisfy them."

Another three essences gone.

"How could one come to an agreement with the offworlders? One could trade with them, but how?"

"There are no more offworlders left in this world, the question is meaningless. Ask something else."

"Nevertheless, I need an answer, for which I am ready to pay. The offworlders had an ability called *Tainted Blood*. After I became more familiar with it, I had an obsessive desire to obtain it. But the offworlders disappeared, and this ability went with them. I want to understand my misstep. Where did I go wrong?"

"This question is meaningless, since the offworlders have left this world," the Abyss answered too quickly. Suspiciously quickly.

"Let me ask differently. Is it possible to obtain the *Tainted Blood* ability now? If so, how can this be done?"

The pause that followed my questions was alarming. Suddenly, ten other essences appeared next to my own.

"The Abyss will not answer these questions. This is compensation for the time spent."

"The Abyss will not answer, even if I offer a

Riftmaster essence in payment?"

"It is a topic that is forbidden. Ask about how to destroy the lithoids."

"Two Riftmaster essences that are level fifteen and above. You will receive them here and now if you answer my question. How can I get the ability *Tainted Blood*? I have already surmised that it remains available in our world. I have also realized that it can harm the Abyss. Can you use it to fight the lithoids? Skron? The Light? Chaos?"

"Never Chaos." The Abyss paused so long that I began to suspect that our collaborative relationship was over altogether. "*Tainted Blood* is the domain of Chaos. An entity of the first order, although, as it seems to me, it is beyond any categorization and came to this planet as an arbiter that maintains the integrity of this world. If you desire information on how to obtain *Tainted Blood*, you should contact Chaos."

"Are you talking about the Interrogator and the Inquisitor?"

"These are just small echoes of Chaos, closely connected with Skron and the Light. Called to bring the world to order. You need true Chaos. I can't say more. Even the Abyss has its weak points, and this topic is one of them."

"So you can't tell me where I can find Chaos either?"

"It cannot be found. It comes itself when it wishes. When a worthy one appears, satisfying certain conditions. Human, you owe me two Riftmaster essences. For the information you just learned, the Abyss can be severely punished."

"What conditions must be met for Chaos to visit me?" As agreed, I pulled out two essences. They vanished as soon as they appeared. The space shook noticeably, as if the Abyss had experienced something akin to climax. Or it was thoroughly irritated and was warning me that the topic was closed.

"The Abyss has no right to give you this information. Neither I, nor the Fog Stalker. Perhaps the answer is in the closed facilities of the ancients. After all, it was they who initially began working with Chaos, which unleashed trouble and strife upon their world. The first force that appeared in this world was Chaos. The rest came later, having received its permission."

"Does the Abyss know the location of the closed facilities of the ancients where I can find answers to my questions?"

"Fifty years ago, there were only three such places left. Two of them are on the opposite side of the world, one in the lands that are commonly called light. If you want to know where exactly this place is, you will have to pay well. Five Riftmaster essences, level thirty or above. This information, if given to you, can destroy me."

There were practically no essences left in front of me. The Abyss, having paid me a penalty for refusing to answer, diligently swallowed all the orbs back, evaluating a cost for almost every word. Yes, I had many essences, but with such a bottomless pit as the Abyss, even my supply would not last long.

"Perhaps that's enough of the introductory questions. I'm willing to exchange a Riftmaster essence for information on how to destroy the lithoids, as well as information on what effect this will have. Will some other force that has been dormant for a millennium suddenly arise? You must answer me in full. Here is my payment."

"Accepted!" The space rumbled noticeably again when the essence disappeared from my hand. It must be something like an orgasm. The Abyss was regaining its strength. "Darkness and lightning. That is the answer to your question."

"Are you kidding me?" I was taken aback. "I need more details!"

"Darkness is a catalyst that separates the soul of a lithoid from its physical body. Before it goes to the progenitor, this soul can be destroyed by lightning, thereby weakening the progenitor, because it and all the lithoids that appeared on the planet are one and the same creature. The more small creatures you destroy, the weaker the progenitor will be. Last time, a man managed to drive all the offshoots into one point with darkness and seal them with oblivion. But he didn't know anything about lightning. He didn't want to pay for this knowledge. Lithoids belong to the weakest, third-level powers. You don't even need to attract the power of Skron to banish them from this world. Darkness and lightning are enough. Yes, you will need strong lightning. At least level thirty. With less damage, you shouldn't even try to destroy the progenitor.

But the result will be achieved. Banishing this creature will not affect anything. It is inferior. Only humans are lower. This is the full answer."

Lightning and darkness? I definitely didn't have lightning. Make myself a *Thunderer* set? Tempting, but no — I wasn't about to give up my mithril armor. I didn't think the handmade set would work on top of Pharapho's flesh. Use one of my ladies? It was strange to even think about. Both Alia and Eleanore were extremely pregnant, and messing around with the stone creatures would not add to their sense of physical or psychological peace. I needed someone who operated with lightning at a high level, for whom increasing the stone to level thirty will not affect their vitality. How stubbornly I beat around the bush, not wanting to name the only person who could help.

Kimal Sarento. The only high-level mage I knew who could quickly adapt to a level thirty magic stone. And, frankly, the only one with significant power whom I could turn my back to without expecting an attack. Both the dark and the light were quite unpredictable in this regard. All that was left was enticing the chancellor and creating five elixirs to increase the level of the stone from level twenty-five to level thirty. I hoped Kimal Sarento wouldn't disappoint me and that his main ability was pumped up to the maximum values that were available to this world before I started actively closing the rifts.

"Why do the lithoids destroy all living things?" I couldn't help but ask as well. It was much easier to fight when you understood your enemy.

"They feed on the souls and essences of living and half-living creatures. This is the meaning of their existence. For almost seven hundred years, the lithoids have been in oblivion. The progenitor is hungry. He wants to satiate his bottomless belly, so he sends himself everywhere where life is felt. The lithoids can feel it, they can absorb it. This is how they grow. This is how they become more numerous. They are like a virus that spreads in all directions, destroying everything in its path. When the world falls, the progenitor will leave and move on to a new place. Your time in the Abyss is over, human. When you have questions, you know where to get answers. But not more than once a week. The human soul cannot bear separation from its world for long. You may cease to be human at all."

Cease to be human? My grandfather's last words came to me. He had no longer considered himself a man.

"Who was Valdemar Valevsky?" I shouted, pulling out three more essences. The Abyss understood my question correctly. The orbs disappeared, and before the space was again illuminated by bright light, I managed to hear:

"By mixing the power of the ancients with Skron, he became what the ancients called one of the infected. He no longer had a soul."

The light disappeared, and I found myself in the middle of a steppe filled with stone monsters. The creatures were running around nearby, tearing up the ground, as if trying to figure out where the source of their precious food had disappeared. The lithoids could not scream, but the way they froze and, realizing that I had returned, rushed towards me was akin to a joyful cry. The noise from the grinding stones was so loud that it was deafening.

The level twenty-five ousel was unleashed and I rushed towards the stone river. I was not going to run from them. On the contrary, I needed to check how the darkness affected the lithoids and how much time Kimal Sarento would have to finish off the monsters with his lightning.

The answer pleased me — five seconds. That was exactly how long the stones lasted before they began to crumble into a shapeless heap. During this time, the lithoid did not move, did not twitch, did not take any action at all. It simply stood and waited for its soul to finally separate from the stones and return to its progenitor. And I didn't even need to stand that close — all I had to do was hold the lithoid in my field for a second for it to start the process of self-destruction. However, I faced the same age-old problem — the radius of my influence was too small. Thirteen meters in each direction, which was a drop in the ocean now flowing towards the Valdez Clan. I looked at the development model again, but I did not find anything there that could somehow increase my aura. The only thing I could latch on to were several key parameters located on the development crystal, but even here there were limitations. By increasing the radius of my aura, they cut its effectiveness by almost three times. What was the point of having a level twenty-five if it was going to act like a level six on everyone else?

Instead, I had to harken back to my time training with the Evil Engineer and sprint, pushing myself nearly to the limit of my capabilities. Another discovery came unexpectedly — the mithril armor not only did not interfere, but also supported my sprint in every way, somehow managing to redistribute the load. Several times I could not resist and tested the stone monsters with mithril. The glove easily entered the bodies of frozen creatures, but did not pull any resources back out. I ignored the lithoids and *Devour*. As far as the little gemstone was concerned, there was nothing of value here.

In the two hours that the dark ones had allotted me, I managed to accomplish the main task: reaching the end of the stream moving toward the Valdez Clan. It was led by such a hulking behemoth that I doubted my aura would be able to reach the top. Evidently some sort of leader. However, my fears were not destined to come true: the stone monster tried to throw a boulder at me, missed and froze once it entered the radius of my aura. Only after I made sure that not a single living lithoid remained, I ran in the opposite direction. I wasn't even able to cut off the entire stream — only the very front. This would not stop the procession of stone monsters.

Surprisingly, I was wrong. When I returned to

the place where I had started my sprint, the lithoids were no longer there. Only some silhouettes were still visible on the horizon. Soon they disappeared too. The creatures, having lost their leader, were trying to return to the main river of rock. The stream that could have carried away the Valdez Clan had been cut off.

Suddenly, not far from where I was, a magical field flickered and disappeared, revealing to my eyes an active portal, a minotaur, and the misty temple servant who had dragged me to this location. I didn't even have words to describe the whole range of feelings that washed over me at that moment. The servant of the Temple of Skron hadn't run away, he had simply moved to another nearby portal to spectate as I destroyed the lithoids. Or as they destroyed me, which was completely feasible.

"The Temple of Skron desires to know where you disappeared to for almost five minutes?" The Temple servant started in on me right away.

"I think I've already said this, but I'll say it again — the Temple of Skron can desire whatever it wants. That is a prerogative and a right that no one can take away. However, just as you have the right to desire, I have the right not to desire. And now I'm seriously considering completely ending all relations with the Temple of Skron. Including removing the portal from Hearth. I always thought that we were partners, but I was wrong. Partners don't abandon each other on the steppes without explanation. You left me without cover, without information that you would be watching me from the side, without communication with the outside world, without information about what the stone creatures can do. The Temple of Skron acted as if I were its slave."

"The Temple of Skron acted with maximum efficiency, providing cover groups in case of an unforeseen situation. If Archduke Valevsky had known that he was being guarded, he would not have achieved the results that we see now. Clan Valdez is no longer in danger. However, the Temple of Skron did not receive an answer to its question. Where and how did you disappear for five minutes?"

Opening the map, I sighed heavily — we were not just far, but impossibly far from the border of the Kerux metropolitan area and the lands of the light. It would take me at least five days to get back to Hearth without a portal.

"The dark aura does not destroy the lithoids. It sends them back to their spawn point, from whence they once again set off on their rampage against all living beings. These beasts are reasonably intelligent — once they realized that they lost their leader, they returned to the main stream. How many such leaders and streams there are is the crucial question now. But one thing I know for certain: the lithoids are no threat to the light ones. Even if all the dark lands fall under the power of stone monsters, they will not come to us. Because I know a way to destroy them once and for all. To do what the first emperor of the Light lands failed to do seven hundred years ago. Instead of trying to negotiate with me, offering me good conditions and enticing me, the Temple of Skron starts interrogating me about my own personal affairs. About how I become stronger. This stone menace can not only be stopped, but completely destroyed. But I cannot do this alone, I need an assistant. And the only person who can help me is Kimal Sarento. Now I ask you to return me to Hearth — I need to prepare to destroy the forty-two infected rifts. Have you already agreed on a schedule with Eleanore?"

"These lithoids have not been destroyed?" If it were not for the fog, then amazement would have appeared on the faceless mannequin commonly referred to as the servant of the Temple of Skron.

"No. The darkness does not destroy the essence or, if you like, the soul of the stone creatures. It sends them back to their progenitor. The main ideological force behind this group. If you destroy it, there will be no stone monsters left."

"This couldn't be done seven hundred years ago. Why are you so sure that the opportunity is available now?"

"Because they didn't know the way to do it. I do. That's why I am sure that the lithoids won't stick their collective lack of nose in the affairs of the Light lands. They won't want to lose part of their life force. These creatures have intelligence, although not similar to human intelligence. But they know how to feel fear, and that is the main thing."

"What do you need Kimal Sarento for? The Temple of Skron can provide you with a much more powerful mage. Do you need lightning specifically, or will any element do?"

"I need Kimal Sarento specifically because he is the only one I can trust to watch my back. I will not trust any dark human you provide to me. Even if it is Two himself."

"We can involve the chancellor of the magical academy in Kerux. He is the only person known to possess a twelve-by-twelve magical field. There is no person in the world equal to him in strength."

"Are his stones level thirty or above? That's the thing, isn't it? They're not. All his abilities, unlimited mana and thousands of gallo enhancements won't make him someone who can destroy the lithoids. Magic stones of level thirty or higher are needed. Can the chancellor of the Kerux Magic Academy boast of such power?"

"No one alive can boast of this. Strengthening the stones to such a level requires resources that are mined from the thirtieth level of the rifts."

"I have laid out my conditions for destroying the lithoids, now it is up to the Temple of Skron to decide whether to accept them or act at its own discretion. Karina Fardi is quite enough to stop these creatures. Let her destroy the leaders. The ones heading the troops. If you want to get rid of this problem once and for all, you will have to attract additional forces. Hearth will gladly meet the Temple of Skron halfway. As I have already said, we are extremely interested in the speedy completion of construction, but without involving converts. And also, regarding that unpleasant incident that happened today — I believe that the Temple of Skron owes me, and I know exactly the thing that will do. Tomorrow I will be married to Naira Jode. I need the perfect gift for my future wife. What this will be is entirely up to you. Surprise me and my future wife, and then I will forget that the Temple of Skron tried to kill me by throwing me to be torn apart by the lithoids."

"How quickly can you come to terms with Kimal Sarento?"

"Me? I'm afraid you're mistaken, servant. I won't come to any terms with him. It's the dark ones who need to destroy the stone monsters. That little stream that invaded the Light lands will be stopped in a couple of days when I get to it. Involve Kimal Sarento, negotiate with him and give him to me for complete control. Then we will be able to destroy the stone creatures. I won't go and prostrate myself before the chancellor."

"The Temple of Skron has heard you. We'll need a few hours to organize everything. We won't return you to Hearth. There's no need for that. Our task is to save Kerux, and we're ready to do a lot for it. Construction in Hearth will be completed in three weeks. An additional mechanoid protection system that blocks catapult shells will be installed. It will form a protective dome around the city. The Temple of Skron will fully assume the resource provision of the construction. Is that enough to ensure your involvement?"

"Mine — yes. The issue is with Kimal Sarento. Without him, nothing will work."

"This issue is already being resolved. Kimal Sarento will be at the Temple of Skron in two hours. The lithoids must not only be stopped, but destroyed once and for all."

Condemned: Book Eight

Chapter 8

"WHERE IN THE WORLD did you drag me this time?" Kimal Sarento said as he stepped into the Temple of Skron six hours later. Also through a portal. The more I associated with the dark ones, the more I understood how bold and insolent they had become! Having an entire network of converts in the capital through which they provided portal transport at any time was already overstepping. At least there was one positive: the coordinator sitting in the capital would very soon lose the ability to communicate remotely with his masters. Twenty days left before the communication symbols disappeared. And then I would catch up and thoroughly mow down all the converts. As long as I wasn't declared a complete outlaw in the Zarak Empire by then. Although, if I installed a *Phantom* for myself, I wouldn't give a damn about that other. I'd pump that stone up so much that no security system and no piece of jewelry would be able to detect me. Only one thing was stopping me from taking such a step right now: I couldn't plug all the holes at once. The essence of a ruler was finding people to do all the work for you, so you don't have to do it yourself.

"The lithoids. The proposal is to go on a heroic mission to their lair."

"I hope not a suicide mission? I don't want a repeat of our trip to the offworlder lands."

"I would like to tell you that this time it will be a walk in the park, but I can't lie to you. I have no idea how everything will turn out. According to the information I have, we can destroy the lithoids without any problems or consequences. What will actually happen is a mystery. That's why I need you. Alone, of course, it's easier, but the advice and help of an experienced person in a difficult situation is worth a lot."

"Valevsky, flattering me? Is it that bad?" frowned Kimal Sarento. "Tell me everything. Preferably also about where you got the information about the lithoids. By the way, there is news — the northern region is almost half destroyed. At this rate, the lithoids will reach Hearth in five days."

"I don't think the Temple of Skron is a good place to discuss these topics. Any news from Count Vyazemsky or General Khabensky?"

"They haven't reached the north yet. For our hero of light to use the portal of the dark ones, he will need permission from the Pope himself, and even then Count Vyazemsky will think twice about whether or not he should comply. He and his team will only arrive tomorrow morning. As for his army, there's not much to say — they're moving at glacial speed and need at least three days to get to the pass."

"Which will become their grave, if we don't hurry." I unfolded the map that the Temple of Skron had provided. "The intel the dark ones provided shows that the mouth of the lithoid stream begins in these mountains. The nearest portal they can send us is here. They'll outfit us with horses there, but it is still at least two days' journey. All nearby settlements have already been destroyed."

"The portal is ready." Any further conversation was interrupted by the Temple of Skron. "Kimal Sarento, everything we agreed on has been fulfilled. Archduke Valevsky, two hundred work teams under the command of Five were sent to Hearth today. The Temple of Skron values cooperation and fully fulfills its obligations. Follow me."

The central region of the Kerux metropolitan area greeted us with a piercing wind. Here, autumn had not only come into its own, it had begun to give way to the approaching winter. Judging by the faces of the representatives of the Nazatil Clan, who ruled these lands, people were scared. They were afraid of the wave of lithoids passing far from them, but they could not leave their lands. The dark ones saw us as saviors. It was quite a frightening scene — for the entire time we spent on this clan's territory, I did not see a single human eye.

Only the darkness of Skron. And this darkness gazed upon the two light ones with hope.

We were not given an escort. All the converts were busy evacuating cities lying along the path of destruction. The most that the dark ones could do was to allocate us four horses. Two for riding now and two replacements. Kimal Sarento was silent for several hours, but during one of our stops, he stood in front of me and demanded:

"Speak. There are no extra ears here."

I had to tell him. I didn't go into detail about where I had gotten the information, but I didn't see fit to hide much either. I presented the situation as it was. Including about the darkness, and about lightning, and about the fact that seven hundred years ago my distant relative failed to complete this job.

"It's that simple?" Kimal Sarento frowned. "Darkness and lightning?"

"High-level darkness and high-level Lightning," I corrected. "I'm tempted to run *Analyze* to figure out how many elixirs you need, but I won't. Instead, I'll ask directly: what level is your *Lightning Strike*?"

"Do you have elixirs that can increase the levels of my stones?" He asked with interest.

"Yes, but in limited quantities. I lack recipes. Nevertheless, I can raise your stones to level thirty."

"That is fascinating to know, but I think, perhaps, I must decline this generous offer," frowned the chancellor. "Level thirty. What do you have against me, Maximilian, that you would like to lower the level of my stones?"

How I refrained from casting *Analyze* right there and then is beyond me. I'm proud of myself, actually. But I'm even more proud that I did not, like a sheep, ask a question that would never be answered. Something like "What level are you?" The chancellor would only laugh and joke at this question, once again casting me in a bad light.

"However, I can trade," Kimal Sarento said unexpectedly. "I can see from your face that you still haven't run *Analyze* on me, so I propose a trade. I inform you of my stone level, you tell me where you got the information. Since you didn't tell me about it in the Temple of Skron, the dark ones don't know about this method of fighting the lithoids. That means it's not them. Who, then?"

"I'm afraid I'm not that interested in your parameters. Now that you know everything, can we move on? Every minute of delay costs another human their life."

"Since when do you care about the dark ones?"

"I'm talking about the northern region of the Zarak Empire. And the dark ones are people too, really. The same as you and me. Except that they were unlucky in their patron god. You can't judge a person by their place of birth."

"You are a wellspring of wisdom, I see," grinned Kimal Sarento. "However, I am still interested in your source of information. How about a little friendly spar? One on one, the loser answers one question from the winner, fully and honestly.

You want to test your strength, don't you, Maximilian?"

"What are your terms? No holds barred?" I asked, hiding my excitement behind feigned malice. Kimal Sarento offered what I had wanted from the moment I got my hands on the mithril armor. How else could I test the maximum limit of Pharapho's flesh if not in a fight with one of the strongest mages in this world? If the chancellor was not being disingenuous, and he was unlikely to be sarcastic in such matters, then the level of his stones exceeds thirty. This meant that my *Golden Dome of Protection* would be swept away in a matter of seconds, no matter how much mana I put into it, and all hope would lie with the armor.

"You know my weak spot, Maximilian." Kimal Sorento even spread his arms out to the sides, bringing me to attention.

"Darkness?"

"Naturally! I'm afraid that if you activate your dark mirror, the fight will end before it even begins. It's unsportsmanlike. We're not going to test your specialty, are we? We're testing your pure strength? Magic against magic, defense against defense. No ousels from the depths of the rift. Essentially, everything is allowed except the dark aura."

Kimal Sarento was honest in this — he couldn't survive the high-level dark influence. The battle at the magic academy, when the Wave had gushed out of the rift, as well as the encounter with the metamorph, were evidence of this. It was unlikely that the rector played this off so beautifully for the public that he almost died in both cases. Everyone had a weak spot, and Kimal Sarento's particular weakness was the dark aura from the rifts. So in a real fight against the chancellor, I would always have a chance. As long as I could get close enough. As for the current offer... Damn it! I really wanted to test how well mithril armor could withstand stone magic!

"One question, answered truthfully and in full," I agreed.

"I suggest we step away from the horses, lest they get caught in the crossfire."

Five minutes later we were standing on relatively flat ground. The grass was knee-high, so running and jumping wouldn't be possible. And there was no need for that. We were planning to test not our dexterity, but the sheer power of our magic.

"On the count of three?" asked Kimal Sarento, stopping ten meters away from me. "Excellent. In that case, three!"

A thick beam of pure energy rushed towards me and, as I predicted, tore down my *Golden Dome of Protection* and zeroed out all my mana in a split second. The blue bar slowly began to fill back up, but I didn't care about such small fry. Because the mithril armor could handle his attack! Sure, I certainly felt it — the armor trembled, like a living creature caught in the cold. However, Pharapho's flesh had held steady against the attack that had turned the chancellor of the guard academy of his imperial majesty into a piece of charred meat.

"Wow, you're still standing." Kimal Sarento's voice sounded out and the flow of energy was interrupted. "Are you even breathing? Say something."

"I'm breathing. Is that all you've got?"

"That, young man, is the most infinitesimal taste of what I'm capable of. You don't think I plan to kill you with the first blow, do you? First, I needed to check how strong your defenses were. How am I going to heal you if I accidentally kill you? And I can't handle the lithoids alone. But now that I've seen your abilities, I won't hold back. Now you'll know the true power of Kimal Sarento!"

He extended his hand towards me, and at that moment I used *Dash*. The place where I had just been standing exploded, scattering pieces of earth in all directions. My armor began to tremble again. And this time quite noticeably. Kimal Sarento used not a stream of energy, but real lightning, which rushed like a snake with a broken back towards the place where I stood, searing everything it could reach along the way. Including me, despite my use of *Dash*. The ability failed me, and instead of finding myself next to the chancellor, I flew off to the side. When the world stopped tumbling, I stared at the *Armor Integrity* indicator that had suddenly appeared on the status bar. And it was no longer at one hundred percent! Moreover, every second of Kimal Sarento's attack decreased the bar by one! I tried to use *Dash* again to move to the side, but again the ability did not work. Or rather, it didn't work as planned — I was once again thrown off somewhere to the side. My *Armor Integrity* dropped below the halfway mark and continued to fall steadily.

"Stop!" I cried, raising my hand. I have to give credit to Kimal Sarento — he reacted instantly. The lightning disappeared, and I found myself in the middle of a huge clearing scorched until the ground had become hard as brick. The chancellor's real strength was truly colossal. But what saddened me most of all was the frozen *Armor Integrity* bar. It did not start automatically refilling! Either more time was needed for Pharapho's flesh to return to its previous condition, or some auxiliary materials would be required. For example, a piece of unprocessed mithril. But all these were small potatoes — the important fact was that my ultimate armor, which was supposed to withstand any misfortune of this world, in fact turned out to be just a strong adaptive piece of iron, which calmly held up the white flag when faced with a truly powerful opponent. Not so pleasant news, in fact, but good that I learned it now, in a duel against Kimal Sarento, and not, say, during a fight with the dark Magister Elor. The Orthodox certainly wouldn't have mercy on me.

"You know, Maximilian, I'm suddenly faced with a difficult decision, " Kimal Sarento said as he came closer. "I have two questions for you, and I'm equally interested in both of them. Where did you get the information about the stone monsters, and how are you still alive? For the first time in a long time, I used all the power available to me against another person. And for the first time in my experience, the creature against whom my full power was used did not turn to ash. Why? Even if we assume that you have several mithril items, it still doesn't add up. Lightning strikes across the entire area, penetrating even the tiniest cracks. But you're alive, and to be honest, this makes me a little nervous. What could have happened if you hadn't used *Dash,* but tried to reach me on foot? Lightning is not as effective in close combat as it is at a distance."

"It may backfire on the caster," I finished the chancellor's thought. "Yes, it was my mistake. Next time I will do just that. Damn it, I would never have thought that you were so strong. Of course, I knew that Kimal Sarento was an extremely complicated man, but such power…it frightens even me. I owe you an honest answer. Ask away."

"Skron be with your source," said Kimal Sarento decisively. "What is, is, and what difference does it make where it came from, right? But your armor…this is something unusual. Something that should not be so. What is it? And where are you hiding it?"

"My only armor is this," I replied and made the mithril armor visible. The clothes that looked like a ceremonial suit, as well as my permanently styled hair, turned into the chic and magnificent armor of the first emperor. Armor that not every emperor should wear, because not everyone is worthy of something of such value. A few moments later, the armor was back on, once again acquiring its familiar guise: a suit fine enough to attend a wedding in.

"I don't even know what to say," Kimal Sarento said after a long pause. "That's...I know that armor. The Temple of Skron once invited me to visit and handed it over, thinking that I was a descendant of the first emperor. To no avail — the armor did not recognize me. Which, I tell you, was quite a shame — I had big plans for the mithril. Actually, it was then, twenty years ago, that I committed perhaps the biggest blunder of my life — I told my partners, as they seemed to me then, about the mithril. The three counts you know. As practice shows, this was a mistake. Why did the armor recognize you? This is also part of the answer, Maximilian."

"Because I am a direct descendant of the first emperor. Although I believe the reason it recognized me was because it was passed down to me by right through assassination. My grandfather, Valdemar Valevsky, killed the first emperor. The Nameless, as he called him. Thus, he assumed possession of the mithril, but for some reason did not take it for himself. When I killed my grandfather, I received the right to do as I would with this set. As if it recognized me as its new owner. Mithril is not a gift of Light or Skron. You know how it is obtained, from the bone armor of the Pharapho sergeants. Mithril is the flesh of Pharapho. It is not metal — it is a particle of the foggy force that has settled in the Black Mountain. I think that sooner or later I will have to pay for using it. It has many limitations — higher entities of any power, be they aliens, lithoids, or even Skron or Light, are inert to this metal. They do not even notice it. It's good against humans, but you can't even go down into the rift with this thing — it lets any and all darkness seep through."

"Nevertheless, it was able to withstand my attack."

"The armor has a new *'Integrity'* parameter, which you have reduced by half. If I hadn't stopped you, there would have been no trace of the armor left, and I would have turned into ash, just as you said. The integrity has dropped to a certain point and will not rise. Apparently, the armor needs some kind of repairs."

"Most likely, you'll need unprocessed mithril," said Kimal Sarento. "So, all of your victories in battle have been due to the armor?"

"I received the armor a little over a week ago. Everything before then...What is that?"

"You hear it too?" The chancellor frowned. The space filled with a familiar, but extremely foreboding crunch of crushed rock. The progenitor of the lithoids had sensed that there was a dark settlement somewhere in this general area and had sent one of its streams to absorb all living things. Apparently, it was reacting to the portal. Incidentally, that was a point of interest — did the lithoids sense and react to portals? I'd have to check.

"That's the lithoids. So, Sir Chancellor, are you ready for a little show? The creatures stand motionless for five seconds. I'll try to be very fast, but try not to destroy me with lightning. My armor is already damaged."

"Let's try," Kimal Sarento climbed into the saddle. Noticing my puzzled look, he explained, "You don't think I'm going to run after you like a goat, do you? I'm not that old, young man. And there's no point in that. Unlike your aura, my magic works at a hundred meters. That will be more than enough to reach the lithoids and escape in time if something goes awry. Have I explained it clearly, or do you need more detail?"

"What do we do with these?" I nodded at the three horses that were tied to the tree. The animals were nervous — they weren't fond of the stone rumbling either.

"I'll take them with me," Kimal Sarento decided and tied the long reins of the three horses to his saddle. "Okay, let's set out. Unlike you, I've never seen stone giants before. I think it's time to satisfy my curiosity."

The process proved quite simple: the stone wave was moving in our direction. Taking a few deep breaths, pumping oxygen through my veins, I ran forward, gradually picking up speed. Thirteen meters. That wasn't enough. Still way too far. The next question I'd have to ask the Abyss is how to increase my aura. Surely there were ways to do that without using development crystals.

The terrible giant leading the army of lithoids forward noticed me from afar. Judging by the fact that the creatures stopped, they really were sentient. And they shared a common memory — they realized what was about to happen, and began to shoot stones at me, trying to stop me in my path! My mana had already been fully replenished, which allowed me to put up my *Golden Dome of Protection* again. If not for its ability to reflect objects, I would have been in trouble. I certainly hadn't expected such a coordinated attack. Hundreds, if not thousands of stones rushed in my direction. Mithril would, of course, protect me from such a rain, but I would be completely buried under the rubble. Now I ran forward, paying no attention to the falling boulders. That said, I still had to jump around a lot. I was constantly staggered by the particularly large stones ricocheting off my shield, which I failed to dodge, but this had little effect on my speed. The leader at the head of the stream stretched all its appendages in my direction and even tried to use something similar to magic, but acted too late — I was close to its side before it could get at me. The stone giant froze, struck by a dark aura, but I paid it no heed. Once the shower of stones stopped raining down upon me, I picked up even more speed, deftly maneuvering between the instantly hardening rocks.

A moment later, I made a discovery that would haunt my nightmares for the rest of my life — the stones could scream. As unbelievable as it might sound, they could scream! They did so because Kimal Sarento was following me, showing off his amplified *Lightning Strike* to the stone monsters. I didn't even have to ask the chancellor where he got the resources for pumping. The answer was so obvious that Kimal Sarento would have considered me a fool if I had managed to bring up the subject. The first emperor's *Devoir!* The magical inventory in which my distant ancestor, the only person to destroy a level fifty rift, kept his supplies. If the nameless emperor sucked up the rift's resources in the same way I do, then the level of Kimal Sarento's stones, at my most modest guess, was at least fifty. The maximum value available to magic stones. Moreover, the chancellor had several stones. For simple things like energy flow, as well as the ultimate *Lightning Strike* that had almost finished me off. A stone for all occasions.

The stone river shook threateningly. I hadn't managed to run even a kilometer before the monsters turned around and rushed back with all their inhuman speed. Back towards the main stream. The speed of the creatures was so great that Kimal Sarento began to lag — I could probably still compete with the lithoids, but they were not stupid animals that would die after ten minutes of such a mad race. I had to stop and wait for the chancellor. However, when Kimal Sarento rode closer, he looked quite pensive.

"What now?" I asked, expecting something bad. The chancellor's thoughtful face couldn't mean anything good.

"I think I've already said this, but I don't mind repeating myself: I often have the thought of finishing you off just to be on the safe side. Because the entire world order, on which our planet has been founded for thousands of years, goes to hell when I start working with you. Not to mention that this is the first time in my life I've ever heard a rock scream. Stones, screaming! Maximilian, could you ever have imagined such a thing? That was a nasty revelation for me too. But that's not what struck me. Screaming stones. Pfft! Big deal. What life really didn't prepare me for was that destroying lithoids would start increasing the level of the ability used for this! You see, young man, it just so happened that I have *Lightning Strike* pumped up to the maximum. To level fifty. It's impossible to go higher. Completely impossible. The parameters of the stone itself indicated that it had reached its maximum. But then you appear, and the entire harmonious system collapses. There is a level fifty-one! To achieve it, you need to destroy several million lithoids, but these are just details. Something that could not initially exist in this world, actually does! It's infuriating. Not just infuriating, it leads to extremely unpleasant trains of thought and decisions that must be made. And I have a question for you, young man. Just don't laugh at me or I'll kill you. Would you like to take me on as your pupil?"

Chapter 9

"PICK UP YOUR JAW. That expression is unbefitting of an Archduke. So what will be your positive response?"

"Pupil? You? Mine?" That was all I was capable of.

"Alright, Maximilian, stop playing the idiot. Yes, pupil. Yes, me. Yes, yours. What's so strange about it that you've suddenly turned into a country bumpkin entering the capital for the first time?"

"Everything! What do I have to teach you?!" No matter how hard I tried, I couldn't shake off my state of shock. I thought I'd seen everything in this life, but no! It still found ways to surprise me. And I couldn't say that I was always thrilled about this.

"It doesn't matter what you can teach me," Kimal Sarento's constant smile had long infuriated me. "What matters is what you can give me. I'm eighty-five years old, Maximilian. The runes that kept me young and long-lived are gone. In a year or two, I'll start aging rapidly — the consequences of using borrowed power haven't gone away. Everything must be paid for. So I suddenly realized that my life was approaching an end point. It couldn't be avoided, so the only question was how to approach that point. Should I moan and groan, run around waving my arms, or should I enjoy the last of my allotted time and visit places I didn't even know existed? What didn't I see at the academy? Students? Teachers? More underhanded games? I'm sick of it. With you, it's a completely different matter. Offworlders. Lithoids. Ancient people. The heir to the first emperor, after all! If I put this on one side of the scale and what awaits me on the other, of course I would like to choose the first. A vivid, crazy life in lieu of one of dull routine, waiting for death. The only thing that makes me happy is that the runes I used for my appearance did not require human sacrifice. Otherwise, the consequences could have been even worse. I suppose Magister Meram has already told you that he has a month or two left to live?"

"He hasn't told me anything," I muttered, still struck by the chancellor's proposal.

"You can investigate further at your own discretion," said Kimal. "I suppose he was released from the Temple of Skron not because the dark ones are such kind souls and always keep their word, but because there is no point in keeping a person who will soon die from physical exhaustion. Moreover, a delayed death is much more terrible than an instant one. When you know that your body is decaying...Ugh! For a second I imagined that it might affect me too. Although, I admit, I still don't understand why Meram is still in Hearth. He has his own house — huge, luxurious. What is he doing at your construction site of a city?"

"Rune magic is gone, but not symbolic magic. My grandfather used it to activate portals. Of course, I was told right away that there was no way to extend a life with symbolic magic, but it seems to me that Meram has not given up hope of coming up with something. No matter how you look at it, he has a lot of personal development. That's why he is still in Kostrishche. Waiting for me to finally return and be able to have a heart-to-heart with him. With all these lithoids and infected rifts, it has been hard to find the time."

"So that's what it is," Kimal Sarento said thoughtfully. "The cunning viper doesn't want to die and is looking for ways to save himself. But what do you need from him?"

"Resources. Over the years, Meram has no doubt collected a ton of stuff. I want to take it all."

"There it is! I knew you had a noble goal, worthy of the ruler of an autonomous city! No selfish sense of humanity. So what do you say, Archduke Valevsky? Will you take me on as your apprentice?"

"It's not so simple. What will happen to the

magical academy? From what I understand, as my pupil, you want to be by my side at all times. Through all my wanderings. Who will manage the academy, your brainchild?"

"What a perceptive young man. You can tell right away that he is a mentor," Kimal Sarento openly mocked me. "That's right. I truly am interested in following you, wherever fate leads you — except the rifts, of course. I am no longer at the age to acclimatize. You can handle those campaigns on your own. As for the magical academy, I have already given it forty years of my life. It's time to retire. Magister Tarra Lloyd is perfectly capable of handling the academy affairs. I have been preparing her for this moment for a long time, I knew that sooner or later I would get bored of sitting in one place, so nothing will happen to the magical academy of the Zarak Empire."

"Becoming a pupil implies complete openness on the part of the pupil toward his mentor. Are you ready to comply?"

"As if you don't already know everything about me," scoffed Kimal Sarento. "Alright, maybe you actually have kept true to your word and haven't run *Analyze* on me. In any case, in that notebook of yours that is synchronized with the entire world, there is not a word about me. For that alone you can be respected. Yes, Maximilian, I am ready to be open. I have explained the motives for my actions. The advantages that you will receive from me becoming your pupil require no explication, I believe. Information, connections, experience."

Kimal Sarento was so convincing that I began to doubt his sincerity. Not this man.

"Okay, what's the catch? I know there is one. There has to be, otherwise I'll be disappointed in the great Kimal Sarento. Yes, I'll take you as my pupil. I'll open your status bar, the ability just refreshed again, but I have to know the real reason behind your actions. All these beautiful words about old age are, of course, captivating and may contain a kernel of truth, but only a kernel. In all the time that I've known you, I've realized one thing: Kimal Sarento never does anything for no reason. Never. There is something else, and I have to know it. Here and now."

"So you'll take me on as your pupil, and we'll officially announce it to the world?" Kimal Sarento asked with a squint.

"If I find out your real motivations, yes. For now — no. I don't want to take on a pupil who just decided he wanted to have some fun in his old age."

"You're evil, Maximilian. Yes, there is another reason why I would like to take you on as a mentor. And this reason is Magister Elor. After our spar, it became clear to me that you are capable of standing up for yourself, so you shouldn't have any problems with him."

"The head of the Dark Orthodoxy?" This was unexpected. "What does he have to do with this?"

"Well...It's funny how difficult it can be to talk about your mistakes. Remember Karina Fardi's beautiful finale in the Citadel? Fire, the coming of

Skron, general panic, the heroism of a single rift conqueror? This was a joint project I had with Magister Elor. I never liked the Citadel, so I decided to significantly weaken them with the help of the dark ones. In principle, it worked. The cardinals died out, two commanders went to meet their beloved Light, a whole group of clerics will never torture ordinary people again. An ideal result, with one small drawback: the new Fardi was born. It was planned that she would simply be a strong dark human, who would never let you live in peace, forcing you to constantly evolve, but fate decided otherwise. After this occurred, Magister Elor announced that from now on our paths must diverge and that our next meeting will be my last. Which, oddly enough, I have almost no doubt about. Yes, I am a stronger mage, but he has darkness on his side, against which I have no response. Some random convert with an ousel could send me to my eternal slumber — and that is the last the world will hear of Kimal Sarento."

"I still don't understand what part I have to play in this."

"The Orthodox, young man, are very sensitive to tradition. You can't touch a pupil while he has a mentor. If you have any complaints about a pupil, you must talk to their mentor. Having become your pupil, I will turn Magister Elor's attack on you."

"Well that's just fantastic!" My shock gave way to anger. "So you decided to expose me to attack at his hands again?"

"What do you mean, 'decided?' You're on his kill list anyway. Didn't Magister Elor practically murder your Alia? As I said, the Orthodox will solve issues with the mentors first. At that point, your mentor was Magister Meram, against whom Magister Elor could not lift a finger. That is why he didn't touch you and instead destroyed those who were near you. Now that your apprenticeship with Magister Meram is over, Magister Elor will have his eyes on you. He will try to kill you one way or another. That is his goal. You will lose nothing by taking me on as a pupil. You stand only to gain!"

"A headache, a powerful enemy, the hatred of almost the entire Zarak Empire," I muttered, realizing what Kimal Sarento was signing me up for.

"Intel, intel and more intel. Everything else is insignificant. Connections, dependent people, resources — all this is vanity compared to information."

"Your story is nice and all, except for one thing. I opened Alia's status bar, making her my pupil. Nevertheless, Elor attacked her. Tradition didn't stop him."

"Alia is your pupil?" The sincere surprise on Kimal Sarento's face did not look feigned. "What interesting news. Does anyone else besides the two of you know about this? Have you registered your relationship somewhere?"

"No," I said, surprised.

"In that case, how would Magister Elor know that she was under your protection? It's not written on her face. Understand, Maximilian, there is no third party in this matter and there cannot be. Either you inform the whole world about your relationship, or you can't be surprised that no one knows about it. What happened to Alia might not have happened if you had informed society about it in a timely manner. I, for instance, do not intend to make such a mistake. As soon as we return from this campaign, I will herald my new status to the entire empire."

"But you understand that by becoming my pupil, you will become the object of close attention from all sorts of forces? The clergy, the Temple of Skron, the entire Zarak Empire, Padishah Bayazid the Third. A whole bunch of people want nothing more than to destroy me."

"Now imagine their faces when they find out who has become your pupil," Kimal Sarento grinned. "Without false modesty, I am the most powerful mage in this world. Well, the most powerful among all the mages I know, because now a new level of magic stone has opened up to me. What if there are creatures somewhere for whom level fifty-one stones are a commonplace thing? Can we rule that out? Of course we can't. But for everyone you just listed, I am a serious force to be reckoned with. And this force will be on your side. A reasonable question arises: will General Khabensky decide to send his army to Hearth, having learned of my new status? Or will the Nocturnal Guild take revenge for your very demonstrative visit to their lair? The capital started boiling before you even left their base."

"Okay, then there's still one more important issue to resolve. The notebooks and how we will synchronize them. And I'm not talking about the fake artifacts designed to confuse. I'm talking about the real ones."

Kimal Sarento's cheek twitched. Apparently, he had forgotten this detail when he offered to become my pupil. Or he was making a deliberate show of his emotions in order to then humbly agree to my conditions, which was also a distinct possibility.

"Dual integration?" he said after a long pause. It was as if he was wringing the words from my body, which made me chuckle.

"So this is what awaits me? Constantly monitoring your facial expressions and analyzing whether they are natural or feigned? My dear Count Sarento, why would I subject myself to that?"

"Because that is the key to survival in this dog-eat-dog world you find yourself in. As a simple baron, piddling his life away in Skron knows what province, you were of no interest to anyone. Now that you are the Archduke of the first autonomous city in history, whether you like it or not, you will have to learn to communicate with the sharks that eat runts like you for breakfast. Monitoring facial expressions, gestures, behavior. Constant analysis of the situation. Incessant collection of information about your opponents and especially about your partners. If you do none of this, sooner or later you will be destroyed. As will everyone near and dear to you."

"So our discipleship will be mutual?"

"Closer to one-sided, but we won't focus on that. To the rest of the world, you are my mentor. And I am really interested in visiting the places where fate will take you. Including...Are they back already?"

Judging by the rumble of stones, the lithoids had regrouped and, finding that we were no longer in pursuit, calmed down. They must have decided that everything that had happened was pure accident, that we had long since gone about our business, and that now no one would stop them from finally reaching the settlement of pathetic humans and gobbling up everyone in sight.

"So?" Kimal Sarento turned his gaze back to me. "Are you ready to delve into a hidden world of discoveries by becoming my mentor?"

"For those of us who still have things to discover about this world," I muttered. "Are you ready to receive your status bar? Or do you already have one? Without it, I cannot make you my pupil."

"I'm ready. And I definitely don't have any of your dark gadgetry. Magister Elor once offered, but his conditions for installing it were such that I had to refuse. When can we do this?"

"Right here and now. Give me your hand! Henceforth, I Archduke Maximilian Valevsky, Hunter of Darkness, take you, Count Sarento, as my pupil. As the Light is my witness!"

"As the Light is my witness," repeated Kimal Sarento and his eyes widened from the monstrous pain. He wheezed and sank to the ground. The binding took only ten seconds, but it was enough for the man to experience all the charm of the process. I had a full description of my new pupil, but the approaching rumble of stone monsters did not allow me to calmly peruse the data I had sought for so long. The chancellor's parameters should be read in a calmer atmosphere, over a glass of good wine. It was certain to be as thrilling as an action novel.

"I've always wondered why students can't stand this process," said Kimal Sarento. "Until now, I've only been on the other side of the process, but now I realize that I was being sarcastic about my lazy students in vain. Not the most enjoyable endeavor."

"You have never been a pupil? How did you study magic?"

"I should clarify: I have not been the pupil of any specific mentor. I've had plenty of teachers. Magister Meram, for example. But for someone to bear full responsibility for me — this has never happened in all my eighty-five years."

"Enough, we'll talk later." I looked at the approaching lithoids. These creatures weren't here by chance — they were moving purposefully toward us. Not toward the dark settlement. The progenitor had recognized the danger and sought to destroy it. Because it wasn't a small offshoot moving towards us, but a full-flowing river of rock, at least two hundred meters wide.

"Where are we going to bury you all?" I muttered, realizing what I was about to face. I hadn't expected such a landslide. And these weren't the common rock beasts that the Wall's defenders had drawn. Huge monsters were coming our way, somewhat reminiscent of the ones who had led previous streams. The elite of the stone army. In any case, I was pleased to think so. Because it was always nice when you found an easy way to destroy terrible creatures, essentially while putting in zero effort. And I didn't have to put any effort in now either. *Dash*ing away from Kimal Sarento, so that he wouldn't accidentally be hit by a stone block from above, I rushed to meet the army. The creatures froze with the same ease as before, only to immediately crumble to the ground as lifeless boulders — my pupil's lightning...damn it the words sounded so strange! Basically, my pupil's lightning left the lithoids without a single chance of returning to the progenitor's bosom. At some point, they even stopped throwing stones at me, trying to catch me with the tendrils they called arms, but how could an elephant catch a fly? I rushed between the monsters in a flash, deftly maneuvering between the statues. Their attack had been cut off at the neck before it ever truly began. The rocks again faltered and turned around, getting away. The progenitor understood that something was happening, but could not even figure out what exactly. Because the information did not reach it. It was simply becoming weaker. Just a little, drop by drop, but noticeably.

"Adeline contacted me," Kimal Sarento rode up

to me as the stone monsters fled, handing me the reins of his horse. "The northern region is in chaos. No one can fight back the creatures. They are slaughtering city after city. I fear that if we do not hurry, there will be no more people in the north of the Zarak Empire."

"Didn't your wife return to her clan?" I jumped on my horse and, checking the map, set off on a direct route to the probable place that the progenitor would reside.

"She had to come back. I needed eyes and ears. I have two groups working in the northern region, they pass on information to Adeline, and she passes it on to me. Count Vyazemsky still managed to get into place in a short time. Apparently, they drove the horses practically to death. Twenty mages launched into battle, three managed to escape. Unfortunately, including Count Vyazemsky himself."

"And the army?"

"They need a minimum of three days to take up their positions at the pass, but if we are to believe the intelligence we have received, the lithoids will arrive much earlier. Count Vyazemsky is being chased. I believe you can already see for yourself how fast these creatures are. There are no details yet, but they fled towards the gorge that connects the northern region with the central one. From there it is a day's journey to Hearth."

"Those bastards," I cursed, referring to Count Vyazemsky and all his henchmen. "They could have just died."

"I sincerely hope that they do, but the fact remains that the lithoids know about the gorge. The progenitor, as I see it, is a rather clever creature. It tries to cover all the space it can. Considering that only the vanguard, the most mobile and fastest, broke through the Wall, they will be near the Hearth much earlier than in a day. I give it twelve hours at most."

"I'm not too happy about your estimations." My cheek twitched.

"You know, mentor," Kimal Sarento said, emphasizing the last word, "it doesn't matter what makes you happy or not. What matters most is how you react. You have to assume the worst. Twelve hours. That's how much time we have. If it takes them longer, great! It's always nice to be wrong. But you have to evaluate your opponent's actions from the worst-case scenario."

"Even if we go back, they won't open the portal for us." Anger began to boil in my chest.

"They won't. We were sent, if not to destroy, then to significantly slow the lithoids down. Perhaps we are succeeding. Perhaps all the forces of the monsters are moving towards us now to grind us into dust. Without information, we must rely on what we see and hear."

"Nonetheless, we need to operate on the fact that we have twelve hours at most," I said.

"That's right. In any situation, Maximilian, you must have at least two plans. One is the most desirable situation, the other is what will happen if everything that can go wrong does. The one where the enemy is orders of magnitude stronger than you assumed. This requires a lot more mental and temporal resources, but if you don't learn to have at least two plans, you will never be the ruler of a city."

"We won't be able to get to the progenitor in twelve hours," I checked the map again.

"What prevents us from doing so?"

"Our speed."

"Our speed or the speed of these lovely little horses? You see my development model. I can run for a long time. A very long time. And quite fast."

My heart started beating wildly when I finally opened the parameters of my new student. What could I say but...Kimal Sarento was a monster. A real one! Similar to old man Meram, the chancellor had pumped up his development model as much as possible, devouring twenty gallos a year and investing development points in all necessary parameters. Magic power, normal strength, agility, endurance. Over eighty-five years, the chancellor had opened up a huge number of key parameters for himself, leveling them up to somewhere around one hundred percent, and somewhere around one hundred units. As for the magic field...

"Ten-by-ten...Considering how much one elixir costs to level up, I'm afraid to even ask what it was you were offering the Temple of Skron."

"Oh don't be afraid, go ahead and ask." He couldn't hold back his sarcasm. "I supplied the dark ones with equipment that is produced in the Fortress. In the Citadel, actually, but that doesn't change anything. Equipment that creates elixirs, in exchange for these very elixirs. It's simple."

"I've always wondered why the dark ones couldn't set up production of equipment for elixirs themselves. The security system they installed in Hearth alone is worth something!"

"If you find an answer to this question, be sure to share it. I, for one, don't know. I supplied the dark ones with equipment, but it was constantly breaking down and malfunctioning. They couldn't service it. No one can, except for the servants of the Light in black robes. No matter how many times I asked this question to both the previous High Priest and the current one, I never received an answer."

"The previous High Priest? Did you know him?"

"Of course. Father Locke was a fascinating man. It's a pity that his reign was so short-lived. They say that during the change of power even the Inquisitor had to intervene. But I'm not certain this is so — I was not in the city then, I do not know the details."

"Father Locke is alive and in Hearth. I took him from a cage in the Nocturnal Guild lair, along with Miralda Lertan. But that's not even the funniest part, my frowning pupil. The funniest part is that he was put in this cage by a man who calls himself Coordinator Number Fourteen. The one who appoints a new trio of killer leaders every nine months, recording all the appointments in a special notebook that has been kept since the founding of the Nocturnal Guild. I saw this notebook, I saw the handwriting. As for Father Locke himself, my still-frowning pupil, this fascinating man was listed in the log book of the leaders of the Nocturnal Guild as Coordinator Number Thirteen. But twenty years ago, power changed hands."

"You know, coming from your mouth, 'pupil' sounds like an insult," Kimal Sarento grimaced. "As for what you just told me, I can say one thing: Hearth is not just in big trouble, it's facing complete catastrophe. If the lithoids don't destroy your city in twelve hours, then the High Priest will do it within twenty-four. I have never seen a more vindictive and dangerous enemy in my life. And another thing…mentor — Alia is his adopted daughter. Father Urg raised her from the age of three, instilling the idea of his own infallibility. I don't want to accuse anyone in advance, but in the next six months I would not turn my back on your personal attendant. Because Father Urg will strike with the weapon you worry least about. And he most certainly will strike."

"So we need to strike first. Alright, let the horses go, we'll do the rest ourselves. The animals are only holding us back. I'll take the water and food. The mithril armor allows me to reduce their weight. Ready? Then let's go. The lithoids won't kill themselves, and we still have to go back and pay someone else a formal visit. I have a long list of questions I've been meaning to ask Father Urg for quite some time now."

Chapter 10

"THIS MUST BE SOME KIND of nightmare," I muttered, nearly collapsing to the ground. *Heal* allowed me to ignore the fatigue, but it pushed me to the limit mentally. We did the impossible — in six hours we managed to cover a distance that would have taken a couple of days at a normal pace. As we approached our goal, the number of lithoids increased. The previous two hours had turned from a race against the clock into a genocide. We mowed down lithoids, not even by the hundreds, but by the thousands! Kimal Sarento could not only move quickly, he could also cast his lightning with perfect accuracy well while running, so the main problem I faced was avoiding getting hit by his branching lightning. I had to squeeze the last drop of energy out of myself in order to dodge and remain in the heat of battle. In fact, the constant vigilance exhausted me to the limit, transforming me into a weak-willed vegetable.

"Get up, lazybones, there aren't that many left," Kimal Sarento said heavily. He was holding up well, of course, but his breathing gave him away. According to the map, we had to run another ten kilometers to reach our destination. Or, at least, to the point that the dark scouts had indicated to us. Kimal Sarento was making full use of his new abilities. The status bar, from what I could tell, had made him the happiest man in the world. While at first he was skeptical about all these "immaterial" things, the more he immersed himself in the functionality, the giddier he became. For example, he used the map constantly. Especially after I data dumped all the maps of the dark lands on him. Without the unnecessary addition of the rift locations, of course. Why would he need those?

"You know, I've even started to wonder if there will ever be an end to these lithoids. I have a feeling that more will come." I looked up at the mountain of stone surrounding us. This was all that remained of the next wave of lithoids that came to apprehend us. The progenitor had clearly begun to suspect something terrible was going on, since his army's attacks had continued without interruption. It had reached the point that Adeline reported that the lithoids in the northern region had begun to act strangely. They had ceased their onslaught, and instead of continuing to pursue Count Vyazemsky and finish the bastard off, quickly rushed back. The progenitor was pulling together all available forces to protect its own soon-to-be corpse.

Another rumble of stones told me that I needed to get up and meet the next batch. With a groan more characteristic of an old man than an almost nineteen-year-old boy, I rose to my feet and frowned. Apparently, the lithoids had decided to go on the final offensive. What was moving towards us could only be called a mountain — a very tall and wide body of rock accompanied by almost a hundred leaders. Perhaps if this mountain got close to Hearth, then nothing would remain of my city — it would crush me and not even notice. But it was not only the size of the living mountain that was most impressive — a dark cloud hung above it, in which lightning flashed. The thing approaching us wielded magic.

"What an interesting specimen," Kimal Sarento stood next to me. "I believe, young mentor, that our great race is over. What is approaching cannot be a simple monster. I believe that this is the very same progenitor of the lithoids, who grants them all strength. Are you ready for the final battle?"

My moral fatigue disappeared as if by magic. The approaching landslide was still far away — several kilometers, but even now the full power of the leader of the lithoids was becoming clear. It is not surprising that my ancestor had not succeeded — it was impossible to destroy such a carcass. The first emperor had already performed a heroic deed by managing to drive it into a pen.

Even if only for seven hundred years. Running the calculations, I smiled. The radius of my dark aura was insufficient even to break through the initial layer of stones. I would jump like a flea on an elephant, trying to gnaw through a bit more flesh.

"Any ideas on how to destroy it?" I asked, surprised to find myself trembling nervously. The looming mountain was overwhelming.

"How would I know? You were the one who met the offworlders, not me." From the tension in his voice, I could tell that Kimal Sarento was also nervous. It wasn't every day that you got to meet one of the leading forces of this world. Even if it was the weakest of all thirteen alien forces. Or twelve, if you didn't count the offworlders.

"Then I suggest we first finish with the small fry so they don't get in the way, and then deal with the main mountain."

"By small fry, do you mean the hundred-strong five-meter-tall stone goliaths over there?" Kimal Sarento turned in my direction, surprised by my calm demeanor. "Are you saying that you have a plan?"

"Of course I do," I replied honestly. "But in order to implement it, we need to get rid of the small fry."

"Okay, let's get rid of the small fry," Kimal Sarento agreed, not insisting that I tell him my wild idea. Which, if I thought about it, truly was wild.

Where had this second gust of wind in my sails come from? The excitement of the upcoming battle was stirring in my body, and, having finally made a decision on what to do, I rushed forward. The progenitor immediately responded — dark clots of some nasty substance flew at me. Disgusting. Something I most assuredly did not want anywhere near me. The shells were forming somewhere on the top of the mountain and looked like classic fireballs. Only they were a deep, inky black. My brain switched off to save me from panic — when the first one crashed into me, popping my *Golden Dome of Protection* like a soap bubble, I realized what the mountain was throwing at me. Dark flame! That was what the lithoids had brought into this world! A terrible weapon, against which there is practically no defense.

But "practically" doesn't mean "none at all." For I was maybe the only human who was not afraid of the dark. The mithril easily dealt with the attacks of the inferior entity. The flesh of Pharapho saw the progenitor's creation as something insignificant, and even the monstrous power that was embedded in the dark flame and formed a huge scorched space around me was not able to harm my mithril armor. It didn't even touch the *Armor Integrity*!

The progenitor's stone army rushed toward me, but Kimal Sarento wanted to have a word with them first. The creatures froze in my aura and immediately fell to the ground. Several dark orbs flew at the chancellor (I had the feeling that I would never get used to calling Kimal Sarento my pupil), but he deftly dodged them, casting lightning unceasingly as he did. And then something happened that forced me to reconsider our battle tactics: reinforcements arrived. In a matter of moments, we had destroyed more than half of the enormous "commanders," but then the surface of the mountain began to undulate as if it was alive, and a new wave of monsters poured out of it. The progenitor did not simply spawn his army, giving part of its power to lifeless stones — it gave part of itself! All the lithoids that ran around our world were essentially one whole! They were all the progenitor!

This realization almost threw me off kilter. Unlike the main mountain hucking black fire, its brainchildren used more banal techniques, namely throwing stones. I had to remember my agility training as I dodged the dark clots, as I needed *Golden Dome of Protection* to reflect the stones.

The "dance," as Gustav liked to call it, had begun. I determinedly crawled forward, moving from one large creature to another, Kimal Sarento filled the space with lightning, destroying the souls of the lithoids, the Progenitor gave birth to new creatures and did not decrease even a fraction of an inch in size. It would probably be possible to calculate how many hundreds of thousands of large lithoids needed to be created to reduce the volume of the mountain at least by half, but I was not up to complex mathematical calculations. Having found a gap in the formation, I rushed forward, deftly slipped between two frozen creatures, deflected several dozen stones and, making a leap that would make most people say, "humans can't do that," I forced my way up the mountain.

The whole area trembled — the progenitor had felt the effects of the level twenty-five ousel on its own skin. The stones on which I stood began to roll down, as if they had lost their connection with the mountain. Huge boulders threatened to bury me alive, but my training with the Evil Engineer once again proved its worth. The stones under me went in one direction, and I pushed on in the hopes of getting closer to the source of black magic. But it was not easy, even with my enhanced agility and dexterity. With each step the avalanche became more powerful. Eventually I realized that I was moving in place, jumping over the stones with inhuman speed. But none of my efforts were bringing me closer to my goal. They were spent simply trying to maintain my position.

The revelation of what I must do didn't dawn on me instantly, but I made it there in the end. I switched off my dark aura. The trembling ended abruptly as the progenitor stopped twitching and sloughing off its "dead skin." The black flame strikes became more active again — an orb crashed into me almost every second. The stones I was jumping on started moving again, only this time they didn't roll down, but turned into lithoids. Paws sprouted from them and tried to grab me to slow me down, but even this entourage didn't stop me from purposefully moving towards my goal — a dark cloud on top of the mountain. The place where, in theory, the progenitor's brain was located.

But could such a beast as this have a brain? Surely it must formulate thoughts somehow?

I guessed wrong! When I reached the top, I found myself on a flat plateau the size of the central square in Hearth. There were still at least thirty meters left to the cloud above my head, but it was absolutely impossible to get there. The top of the progenitor seemed to have been shorn off by a huge sword, that was how flat it was. Not a single pebble, not a single ledge that I could climb and try to reach the cloud with my aura. However, the cloud faded into the back of my mind when I noticed what was in the center of the flat area. A mouth. An actual mouth! Some dark clots periodically fell into it from the cloud, which the progenitor chewed and spat out at me in the form of a dark flame. Moreover, he spat them out from somewhere below — the clots rose along a strange trajectory and fell on me, ineffectively flowing down my armor.

Looking at the cloud again, then at the spot where Kimal Sarento should be, then back at the cloud again, I raced forward. The original plan, as expected, was not working. If the cloud was the progenitor's brain, it was well protected. But were its insides just as well fortified?

I knew that what I was about to do was closer to madness than reason. No one in good mental health would think to climb into the mouth of a huge monster. But I didn't see any other way to get to the vital organs of the twelfth most powerful creature in this world. Once again, I activated my dark aura, and the progenitor twitched. This time, the stones had nowhere to roll. The edges of the plateau began to collapse, but I was already too close to the center to pay attention. Another black clot fell into the monster's mouth, and, gulping, I dived after it. The stone gullet shrank, trying to crush me like a bug, but *Golden Dome of Protection* showed its might, in all its glory. The stones cracked, crumbled and broke, but they could not get through the barrier. Moreover, the stones themselves were already lifeless — the dark aura destroyed any hint of life.

The Progenitor jerked once more, and the space beneath me disappeared. Waving my arms, trying to grab hold of at least something, I flew down. There was impenetrable darkness all around, but soon it dissipated into a gloomy, bloody light. My hand caught on some ledge. I hung there and immediately struck the rocks with my other hand, creating a support ledge for myself. Arching my head, I saw the pulsating sphere far below that was the source of the dismal lighting. Dark lightning ran across the sphere, dark clots of flame flew off. If I was looking for some sort of vital life center within the progenitor, I couldn't place a better bet than this.

The dark aura didn't reach the sphere, so I had to descend. I had no desire to land on this bloody sphere. It looked too creepy. The progenitor was going crazy — the space was shaking as if the mountain had gone mad and was running around like a chicken with its head cut off. At times, I was moving more horizontally than I was vertically, as if the creature had fallen on its side. This allowed me to detach myself from the rocks and approach the bloody sphere with a few jumps. The dark aura finally reached it, plunged inside and...there was an explosion.

I was stunned. Maybe even concussed. The *Heal* I kept pouring into myself was of little help for some reason. The dust settled, and I realized that I was lying on the rocks under the blue sky. The explosion of the bloody sphere had torn the progenitor into several pieces, but it had not killed it! Judging by the fact that the rocks continued to move, there was still some life left in them. One of the lithoids rushed towards me, but stopped abruptly after falling within my aura. And then it crumbled into pebbles as a bolt of lightning crashed into it.

"There's some power source lying twenty meters away from you! You must finish your task!" I heard Kimal Sarento scream, which sounded like it was coming from a deep well. It was hard to move, but the chancellor's insistent demands, shouted over and over again, were infuriating. The only way to get rid of this muffled scream was to do what was required of me. Maybe this would at least shut him up.

Turning over onto my belly, I crawled forward. I couldn't get up. Despite the protection offered by my dome and armor, I had still taken a pretty heavy blow. My brain couldn't even fathom what was happening. Where was I? Who was I? What was I? No — if I strained, I could answer all these questions, but it would take a lot more effort than usual. Another bolt of lightning flashed, space twitched again, as if trying to fold itself into another dimension, and then everything went silent.

"Remove your aura so that I can come closer!" The incessantly irritating man did not let me rest. I had to obey this time too. For some reason, lying on my stomach was painful, so I rolled over onto my back, almost losing consciousness from the pain that overcame me, and peered through the fog in my eyes at the approaching Kimal Sarento. My pupil (Oh! For the first time I calmly called him a pupil without that feeling in my gut) was quite a sight. He was completely gray from the dust, and only his eyes stood out from his face.

"You alive?" he asked.

"Doubtful," I replied. Or rather, I tried to reply, but didn't have the strength to do so. Instead of words, a groan came out, and then a cough. My lungs were burning, and I had to urgently cast *Heal* on myself again. It helped — only very slightly, but it helped.

"You don't look so good," Kimal said as he approached. The thick layer of dust on his face didn't mask his sincere concern.

"Is it that bad?" I wanted to ask, but again only wheezing came out.

"Don't waste your strength, you'll need it later," he said and picked me up. A wave of sharp pain ran through my body, which I had to relieve with *Heal.* My body was acting strangely. It seemed like there was no damage, but at the same time I felt as if I had been put through a meat grinder. Several times.

"Alright, I see that you're trying to make your face into a frown, so I'll explain what's going on. You have barely a memory left of your mithril armor. It hangs on you in shreds. Only the belt and part of the chestplate remain. Everything else is destroyed. Along with your limbs as well, most likely, but you have already restored them. Your body is now one big burn. Which cannot be removed by your *Heal.* It looks like you were dipped in a vat of dark fire and thoroughly boiled. The damage is apparently not only on the outside, but also on the inside. That is why you cannot speak. Do not close your eyes, dear man. You are strictly forbidden to sleep now. How you are still alive, I cannot say. Apparently, you are holding yourself in this plane by constantly using *Heal.* The only chance to get you out is to urgently deliver you to the Bartolomeo Clan. As far as I know, they are the only ones who have a device that eliminates the effects of the dark flame. But we still have to get to them. So don't stop healing yourself. Heal, Maximilian. Your life depends on it."

"Look!" I croaked. Again, it came out as unintelligible, but Kimal Sarento understood me. He switched to a light trot, holding me in such a way that I did not feel his footfalls at all.

"I already checked — there was nothing there. The progenitor vanished without leaving anything behind. At least, *Devour* didn't find anything. Maybe if we passed over it with the mithril gloves, we could get something, but where are we going to get a set of gloves now? Yours are gone, I don't have any yet. So all we can do now is hastily get back to the Bartolomeo Clan. Adeline has already been warned, they will be waiting for you. Don't you dare croak along the way. *Heal,* Maximilian, don't stop casting *Heal.* And don't you close your eyes! We have plenty of fun adventures awaiting us, you must not die now."

* * *

The Kerux Metropolitan Area, central territory

Kimal Sarento ran towards the nearest settlement of dark humans, periodically glancing at his load. Maximilian was in a semi-delirious state, balancing on the edge of life and death. Any ordinary person left in the condition this young man had been after the battle with the progenitor of the lithoids would not live, but this one held on. He wheezed, suffered greatly, but continued to restore his dying body. The dark fire that had since disappeared from this world had used its last hurrah on the young archduke, turning him into a piece of burnt meat. Maximilian managed to restore his arms and legs. Judging by the fact that they were virginally clean, the young man had managed to grow them anew, but he could not do anything with the rest of his body. He needed a neutralizer, which

164

the Bartolomeo Clan had, and Kimal Sarento really hoped that he would be able to deliver his new mentor there alive.

A new mentor. The man decided to keep quiet about the fact that there were others. As well as about the fact that he'd already had a status bar for the past hundred years. And even at his current age, Kimal Sarento was not going to initiate Maximilian Valevsky — at least not in the near future. Because fate, such a funny bastard, once again demonstrated that it can turn tricks nastier than anything you could imagine in your worst nightmares. The man even shuddered, remembering the recent notifications that appeared before his eyes, which, in fact, had sentenced him to imminent death:

The offworlders have left this world.

Rune magic has left this world.

Fifty-eight human souls are attached to you. You must fuse them within 30 days, otherwise your body will reject them and return to its original state.

Words could hardly describe what the man felt at that moment. By the age of one hundred and thirty, he had had to repeatedly employ Magister Meram's services to maintain the familiar appearance of a forty-year-old ladies' man. Emergency solutions were required, bordering on outright madness. Because there were no longer any standard ways to respond to these circumstances. The human body was not designed to live for one hundred and thirty years. If his current body was returned to its "original state," it would die. Instantly and irrevocably. The dark ones could not help in any way. The Citadel was essentially useless. Kimal Sarento began to experience a long-forgotten feeling of despair when the lithoids and Maximilian Valevsky appeared. The man clung to it with all his might, realizing that only the impossible could help him now. And impossibility was the constant companion of the young Archduke.

What had happened next took Kimal Sarento by complete surprise. Reaching the fifty-first level of the stone was, of course, an exciting new development, but not as much as the message that appeared after the first battle with the lithoids:

Fifty-eight human souls have been temporarily fused.
Fuse time: 5 days.

Destroying the lithoids somehow extended the life of Kimal Sarento himself, and at that moment the chancellor made another leap of madness. He decided to bind himself to Maximilian Valevsky. Because that was where he saw his salvation. The man was not mistaken — his new mentor turned out to be an extremely fascinating person. The fact that Magister Meram hadn't given up yet spoke of hope for symbolic magic. So, Kimal Sarento needed to be as close to Valevsky as possible in order to be the first to receive the benefits.

However, he had to act carefully. Count Sarento knew the specifics of this young man very well — he hated those who mercilessly used the lives of others. Apparently, his time as a doomed soldier had left its mark. Therefore, the chancellor had to lower his age. Eighty-five years was a completely accessible age for a human and wouldn't raise unnecessary questions. That was the last thing Kimal needed now.

The lithoids have left this world.
Dark fire has left this world.
You have absorbed the power of the lithoid progenitor. A stable soul fuse has occurred. Your current age is forty years old.

New messages appeared as soon as Kimal Sarento finished off the strange dark clot that was pulsating near Valevsky's twisted body, and then stepped on it with his mithril boot. The human body was not able to accept the full power of the alien creature, but it still reacted. The man barely refrained from screaming with joy, which he had not done for a long time — the issue of the borrowed souls had been solved! But the issue of longevity was still relevant. Kimal Sarento was not going to limit himself to, say, sixty years. But this was why Valevsky was needed — only by being near him could Sarento receive bonuses from symbolic magic. He would have to demonstrate his usefulness and protect this blockhead boy from enemies.

But before any of that, Valevsky must be saved. That meant running, running and more running. Kimal Sarento had returned to his usual state of affairs — when his life depended only on himself and his actions. And he really didn't want to give up this sweet feeling. As for Valevsky...Someday he would learn the truth. But definitely not today.

Chapter 11

THE NEXT FEW DAYS were a vague blur. I had the impression we were running somewhere, teleporting somewhere, someone was negotiating something with someone, and I was laid down somewhere to rest. The only thing that stuck in my memory, and apparently for life, was Kimal Sarento's incessant demands. My pupil had demanded the impossible from me — not to sleep and to keep casting *Heal* on myself. He even slapped me on the cheeks when I wanted to fall into sweet oblivion. My body was burning like it was on fire, and *Heal* helped only for a few moments to relieve the pain. Then it returned, and it was so mind numbing that I wanted to howl like a wolf. Which I would have gladly done, but my throat had not yet recovered. So I had to wheeze and endure my pupil's bullying. I was allowed to rest only after an eternity, when a strange device enveloped me in white foam and the same foam was shoved into my mouth, forcing me to swallow, then the pain suddenly subsided, and while Kimal Sarento was off somewhere else, I fell into unconsciousness.

Those were the only memories that stuck.

Opening my eyes, I stared at the white ceiling. The air was light and smelled of flowers. Some kind of alchemy. There was no pain. I clenched my fists — my fingers worked perfectly. I bent my knees and they also worked perfectly. Pulling off the sheet and tilting my head, I saw a smooth body. There were no terrible burns that once covered my chest. For some reason, I was naked. I didn't even have mithril armor on. This was a vulnerable sensation, so I almost instantly formed *Golden Dome of Protection* around me. By a strange coincidence, I found myself in an unfamiliar place completely unprotected. Although was it really that unfamiliar? A map appeared before my eyes. Zooming in, I chuckled — we had made it back to the estate of the Bartolomeo Clan. Yes, Kimal Sarento had said something about the clan of my future wife, but, to be honest, I didn't recall his words at all. Only that this clan was mentioned. In fact, I didn't remember much from the final minutes of the fight. There was an explosion, and then everything was a fog. Some incoherent fragments and a clear understanding that we had done it. There were no more lithoids left in the world.

I found my clothes on a chair, next to the bed.

On top was my breastplate, mangled as if it had been in a smelting furnace, and my belt. Having dressed, I put on the remains of the mithril armor and they begrudgingly dissolved, assuming the appearance of ordinary clothes. Straining, I remembered Kimal Sarento's explanation and my soul fell — again, I had lost almost everything. The immaterial backpack, for example, was now also inaccessible to me. And if I remembered correctly, that was where I had kept my wedding gift for Naira Jode. A beautiful set of precious stones. I thought about giving it to her after the trip to the lithoids, but it didn't work out. I was glad that I'd had the foresight to unload everything before the trip. I couldn't imagine how I would have coped with the loss of everything that I took from the Nocturnal Guild's lair.

Habitually clenching my fist to activate the katars, I looked at my hand for some time in bewilderment as the blade did not appear. The realization that I no longer had the mithril gloves came late, accompanied by a sense of panic. Not panic — horror. I didn't care about the katars and crossbows, I could make more. The important thing was that my four exclusive rings are gone! Moreover, three of them had increased my resistance to darkness, allowing me to calmly travel through level thirty rifts, and one blocked the influence of rot! Now this infection would corrode my items. The horror! The damned horror of it all!

I said the last words out loud as a maid looked into the room.

"Oh, sir, you're awake! Wait, I'll be right there! He's awake!"

These last words the maid screamed out the doorway. I wasn't a masochist, so I followed after her. The longer I stood still, the heavier my thoughts became. Why the hell had I agreed to destroy the progenitor? Where will I find more rings for myself now? I needed at least four uninitiated, and as practice showed, these were a very rare find. Among the sealed rifts that I had to destroy, only three contained metamorphs. Would I have to delve into my stash? I still had an uninitiated ring and amulet in my inventory. I thought that I would be able to activate them at level forty, when I got to the invert levels, but apparently fate once again mocked my plans.

"Sir," a guard met me at the door. The dark human was dressed in full armor, as if he was not there for show, but really was carrying out some important mission. The unsheathed, razor sharp combat spear only confirmed this suspicion. He did not stop me, but followed me, keeping his distance. Strangely, I was not going to argue with the clan's rules. Maybe that was just how the Bartolomeo Clan did things.

Soon, another maid arrived and I was escorted to a guest room. They brought food, and, catching the enchanting smells, my stomach sang a mournful gurgling song about how it had forgotten when it had last eaten. I had to give in to my most primal desires and completely chow down. For what I was doing couldn't be considered "eating" — as soon as

I took the first bite, I nearly lost my mind trying to stuff as much food into my mouth as possible. My body was behaving extremely strangely. I had never experienced full-body shakes at the sight of a strange-looking stew that I normally would never have batted an eye at. I lapped up every single drop!

"A healthy body with a healthy appetite," I heard Kimal Sarento's sarcastic voice. I ignored my pupil, scanning the trays for any remaining crumbs. The large bowl of stew only whetted my appetite, without filling me up at all.

"More!" I said, looking up at the maid standing nearby. And my tone made the girl turn white and retreat, hiding behind Kimal Sarento's back.

"This is all you have been allotted for today," said my pupil. "You need to be extremely cautious with food after a cleansing. Especially such an extensive one. Tomorrow you will get another plate."

"Are you kidding me?" I had to make great efforts not to pummel the chancellor with my fists. "Bring me some food! I'll starve by tomorrow!"

"You won't even make it until then," chuckled Kimal Sarento. "They'll kill you first."

"Who?" I said, taken aback. My hunger faded into the background. It was still there, but my personal safety intercepted control of consciousness, allowing me to gain at least some reason.

"A lot of people," Kimal Sarento shrugged. "After I hauled you all the way to this lovely little estate, the Bartolomeo Clan received four letters demanding, not asking, that you be handed over to be torn to pieces. Three were from the Orthodox, including Magister Elor, the fourth was from the Gourfan Clan."

"What did I ever do to them?"

"Deprived them of their personal weapons. Gerard Moises was known as one of the best adepts of dark fire. In this he was inferior only to Magister Elor. But you went and tore out these snakes' fangs. They are still dangerous — they can squeeze you to death, but they can no longer en-venomate you. That's why they're beside them-selves with rage."

"*We* tore out their fangs," I reminded him. "The final blow was struck by your lightning."

"The pupil was fulfilling his mentor's orders," Kimal Sarento was clearly extremely satisfied with himself. "So I have nothing to do with it, all the blame for the fact that there is no more dark fire in this world lies with Archduke Maximilian Valev-sky. You were even given security. Appreciate it!"

"We were both fulfilling a task set by the Tem-ple of Skron. All complaints should be directed to them."

"So the Temple of Skron are also among those who are dissatisfied with the current state of things." Although it seemed there was no more room on his face, my pupil's smile grew even wider. "Four has already arrived at the Bartolomeo Clan and wants to meet with you. The misty servants have complaints about you, mentor. They do not like the fact that every time you go on an important and responsible mission, the dark ones lose something. Runic magic, then dark fire, which the Temple also used. Basically, the dark ones have mixed feelings about you. Thanks to you, they survived, but they also lost a lot. Incidentally! Information that it was you who defeated the stone-like creatures, and not some Count Vyazemsky, has already been sent to the Citadel, Fortress, Stronghold and all three imperial chanceries. Here, I admit, I tried. Because an act like that cannot be hushed up. We will make you the savior of the world, not a whipping boy for the powers that be. Now, if someone touches you, he will have to explain to the Pope and all three emperors why he decided to do it. Politics, mentor, that's what it is."

"How much time has passed already?"

"Since the destruction of the lithoids? Four days. I spent two days dragging you to the portal, a day cleansing you from the effects of the dark flame, a day recovering. In fact, you should have come to your senses only by evening. Apparently, your strong young body coped with the stress much earlier. Alright, before the main show begins, I want to return something to you."

Kimal Sorento put his hand in his pocket and pulled out four rings that emitted a red aura.

"Don't look at me like that. Of course I checked them. How could I not? In principle, they're not bad rings, but without them, as I understand it, you'll be a little sick in the high-level rifts. Or, to put it bluntly, you'll die. Personally, that would complicate things for me. I just got a mentor, I can't lose him just like that."

"Where did you get these?" I gulped. I certainly hadn't expected that.

"They were lying next to your body. Apparently, the dark flame that ate through the mithril was powerless against Skron's artifacts. Of course, I took them away, assessed them, tried them on to see if I could use them myself, and realized that I would have to return them. Protection from mental attacks is, of course, interesting, but not so much as to deprive you of the dark influence block. So here you go and try not to lose them next time. I won't always be there to back you up."

It was only after I put the rings back on my hand that I felt an incredible sense of relief. It was as if a part of me had returned. The rings themselves weren't as attractive as what they did for me. They transformed me into a high-level rift conqueror, not just a common human who could avoid dying at the hands of rift creatures.

"Follow me and try to control yourself. Remember, we're guests."

"Where are we going?"

"What do you mean, where? To your wedding."

"Now?" I involuntarily glanced down my clothes, only now realizing what they looked like. The formal suit was clearly not suitable for long journeys. I was so used to this look in mithril armor that I hadn't immediately noticed.

"What's the point of dragging it out? After what you've done, the Bartolomeo Clan will sink their teeth into you and won't let go. And why would they? The Savior of the Dark Lands! To be honest,

I had a hand in that title too. In my opinion, it is still excessively modest. Since you do great things, you should be treated as a great man, not an ordinary person. So enjoy your fame. Today is your day."

"Fame is always accompanied by envy," I muttered, unsatisfied.

"And where would we be without it?" Kimal Sarento grinned. "Dozens, if not hundreds of dark orthodox now consider you the main source of their troubles and will do everything to finish you off. First rune magic, then dark fire. If you also get rid of magic stones, the whole world will turn against you. I was joking about the stones, just in case you don't realize. I know you — you're already thinking about how to do it."

"It would be harder to get rid of the stones," I replied. "To do that, I'd need…"

"Whatever you'd need, tell me in Hearth. After the wedding, we will return to your city, where we will solemnly receive a delegation from Turb. The emperor sent you a gift as a token of personal gratitude for saving the inhabitants of his empire. After Count Vyazemsky shamefully fled from the front line battle with those blockheads, saving his life at the expense of the inhabitants of the Northern and Central Regions, Archduke Valevsky became a very popular figure. So far, just among ordinary citizens, but my people are working to ensure that word of your glory penetrates into the higher echelons. There is still a lot of work to do, but in any case, for four days the result is more than satisfactory. Adeline works real miracles. Alright, let's go."

"You yourself said they didn't expect me to wake up until evening. Why are we having the wedding now?"

"Because the dark ones don't usually have bright and beautiful ceremonies. You'll see for yourself now."

I had to obey and follow Kimal Sarento. I was taken to the very hall where I first saw Naira and almost went crazy as I fell under her perfumed spell. There were quite a few people in the hall, despite what my pupil had assured me. Their vestments were clearly not of an official nature. Everyone was dressed in something casual, but not in any way ceremonial.

Cedric Jode, head of the Bartolomeo Clan, sat on a throne surrounded by his advisers. Naira, clothed in a beautiful blue dress, stood next to me. My heart began to beat wildly — the girl was stunning. So much so that a fire of passion flared up inside me in anticipation of our wedding night. Again the effect of her perfume? Unlikely — everyone else was gazing at Naira with unclouded eyes. Had I really grown accustomed to the idea of having a bride, and begun to look at Naira not as an enemy, but as my wife? In any case, I would not forget Alia! And this issue would definitely need to be clarified somehow with my new bride.

Not far from the throne of Cedric Jode there was a group of dark humans who rubbed me the wrong way from the start. The dark pits of their eyes stared at me point-blank, and from the expressions on some of their faces, it could safely be assumed that they loathed me. Could these be the Orthodox who wanted to finish off the man who banished dark flame from our world? Then why did they not risk their health and attack as soon as I appeared in the hall? Ah, that was why!

The reason was standing not far from the group. The foggy servant of the Temple of Skron was motionless as a statue, however, his presence alone stopped any attempts to harm me. The dark one was holding some kind of box and, as soon as I approached the throne, he came up to me.

"The Temple of Skron fulfils its obligations, Archduke Valevsky." Four was hiding under the mask of a simple Temple servant. I accepted the box he extended to me, opened the lid and my heart began fluttering wildly again. A miracle lay there on the red velvet. The beautiful five-piece jewelry set couldn't be described any other way. The two rings, earrings and necklace were made of white gold of the finest craftsmanship and were adorned with a smattering of large diamonds.

"The rings were sized to Naira Jode's fingers, " he added. "The Temple of Skron considers the incident with the lithoids closed. We will discuss the rest of the details after the ceremony. Clan Head, he is yours."

Four retreated to his post, continuing to shield me from the Orthodox. Cedric stook up and a servant immediately ran over to his side, holding a long, massive chain on another pillow.

"The Bartolomeo Clan is not accustomed to long wedding ceremonies," said Cedric. "This is a celebration of the newlyweds, not for those around them. All we can allow ourselves is to witness the bond between Master Naira Jode and Archduke Maximilian Valevsky. Please come closer."

I handed the box to Kimal Sarento, who was standing nearby, and approached Cedric Jode. Naira stood next to me. A pleasant aroma hit my nose, completing the overall impression and making her even more tantalizing.

"Hands," demanded Cedric. Naira extended her hand forward. No one explained the procedure to me, but logic told me what to do. I repeated the girl's movement, extending my hand forward and joining our palms. Our fingers intertwined and clenched into a single fist.

"As head of the Bartolomeo Clan, I now pronounce you husband and wife! Naira, from this moment on you have lost the name Jode, but the clan's doors will always be open for you, Naira Valevsky. The same is true for your husband and children," Cedric said, after which he wrapped the chain around our hands. A few moments of silence passed, after which Cedric sat back down on the throne and looked at us in bewilderment:

"How long are you going to stand like that? That's it, the ceremony is over, you can leave. Just give me the chain back."

I enjoyed this ceremony. My older brother's wedding had been held according to all the conventions of the Zarak Empire — lavish, grandiose, and with an incredible number of guests. Everyone partied for several days straight, getting drunk at our expense. I didn't even want to recall how many duels and fights we broke up — my father had gotten angry, but could do nothing. The traditions that he himself instilled in everyone required turning a blind eye to any violations or destruction. I never wanted anything like that for myself, so I was already primed to enjoy the dark ones' lack of ceremony. The servants unwrapped the chains, and as soon as Kimal Sarento thrust the box at me, I turned to my wife.

"May I?" I pulled out the rings and showed them to the girl. Judging by how her eyes widened, and everyone who was near us fell silent, the Temple of Skron had really pulled out all the stops.

"Of course." Naira extended her hand to me. Surprisingly, it was visibly quivering, as if she couldn't believe what was happening. I placed both rings on her fingers and fiddled with the earrings a little, unable to resist kissing my wife on the ear, then took off her old necklace and put on the new one. The diamonds fit her image perfectly, complementing her blue dress with the cold sparkle of the stars.

"It suits you," I said and for a while lost touch with reality. Naira's gentle lips touched mine, and the main hall of the Bartolomeo Clan ceased to exist for me. The nasty voice of Kimal Sarento intervened in this sweet moment:

"Mentor, please, have a conscience. You are not alone."

"Oh." Naira moved away from me and blushed deeply, glancing guiltily up at the throne. Cedric Jode was making a show of minding his own business and not paying any attention to us.

"I would like to propose we take leave of this lovely estate and head back to Hearth." Kimal Sarento kept calm, but a few small details showed that he was nervous. Following his eyes, I began to grow anxious as well. New faces appeared among the Orthodox. Dark Magister Elor and Karina Fardi. Until that moment, I had never seen Elor in real life, but I had no doubt that the one standing next to the girl emitting pure darkness was him. The couple purposefully moved in our direction. Four tried to stand in their way, but Fardi's gaze riveted him to the spot. Karina stopped a few steps from me. The heavy gaze of the dark holes of her eyes was oppressive. I had to make an effort not to take my eyes off the girl and not fall to my knees in front of her.

"Valevsky." Karina's voice changed. It had lost any hint of humanity. A large empty space formed around us. The dark ones hurried to get away from the resonant and unpleasant sound. And just being near Karina was terrifying. Even for me, using the dark mirror. Not to mention Naira, who clung to my hand with a vice grip. My wife could barely retain consciousness next to this monster, who, by some strange whim, still bore a human name.

"Skron," I nodded, greeting the higher power.

"You're funny," grinned Karina. "He's not here right now. Just me."

"What are you doing in the Bartolomeo Clan? As far as I know, they don't like the Orthodox. Especially those who burn my pupils with the dark fire. If you come near Alia, my pupil, again, I'll tear you to shreds. I'll do the same to you as I did to the lithoids."

I said the last phrase as I stared into Elor's dark eye pits. He frowned, but said nothing. I returned back to Fardi, waiting for an answer.

"What am I doing here? I came to see the one who saved my lands."

"Since when did the Kerux become yours?"

"Just now, it became yours. I realized that the Temple of Skron is too kind to freaks like you. Too kind to the light ones. Fawns before them. Behaves unworthy of the true servants of Skron. It is time to correct this mistake and show the whole world that the dark ones are the dominant force. Show the light ones their true place."

I looked over at Four, who was standing nearby. He did not interfere in our conversation, but I had no doubt that active negotiations were currently underway between him and other representatives of the Temple of Skron.

"Did you just come to watch?"

"Why not? Now that I have realized my mission, I want to tell you what I could not before. I liked you, Valevsky. I liked your tenacity, your willpower, your attitude. At some point, I even began to think that we could be together. But then you betrayed me. Killed me. Yes, I took revenge by killing you in retaliation, but that was when I saw the light. I liked not you, but the strength within you. Now that I have received much greater power, I look upon you as a small rodent. Useful in destroying various cockroaches, but nevertheless small and pathetic. Which is what you have always been. I am ashamed that I wasted my time on you. I tried to think of a way to destroy you. It's all insignificant. Petty. You destroyed the cockroaches that wanted to occupy my lands, so now you will live. I can be kind, too. Neither I nor any other true follower of Skron will touch you or your pupils. That is my will. But this will only last until you cross me. Sit there in Hearth and keep a low profile. You are no longer welcome in my lands. The only place you are allowed access to is the lands of the Bartolomeo Clan. I give you the right to accompany your wife. If you appear in the lands of any other clans without my permission, I will perceive this as an open act of aggression. In this case, you will become the lawful prey of my servants and me. Farewell, Valevsky. I hope never to hear from you again."

Karina Fardi turned away from me with no concern that I might stab her in the back. She turned toward the Temple servant.

"Four, I wish to speak with One. It is time to call the Temple of Skron to account for everything that you have allowed into this world."

The dark delegation left. Kimal Sarento approached, seeming outwardly unperturbed, but his gaze indicated that he was uneasy.

"Something tells me that the Temple of Skron

will soon regret that they gave birth to such a monster. I suggest that we leave this celebration of life
before some other forces become interested in us.
I think that the dark servants have no time for you
now, mentor. And, as it seems to me, they won't
consider you or your feelings again for a long
time."

Chapter 12

"MAX, THEY'RE WAITING for us." Naira sat up, making no move to pull the sheet over herself. Against my will, I opened my eyes. Yes, I'd seen that naked chest more than once over the past twelve hours, but I still couldn't resist enjoying the beautiful view once again. Like Alia, Naira's chest fit perfectly in my palm, making me reach for it even now, after such a tumultuous and unforgettable night. The girl didn't move away. On the contrary, she reached out to me herself, brazenly tearing me out of the embrace of my short sleep. Using *Heal* to remove even the slightest hint of fatigue, I forgot about all the troubles of this world for a while. Say what you will — right there, right then, I had the most beautiful girl in this world in my arms. And I wasn't going to refuse a little joy.

"Now we definitely have to go." Half an hour

later Naira finally broke free from my embrace and began to dress. "You and I have our whole lives ahead of us, and representatives of your emperor don't show up in Hearth every day. As the ruler of the city, you need to meet him.

All I could do was sniffle discontentedly. Naira was right — Zurgan the First's personal assistant, who had come to Hearth, could significantly influence the balance of power in the Zarak Empire. Archduke Valevsky could cease to be evil and instead become the savior of the empire. To do this, I had to show a little politeness and sensitivity. Show that I was glad for such an honor and was ready to continue to benefit the Light lands. Kimal Sarento had wasted four hours yesterday forcing me to rehearse a smile, a greeting, and a majestic bow. And I had no opportunity to push this procedure onto Eleanore. At this level, only personal presence was required.

"Max, wrap it up, they're waiting for you," Alia's words appeared in my head. We both carefully avoided discussing what had happened. My personal attendant understood perfectly well that as long as she was part of the church, our marriage was impossible, so she calmly reacted to the demands of the Bartolomeo Clan. Jealousy was generally uncharacteristic of Alia. Her obsessive desire to return to the Fortress infuriated me, but I couldn't solve this problem now. Even Alia's conversations with Father Lock, the former High Priest, didn't help. Okay, these were all problems for my future self. I'd come back to them later.

"Coming. Already getting dressed," I answered, putting my hand on my thigh. There were still two symbols on my body, but with each passing day they were becoming less noticeable. Somehow faded. I urgently needed to study *Author* to figure out the remote connection. It was a convenience I wasn't willing to give up. The very same Magister Meram, who was hanging around Hearth, almost knocked down the doors yesterday when he found out that I had returned. He had clearly wanted to talk to me, but I was a little preoccupied with Naira and my wedding night.

The maids arrived. Almost all of them were busy with the disheveled Naira, but one was still assigned to me to style my unruly hair. With the mithril helmet, I always had a perfect hairstyle. Without it, I was little different from ordinary people.

An hour later I was sitting on my throne, ready to rule and administer. Eleanore stood on my right hand, Kimal Sarento on my left. Alia and Naira were standing behind the throne. I had taken a wife too quickly, so her throne was not yet ready. The hall was crowded. The symbols shining above their heads told me that most of them were guests in the city. The representative of the emperor, as a person of high rank, had no right to travel around the Zarak Empire without an escort. Several dozen nobles of various stripes had to accompany this man, demonstrating his status. Finally, a herald entered the hall and solemnly announced:

"Authorized representative of His Imperial

Majesty of the Zarak Empire, the Duke of Odoev-sky!"

The rules demanded calm and patience from me, but the emotions that were overwhelming me were eager to break out. The bastard who killed my family dared to come to my house? Count Fardi entered the hall, his head held high. This bastard was afraid of nothing. His status as the Emperor's representative protected him from both attacks on his life and insults. For here and now this man represented Zurgan the First personally. And any sidelong glance at him was a crime against the crown.

"You knew, but you didn't say anything?" I whispered, turning to Eleanore. Kimal Sarento coughed to my left, signaling me to calm down, but I didn't heed him.

"If you had known who the Emperor's representative was, would it have changed anything?" she asked point blank.

"Yes. Yesterday I would have come up with some urgent and mandatory matter for myself somewhere in the Kaliman Empire."

"Your meeting with the authorized representative of the Kaliman Emperor will take place immediately after accepting Emperor Zurgan's gratitude," Eleanor replied. "You had no opportunity not to attend this meeting."

"Look at the bigger picture, mentor," Kimal Sarento realized that a simple cough would not calm me down. "Count Fardi knows very well who you are and what you want to do. Which, in principle, you already did to his daughter when you put a crossbow bolt through her forehead. And despite this, he came here to bring you gratitude on behalf of Zurgan the First. What a blow to his pride!"

"I am more concerned with the question of why the Duke of Odoevsky has come to Hearth." Eleanore did not take her eyes off the slowly approaching man. "The emperor has plenty of assistants. Why Count Fardi?"

"A pure provocation," answered Kimal Sarento. "Someone sincerely hopes that Maximilian will not be able to cope with his emotions and will attack a representative of the emperor, thereby signing a death sentence for himself and the entire city."

"Count Vyazemsky?" Eleanore frowned.

"Who else? He needs to rehabilitate his image after the incident with the lithoids. The best way to do this is in the context of the fight against Hearth. Alright, everyone, enough chatting. It may be construed as disrespect for a representative of the emperor."

The Duke of Odoevsky approached an invisible line and stopped. The experienced politician knew perfectly well where personal space began and did not plan to violate it. For in this case, even the emperor's protection would not help him.

"I greet the representative of His Imperial Majesty Zurgan the First in the autonomous city of Hearth," I said, repeating the obligatory phrase. This was the protocol. My personal attitude towards Count Fardi should not affect the city.

"His Imperial Majesty Zurgan the First expresses his gratitude to Archduke Maximilian Valevsky for the destruction of the lithoids and the salvation of the inhabitants of the northern region of the Zarak Empire," Count Fardi said solemnly. "In gratitude for such a great deed, His Imperial Majesty invites Archduke Maximilian Valevsky to take part in a competition to determine the representative of the Zarak Empire in a tournament of the three empires."

"Wasn't this honorary role awarded to me based on the results of the previous tournament?"

"The results of the failed tournament were declared illegitimate. The winner was chosen not by the results of the competition, but by the decision of the participants. Due to the fact that the tournament of three empires was postponed to a later date, His Imperial Majesty decided to hold new qualifying competitions. They will take place in a week in the vicinity of Turb. The schedule and invitation to participate were handed over to Hearth's chancellery today."

Chancellery? I had one of those? I didn't like the expression on Count Fardi's face. Not even his expression, but his eyes. They clearly showed that I was in for some big trouble at the upcoming competition. What would it be? Why did this man look like he had won, even though he had come to thank the man who would kill him? Everything looked extremely suspicious. It smelled like another setup a mile away, but I had no right to refuse such an invitation. The emperor's representative had publicly declared that said emperor wanted to see me at the competition. No matter what it took, I had to show up for the tournament. Because people would misinterpret my refusal.

"I accept the invitation of His Imperial Majesty and will arrive at the competition at the appointed time," I replied. A victorious smile appeared on the Duke of Odoevsky's face. Everything was going according to the plan set by this man's master. Count Fardi spun around, getting ready to leave the hall, but this did not suit me. It was not good to leave the last word to the opponent.

"I didn't release you, Duke of Odoevsky," I said. Kimal Sarento coughed again, but I ignored it. Karina's father turned around and, raising an eyebrow eloquently, asked with a grin:

"Does Archduke Valevsky wish to say something to the voice of the emperor?"

"I do," I said, looking into the eyes of the man who ordered the assassination of my family because of three unregistered rifts on our lands. "I request that a representative of the Citadel come forward."

Brother Lou, whose eyes were filled with light, approached the throne. The Citadel had not been petty and sent Brother Lin's deputy to Hearth. The man wearing the red robe of an investigator had combed my city up and down, looking for hidden dark ones or those with whom we could work outside the control of the Church of the Light. But there were none. Hearth lived strictly according to the laws of the light world, not giving even the slightest reason to doubt our loyalty. Three days ago, for example, when Kimal Sarento was bringing me to the Bartolomeo Clan after the battle with the lithoids, Viscount Kurpatsky shot several dark humans he found on the street. They didn't say a single word to them — there was no pillar of light above their heads and the Viscount himself did not know them, so he gave the order to shoot to kill. Analysis of the corpses showed that converts had descended on Kostrish. The rapid response team, which included Brother Lou, discovered the dark ones' secret hideout and destroyed them all. Five less people in our city and a slew of questions about our security system. We desperately needed the same pillars of light over the dark ones as we had over the light ones.

"I am listening, detector of darkness," the cleric said. The representatives of the Church of the Light only referred to me thusly. One who can detect darkness in a person, regardless of the degree of his preparation or protection.

"The man who stands before me has immunity. I have no right to accuse him or punish him. I have no right to even look askance at him, because now he is the voice of his imperial majesty of the Zarak Empire. However, I have the right to tell the representative of the Citadel one fascinating story about Countess Fardi, the daughter of an untouchable man."

"Karina Fardi is dead," Brother Lou reminded me. "What's the point of telling the story of a woman burned at the stake in the Citadel's yard?"

"Karina Fardi is alive and continues to serve Skron, giving her body over to him as a vessel," I said, deciding not to beat around the bush and immediately blurting out the truth. The fact that the Citadel did not know about Fardi was the Citadel's problem, not mine. "She has ceased to be a human in the usual sense of the word. She is not even a convert. She is a vessel. Dark, capable of withstanding the darkness of Skron and manifesting it through herself. Karina Fardi embodied Skron and destroyed the offworlders, after rune magic left the world. Karina Fardi successfully attacked the lithoids and prevented them from entering Kerux. Karina Fardi has now shown up at the Temple of Skron and demands that the dark ones take active steps to destroy the Light lands. My words are not unfounded — there are two witnesses here who saw her conversation with the Temple servant. Karina Fardi wants to destroy the Church of the Light and will do so as soon as she gains the strength."

"I hear you." The tone of his voice told me that the news was not the most pleasant for Brother Lou. "However, I don't understand why you told me this. As far as I can see, the girl in question is not among those present here today."

"Karina Fardi is a student of the dark Orthodox Elor. Three months ago, she was in the Citadel, where she was trained by the servants of the Light. There was no darkness in her then. I have a question for you, Brother Lou: where and when could the young countess have met the orthodox

Elor? Who brought them together? Who gave birth to a monster in this world capable of destroying the Church of the Light, as she did with the offworlders? I cannot voice the answers to these questions — I do not have the right."

"But I can." Brother Lou turned his gaze to the Duke of Odoevsky. The malicious grin disappeared from Count Fardi's face, and he turned into a motionless statue without any hint of emotion. "I need proof that Karina Fardi is alive. Who is a witness to this?"

"If you'll permit me to speak, I am," Kimal Sarento said, bringing attention to himself. "Yesterday, at a reception in the Bartolomeo Clan, we crossed paths once again. I will have to make some clarifications to my mentor's story. Karina Fardi came to the Citadel already as a pupil of Magister Elor. The dark one told me this information personally when he announced that he was going to destroy me soon. For some strange reason, Magister Elor first wanted to meet with his enemies before taking any action against them. Magister Elor was extremely pleased with the fact that his pupil had made it into the Citadel and passed all the checks, even though she already had an open status bar by that time. The dark one also told me where he met his future pupil. At the Fardi estate. He was a frequent guest of this house. And long before he became interested in Karina Fardi. What he was doing there and why is clearly not a question for me, but for...Unfortunately, I have no right to name names, as dictated by the law on representatives of the emperor."

"Throwing around accusations without proof is a direct path to the stake." Brother Lou's voice dropped and the Light in his eyes seemed to incinerate my pupil. But it was impossible to impress the seasoned schemer with such trifles.

"That was why I, completely by chance, preserved the transcripts of conversations that took place in the Fardi estate between Magister Elor and...You understand, Brother Lou, that I have no right to name names? The law of the Zarak Empire forbids me from doing so."

"I do not intend to stand here and listen to unfounded accusations against me!" The Duke of Odoevsky declared. "His Imperial Majesty will be notified of what has occurred. Violation of the law..."

"One more word, Count Fardi, and I will order you to be shackled and have your mouth filled with molten tin." Brother Lou's voice was filled with the terrible power of a man who was capable and empowered to commit such terrible deeds. The Duke of Odoevsky understood this too — he continued to stand with his head held high, but all the arrogance with which he came to my city had flown away. It is hard to argue with a man speaking on behalf of the Light. Even the emperor could not do anything to a man like Brother Lou.

"Is the stenographer who was present for the meeting still alive?"

"Yes. He is currently on assignment, and I can make him available for questioning within three days."

"Where are the documents?"

"They're not in Hearth. They're in Turb, hidden away in a secure spot."

"The Church of the Light wishes to receive these records," Brother Lou said. "I ask everyone present to leave the hall! Count Fardi, you stay here." The other guests clearly did not want to leave the place where such a fascinating spectacle was being played out, but no one wanted to argue with the churchmen. For quite suddenly, ten servants of the Light dressed in red robes appeared in the hall. I didn't even know that there were so many investigators in Hearth. Once everyone had finally left the hall, Brother Lou turned to the Duke of Odoevsky.

"Count Fardi, as the pope's official representative in the Western lands, I suggest you repent your actions. A sincere confession will be a mitigating factor and may save you from the stake. Karina Fardi is an adult and will answer for her actions herself. The Church of the Light wants to know how she became dark. At what point? What knowledge could she have taken from the Citadel? What could she have done or arranged? The Citadel is still dealing with the consequences of the discovery of the Wave in its home base. Many valiant servants of the Light, ordinary citizens, have died. The pope wants to understand why everything happened this way. We will check Kimal Sarento's testimony, make sure that the shorthand records taken of the conversations are genuine, so that sooner or later we will get to the truth. With one specific note. If you really were instrumental in turning your daughter dark, you will be burned. The punishment is severe, but I do not find it to be radical."

"I will not speak in the presence of this person," Count Fardi replied after a pause. He was staring, of course, at me. "Karina decided to become dark due to him!"

"We'd like to find out that too," Brother Lou gave me an unkind look, then turned to his team. "Arrange for the Duke of Odoevsky to be transferred to the Citadel under heavy guard. If there is an attack, destroy the entire facility. Inform Zurgan the First that the Citadel has arrested Count Fardi. Send investigators to the Fardi family estate. Search everything. Move!"

His Imperial Majesty's representative was taken away, and not through the front door. Brother Lou did not want the crowd of hangers-on that had come with Count Fardi to accidentally rescue him or see their patron in such an unflattering light. It was not every day that the Church of the Light arrested someone. Especially someone of his stature.

"I need the documents and your man," Brother Lou turned to Kimal Sarento.

"As I said, for this we need to go to Turb. I believe that my mentor and I will do this today. The personal invitation of His Imperial Majesty cannot be ignored."

"I am going with you," the cleric stated definitively. "How much time do you need to get ready?"

"We'll be ready right after the meeting with the representative of the Kaliman Emperor," I said, looking at the list of guests who were waiting to meet me. Eleanore can take care of the rest of the crowd, but I'll have to accept this one. By the way, I don't think I've met the Kalimans yet. I'm quite eager for the experience."

"I hope you won't accuse them of having ties to the darkness," said the cleric and went over to stand by the wall. I wasn't too happy about his remark, but I didn't react. Another cleric opened the doors and the guests filled the hall again. They glanced left and right, trying to find the Duke of Odoevsky, but he was no longer in the palace. I suppose the clerics were already galloping towards the main gate, trying to carry out the order of their superiors as quickly as possible. Murmurs and timid questions about where the duke had gone fell silent when the herald introduced the new guest:

"Authorized representative of His Imperial Majesty of the Kaliman Empire, Emir Haji!"

Emir? I exchanged glances with Eleanore. The Emperor in the Kaliman Empire was also called the Sultan, he had only four emirs, and they ruled the four regions into which the southeastern empire was divided. The fact that the Duke of Odoevsky, one of the nine heads of the regions of the Zarak Empire, was sent to me in Hearth does not say anything at all — Count Fardi's presence here was a provocation. And he had certainly achieved his goal — there would be gossip about the event for a long time to come. But there could be no claims against me. Address all questions to the clergy. As for Emir Hadji, he was a strong statement.

A dark-skinned giant, who was a head taller than everyone else, floated majestically into the hall. The emir was dressed in strange, vividly dyed garments. Initially, I didn't realize that it was one huge swath of cloth wrapped around his body. Emir Hadji held the end of the cloth majestically in his hand, as if it were the most precious thing. The Kaliman was remarkable not only for his height, but also for his size. The man clearly loved to eat. However, he didn't look like our emperor — he had no drooping cheeks, triple chins, or thick, fleshy fingers. Everything about his image was neat and harmonious, but also substantial.

"May the Light come to your home, Emir Hadji," I said, repeating the greeting Eleanore had taught me.

"May the Light never leave your heart, Archduke Valevsky," the ambassador replied, somehow bowing in such a way that neither bent his back nor showed respect. "The great Sultan of the Kaliman Empire, Emperor Boro, sends you his regards and these modest gifts."

The emir raised his hand and snapped his fingers. The doors opened again, and a group of swarthy servants brought in several dozen huge chests. Placing them next to the emir, they opened the lids, and a muffled whisper rolled through the hall. The chests were filled with gold, precious stones, jewelry, and among them was a small chest with three artifacts. Magical, very simple, but considering the number of artifacts in the Light lands, the gift was truly imperial. The ruler of the Kaliman Empire was buying my favor, and doing so openly and in front of witnesses. And, let's face it, I knew perfectly well why he was doing this. Those two rifts with metamorphs would not destroy themselves. One of the rifts was only level nineteen, but the second had reached the twenty-sixth and was confidently delving deeper, forming levels with rot. The Gourfan Clan could easily cope with such a disaster, I believe, but who would let the dark ones into their lands?

"I thank the great Sultan Boro for such a generous gift, but sadness and sorrow darken my soul, so I cannot respond so generously to such a gift. Emir Hadji saw with his own eyes the construction in which my city is mired. All resources are spent on turning Hearth into the pearl of the Zarak Empire. I can only say that Kaliman merchants will always be welcome guests in my city."

"Archduke Valevsky's wisdom is a pleasant surprise. I see a young man, but I hear a wise ruler," the emir nodded. "The Kaliman Empire is interested in the trade represented in the autonomous city of Hearth. On the way here, we saw many construction crews whose workers were true dark humans. At the same time, I see a monitor of the Light modestly standing by the wall and not sending the dark ones to the righteous fire. Human rumor speaks the truth — Hearth is a hub of trade with darkness. New markets are always compelling. We have something to offer Kerux. But I came here for another purpose, Archduke Valevsky, known to many as the rift conqueror."

Emir Hadji fell silent and I smiled. I was quite fond of this man. Even though, according to the *Analyze*, he was one of the most dangerous humans in this world. I no longer considered myself and Kimal Sarento to be humans. But Emir Hadji could give Count Vyazemsky or Count Shub a huge head start and still defeat them like little children. After the twentieth level, each new increase in stones significantly strengthened its wielder, and if the stones had already made it to level twenty-nine, the maximum accessible level in the ordinary world, then this person had ultimate strength.

"I can guess why you are here, but I would like to discuss the details."

"That is why I came to Hearth. As the great Sultan Boro says, trade is in my blood. Shall we discuss the details here, or can we go to a more private setting? I believe I have something that may surprise the ruler who has taken the sun herself as his wife."

Chapter 13

"I WANT TO BE THE RESPONSIBLE ONE here and say that this doesn't seem like a good idea to me!"

"Young man, where is all this passion coming from?" Kimal Sarento was clearly enjoying himself. "Even if nothing comes of it, what do we have to lose, besides money and a little peace of mind?"

"It is, in fact, a waste of money and sanity," I answered, looking with disbelief at the servants dragging the Pharapho bone armor into the room. And not just one or two pieces, which might seem perfectly normal, but every scrap I had at my disposal. One hundred and thirty-one pieces. A closed-off and well-protected testing ground had been on my short list of demands for city infrastructure. I needed a site where I could study my abilities without unnecessary witnesses, spar, and also create mithril from bone armor, while keeping the production secret. The room had fortified structural elements in the walls and, as I was told, was currently the strongest place in the city. It would not be possible to dig a road here from the outside — the walls, which were a mixture of stone and metal, were ten meters thick.

Kimal Sarento ignored my remark. The servants had already fled the training ground, so the chancellor (still the chancellor) had to work on his own. Grabbing two bone armors from the pile, he dragged them to the center of the room and leaned them against each other, after which he fastidiously assessed the result of his work, grunted with satisfaction and returned to me.

"Stabilize. And try not to lose anything."

Lightning shot out from Kimal Sarento's hands and crashed into the bone armor. There was a burning smell — the integrity of the training ground was being tested for the first time, and with a level fifty magic stone. Before testing his theory, Kimal Sarento explained his idea to me. This allowed me to prepare — remove the *Abyss* gem from the development model and insert a development crystal with the *Split Consciousness* parameter, which allowed me to operate two abilities at the same time.

The race began. The level fifty *Lightning Strike* put the bone armor through the ringer. It made holes, melted it, saturated it with energy while I tried to keep the armor stable and in one piece. I had huge doubts about the possibility of creating mithril with lightning alone, which I repeatedly told my student, but he did not listen to me. When it came to testing, Kimal Sarento was unstoppable. So I had to sweat, distributing my consciousness across two objects at once and pouring an insane amount of mana into them. The good news was that it was restored much faster than it was spent.

I missed the transition, as all my attention was focused on not losing my mind as I cast two streams of magic at once. Two iridescent orbs appeared above the scorched floor. They did not intersect, did not unite, but did not fly apart either. As if something held them together and at the same repelled them from one another.

"Precisely what we needed to prove," Kimal Sarento grinned. "It's not about how many types of magic is used. It's about how powerful the magic is. Mine was enough, and I didn't even have to strain. Go, take the orbs and come back. We don't have much time to waste on your slack-jawed gaping. Sending you to Turb without protection is pure suicide. And I could use some too. Count Vyazemsky will likely use vyrma against us."

"One clarification," I said. "You didn't guess — you knew it would work. How?"

"Isn't it obvious, my untrained mentor?" Kimal Sarento emphasized the last word. And he said it in such a tone that it made me want to smack that grin off his face with something heavy. "The first emperor had a huge problem — he was a lone wolf. He had no inner circle. No friends or companions. Only strength, power, and servants. A whole world of servants. If I'm not mistaken, he was a shepherd before he gained strength, right? So he remained a shepherd after he became all-powerful. Humanity was his flock. The Nameless One would never have involved anyone else in the creation of his armor. He did everything himself. Thanks to the *Split Consciousness* he simultaneously used magic and healing to keep the bone armor in a stable state.

"Then why did you distribute the knowledge of how to make mithril to others?" I frowned, confused by the logic of the chancellor's actions. "If you wanted to conduct testing, we could have done it together."

Kimal Sorento grinned.

"Isn't it obvious? From your face, I surmise it isn't. Okay, let's take the long way around. Tell me, my slow-witted mentor, what is needed to make mithril? Don't bother, I'll answer myself. You need bone armor, a healer, and magical power comparable to a certain level of magic stones. And not level fifty, either — much lower. Which of these is freely available? Magic power? Yes. A healer who doesn't lose vitality when healing? Yes, albeit with some limitations. *Reflection Blocker* is not a unique stone. It's hard to get, but still possible. It's not a rift stone. That leaves bone armor. And then the realization suddenly arises that the only person capable of getting this armor is you. Not Count Vyazemsky, not the Temple of Skron, not the Citadel. You. Maximilian Valevsky. We conclude that if someone needs mithril armor, they should contact you and only you. There are no other options. By passing on the information on how to create mithril, I increased your value, dear mentor. It was reasonable then. No one planned to turn you into an archduke, and me into your disciple. Unfortunately, I am not gifted with the ability to see the future."

"That's why they wanted to rob me," I nodded at the mountain of bone armor. An incident after which I had to install a defense system, because there were Faceless traveling around my city as they pleased, poking their noses wherever they wanted. Including the treasury.

"You need to think long and hard, my careless mentor, about how to protect the city from the dark ones. Or do you think that only light humans have *Phantom*? There are enough dark *Phantom*s in Hearth to make you sweat. Including in your treasury."

I could only sigh heavily, admitting my own impotence. The dark humans could do whatever they wanted in Hearth, that was a fact. And I couldn't do anything about it — I simply didn't have the resources. Kimal Sarento delivered the final twist of the knife:

"Since returning to the city, I've discovered four invisibles. Their stones have already been removed, the bodies destroyed, but how many more agile and capable specialists are running around here? You can't rely on the idea that your treasury defense system is infallible. As I said, in any situation you need to have at least two plans, my thoughtful mentor. Someday you'll get used to the idea."

"So you have a plan?"

"Naturally. I'll tell you all about it after we're done here. Take the orbs and integrate your new armor pieces. They're anxiously awaiting us."

How nice it was to work with other mages who were used to operating with magic of the highest order. The bone armor disappeared one after another, transforming into iridescent orbs, and we continued our work without any special difficulty. Although the only reason I didn't have any problems was because as soon as my head began to spin, I used the dark liquid obtained from the offworlders, saving myself from losing life force. Of course, I had precious little of this dark liquid, but now was that rare occasion when I was not going to spare them. Because I understood the importance of this work.

In order to create a full mithril set, twenty-five units of bone armor were required. I, who already had a belt and a chest plate, needed twenty-four — one armor piece had gone to repairs. Kimal Sarento needed the same amount. He had never removed the boots he made earlier. And seventy-five mithril orbs were spent to ensure the safety of my ladies. While Alia reacted calmly, as she had known about the existence of mithril and how it worked, Eleanore and Naira were truly astonished. When they learned to control the appearance of the armor and fully comprehended the power it contained, including the ability to hide very large objects and use an immaterial backpack, they were thoroughly impressed and battered me with questions about what it was and how it worked. I had to explain that mithril armor was the most valuable resource of Hearth and no one should know about it. Even the head of the Bartolomeo Clan, for it was immediately clear from Naira's face that she was about to tell Cedric about her new acquisition. Surely our family must have its secrets?

"Alright, what's this plan of yours?" I collapsed, exhausted, into a chair. Destroying such a large quantity of bone armor was not easy for me. There were only eight units of this most valuable resource left in my reserves, so I would soon have to walk through the abandoned ruins of some ancient city to find more. Preferably ancient ruins in which the Fog of Pharapho had settled for five or six hundred years. These spots were sure to contain shimmering artifacts. As everyone knew, the more ancient the location, the more valuable the artifacts in it. This was a universal truth.

"You won't like it, but I don't see any other way," Kimal Sarento sat down opposite me. "It's time to tell the whole world that mithril exists. You're protected. Your inner circle is protected. I'll acclimatize to how everything works around here soon, and I'm sure I'll be able to find a communication channel. The Pharapho sergeants communicate with their master somehow — they start avoiding you when you start actively mining armor. That means there's a way to transmit information both ways. Therefore, the Pharapho flesh should provide this for us too. Alia, Naira, and I already have a status bar, all that's left is to open Eleanore's. Even if one of them is kidnapped, the armor won't be able to be hacked. The map will tell you the exact location, the armor itself will protect you until help arrives. But! All this may be rendered moot if the world learns that mithril can be tied to a specific person. You need to demonstrate Hearth's power. Show that there is no point in attacking. The tournament you were invited to is the perfect place to demonstrate your armor to the entire world. Not only to the light, but also to the dark. The clan leaders and the highest aristocracy must once again see your value. They must understand that they need to negotiate with you. That they need to be friends with you. Now Hearth is known only as a place for trading with the dark. You are a conqueror of rifts. Neither of these things are interesting to the higher ups. You need to show them a piece of candy. One that cannot be taken away. Only earned."

Kimal Sarento fell silent, allowing me to consider his proposal. Mithril was a strategic resource of Hearth, and one I was placing a certain bet on. None of my people could be killed and must not be attacked. This was a core value for me. But people would always be people. I had a limited amount of armor now — only five sets. These were for my loved ones. I could also find ten people who were highly likely not to betray me. Gustav, Flask, Rabblerouser and others. Those who owed me their lives. But what to do with the rest? Many of the guards had families in the Zarak Empire. This was a means of control and pressure. They could put pressure on them and force them to part with their mithril armor. Even posthumously, but their family would live in abundance. This issue must be discussed with Eleanore. The families of the guards, artisans, and all the vital workers in Hearth must stand before us for vetting. Now the next important question: what would happen if the world found out about mithril? About how to produce it? I didn't think Count Vyazemsky would keep this information hidden. This bastard was actively trying to cause harm. So the world would find out. The cons? They would close my access to ruins infested with the Fog of Pharapho throughout the Zarak Empire. But that meant nothing to me. There was always the opportunity to negotiate with the Temple of Skron. Damn it, I forgot about Fardi! They would not let me into the dark lands, only into the Bartolomeo Clan. Then another question: how many ruins with fog were on the territory of my wife's clan? This point definitely needed to be clarified, but for now, any trade with dark humans was closed to me. If there was no bone armor, there would be no mithril. But was armor really necessary? This question arose a long time ago, but it took shape only now, after all my long and fruitful work creating mithril.

"Before we give the whole world new knowledge, we need to conduct one more experiment," I said, gathering my thoughts.

"There's too little armor left to throw it away," the chancellor reminded me.

"Thought experiments are elementary and do not require resources. Let's think out loud. Why are sergeants good for mithril? Because they have armor? Debatable. What are soldiers, majors, small fish, for, anyway? Pharapho gave birth to a bunch of creatures, but sergeants are the only ones that can make mithril. And not even from their corpses themselves, but from the armor that remains after long and tedious extraction. Why is it so difficult? And who decided that armor is required to obtain mithril? Why can't you use the whole creature? The fish are also Pharapho's flesh."

Judging by the way Kimal Sarento's lips tightened, he wasn't thinking that way. Slowly, as if tasting each word, he joined the discussion.

"Destroying the rifts is no problem, as well as gathering several high-level mages and a healer in one place. It's possible to protect yourself from the dark spheres that the soldiers throw. Concentrate the abilities of several high-level mages on one creature, stabilize it with a healer...The mass of a conventional Pharapho soldier may well be enough to replace two or even three armors. There will be a lot of mithril. You are right — additional tests are needed. And not just one. If you look at it this way, you can't discount another factor: the dark ones. If the Gourfan Clan strains itself, it will be able to drag a level fifteen ousel up to the surface in a box. Of course, they will lose a lot of people fighting the flying death, but the result will be achieved. They will have an ousel in a cube."

"The dark ones don't have anyone who can mirror darkness," I objected. Apparently, my ego and jealousy were tied to my unique ability. I was the only dark mirror, period. Dark. Mirror. Skron damn it all! Why did this completely natural thought occur to me only now?!

Kimal Sarento had no idea the storm raging in my chest and continued:

"They won't need a mirror. The cube will be made in the form of a cage. And they will work at night, so that the ousel doesn't die in the sun. The spawn of Pharapho will be blocked, the dark ones will cut out the bone armor, give it to be melted down, and literally in two or three months we will face not only Karina Fardi, but also an army of fighters clad in mithril. Against whom no one will be able to do a thing. Not even me. All that protects us now is the dark ones' lack of information on how mithril is made. As soon as they get it, and they certainly will if we start showing off a bunch of sets, there will be trouble. A lot of trouble. Apparently, the idea of sharing information from the records of the first emperor was not the best. This problem needs to be solved now. Count Vyazemsky has been balancing on the edge for a long time, as has Count Shub. The situation with Count Kuzmin remains unclear. I would try to negotiate with him. The old man is fond of unique items and artifacts. He can be bought. The other two cannot."

"Can they be eliminated?"

"They can," the man nodded. "The only problem is that you destroyed the people who could do this work. Of course, we could try to do it our-selves, but I wouldn't risk it right now. We're not ready to wage war with the entire empire. We need to think. Now I want to hear, my mentor who can't hide his emotions, what came into your head when you said the phrase about the dark mirror? Your face changed, as if the Light had descended upon you."

"When I first came to the academy, Father Nor said that the Fortress knew of cases where a light mirror appeared among the dark humans."

"Yes, it is a well-known fact," confirmed Kimal Sarento. "It doesn't occur very often, but in certain families such ability arises. Extremely unpleasant individuals — the magic of the light does not work on them at all. If such people appear in our area, then...Oh, come on now!" The chancellor uttered the last phrase as he looked at my sarcastic face.

"Brothers and sisters?"

"If it's true, then they're just relatives. Distant ones, but relatives nonetheless. Either the first emperor, or his sons, or my grandfather — one of them clearly had a good go at the ladies in the dark lands. But none of that matters. What's important is that we mustn't hand over the mithril now. It's too risky."

"That's true," said Kimal Sarento. "I'll think about how to solve the problem of keeping the mystery of the production process under wraps and exclusive to Hearth. It's my mistake, and I have to fix it. Maximilian, you must meet with Magister Meram before we leave Hearth. I would like to be present during the conversation."

The old man appeared in the office a few moments later, as if he had been waiting behind the door. The servant I had invited had not even had time to properly leave the room when the former runescribe burst in. Judging by his appearance, the seals had begun to dissolve much earlier than Magister Meram had predicted. I had not seen the old man for several days, maybe a week, and in that time he had aged at least twenty years! And he hadn't exactly been a spring chicken before.

Nevertheless, his agility and energy hadn't disappeared. Casting a displeased glance at the grinning Kimal Sarento, Meram sat down on the chair and, nervously tapping on the table, asked:

"Your conditions? What do you want in exchange for giving me the *Author* skill? For me to become your pupil?"

"Everything," I replied. "Everything you have. Gold, resources, connections, contracts. All the developments you will make using the skill. I want everything."

"Unacceptable!" he cried. "What's the point of living if you take everything I have?"

"What is the point of having anything outside of Hearth? What is the point of an estate in the Shurgan Empire if you are going to live and practice your craft here? All my pupils must either be by my side or on my estate. There is no other way."

"Is this your doing?" Magister Meram turned to Kimal Sarento, but the man only raised his eyebrows, pretending that he had nothing to do with it.

"These are my requirements," I answered calmly. "Having the skill does not guarantee a result. *Author* works differently than *Runescribe.* It requires words and sentences that you need to know. Plus the expenditure of life force. I don't have a dictionary, but I have this." I embodied one piece of dark liquid that was mined from offworlders. The frowns on both men's faces told me that they had no idea what it was. I had to explain.

"Dark fluid. A resource mined from high-level offworlders. Thanks to this, you don't have to waste your own life force. One unit was enough for me for several three-syllable words. The supply is extremely limited, there are twenty-three units left, including this one. I get everything, you get five stones, the skill, and the ability to create. I need a dictionary, and you will create it for me."

"Do you know what's happening to me? What will happen if I fail?"

"I do. That's why you have the perfect motivation. You'll keep your nose to the grindstone. Three weeks is plenty of time to invent an aging blocker."

"It's called a soul fuser," Kimal Sarento corrected me. "In order to stop aging, a fuse is required. Otherwise, the body will return to its original state. How old are you, Magister Meram? About three hundred years old? The human body is not designed to survive so long."

"If I were you, I wouldn't be so smug, Sarento. If I don't succeed, you'll die too!" Magister Meram said angrily. He clearly didn't like where the conversation was heading. Apparently, he had been counting on a gentler approach.

"Sooner or later, we all die," the chancellor noted philosophically. "Of course, I'd like it to be later, but the ways of Light are inscrutable."

"We are wasting your time," I said, steering the conversation back towards the topic at hand. "You will give the order to move all the resources you have to Kostrish. What cannot be moved must be sold. I need everything you have. Only under this condition will I pass on *Author* skill and the dark liquid. I need a dictionary, not a master lying around exhausted.

"Your mentor did not pass on the dictionary?" Meram's voice became tense.

"Only a bare skill without any explanations. You will have to solve the problem yourself, without anyone's help. But only if we come to an agreement. Now, from what I can see, we have no such agreement."

If my grandfather's last words were to be believed, all the information I needed to know about the *Author* skill could be found in the ruins of the ancients. How to use it, how to apply symbols, how to create sentences and some sort of dictionary. But my grandfather did not give any guarantees. He just said that there might be. But there might not be. After all, there are only three points left untouched by the Fog of Pharapho. For the last two, I still had to actively trade with the Abyss. The greedy seraphim would definitely squeeze out all the essences I had. I urgently needed to close rifts, but the order of Karina Fardi, given to the dark ones, left no room for interpretation. Valevsky was not welcome in Kerux. How timely was the arrival of the representative of the Kaliman Empire! And how well this man knew how to bargain! I was sure that if he had a little more time, he would have flipped the script so that I would have had to pay extra to pass through the rifts. A very cunning and dangerous man, this Emir Hadji. Good thing I had Demitr Turbin! My former Number One, a merchant, a man who knew how to find a loophole where not only I, but even Eleanore and Kimal Sarento, could find nothing.

"Good." Magister Meram's cheek twitched. "You will receive everything I have."

"I am unable to accept you as a pupil right now. I don't believe in oaths. We have a contract, and everything must be recorded in writing. Eleanore, I need to draft a contract with Magister Meram outlining our terms."

My estate manager appeared with her assistants. The cheerful Demitr and Bagration Rubinsky, the lawyer of Hearth, who had once been Two in my doomed soldier group. I had no other personnel, but these were enough. People who owed me their lives would do everything they could not to betray me. But they were also capable of betrayal. I couldn't trust anyone in this life but myself.

"Are you coming?" Brother Lou appeared, disgruntled, in the doorway to my office. The red robe was infuriated by our slowness. He urgently needed to go to Turb to take Kimal Sarento's notes and finally put pressure on Count Fardi. It was hardly the first time I was in solidarity with the Citadel from start to finish. Lay it on him until he cracked. All the Fardis. Including that freak who read the execution order with such pleasure. I wanted to kill him personally.

"I'll be there soon, I think." I looked at the gloomy Magister Meram, who was reading the draft of our contract. "You're not the only one whose time is valuable."

Chapter 14

"FROM HENCEFORTH, I appoint Tarra Loyd chancellor of the Magic Academy of the Zarak Empire! Wear this title with honor!"

"The magical academy is in good hands, Your Imperial Majesty!"

Shock. This was the state the entire capital had been mired in for the last twenty-four hours. Kimal Sarento had kept his word. After he handed over all the necessary documents to Brother Lou, and also provided him with a man nicknamed *Phantom,* it was time to resign from his high position. As my pupil said, never before in the entire history of the magic academy, either in Zarak or other light empires, or even dark ones, had there been a case in which the chancellor had voluntarily resigned. Especially Kimal Sarento, considering how much he had to learn during this time and what adventures he had to take part in. Magister Tarra Loyd, like Magister Meram, had significantly lost her shine. The once perfect woman had begun to age. The changes were still subtle, but no one would have placed the dance teacher at even twenty-seven anymore. Closer to forty. In the twenty days that remained, the final transformation would occur and Tarra Loyd would become the sixty-year-old old woman that she actually was. Well-groomed, refined, youthful, but still an old woman.

At first, the emperor did not believe it, thinking that this was another of Kimal Sarento's inventions. The letter he sent to the chancellery was reviewed, but not accepted or put into action. I had to waste time and visit the palace in person. That was when the empire plunged into a state of complete confusion. Even now, when the emperor officially announced Tarra Loyd as the next chancellor, everyone looked at Count Sarento, waiting for him to laugh and say that everything that was happening was just a prank. But it was no prank, and the Magical Academy of the Zarak Empire had been appointed a new chancellor.

"Maximilian, will you allow me to steal you for a few minutes?" The High Priest caught me right after the ceremony. A surprisingly quick ceremony — Zurgan the First had fled almost immediately afterward. As for Father Urg, he was almost the only person outside the inner circle who had the right to call me by name, without mentioning my titles. Or at least, that was how he saw it.

"Pupil, don't go off on your own, you're needed." I turned to Kimal Sarento, who was standing next to me and flashing charming smiles to numerous beauties.

"Pupil?" Apparently, information from Hearth did not reach Turb instantly.

"Pupil," I confirmed.

"I'm even afraid to ask what you plan to teach such a respected gentleman." Father Urg clearly had not expected such a turn of events.

"You know, a little of this, a little of that. Apprentice, we need a canopy of silence."

"As my safety-loving mentor says," Kimal Sarento was clearly enjoying what was happening. The High Priest wasn't the only one who heard about my new pupil. Everyone around us had heard as well, and now this information was spreading through the main hall of the imperial palace at lightning speed. The way their faces fell at the astonishing news caused another fit of merriment in Kimal Sarento. But he was the only one having any fun. I, for instance, was not in the mood for laughing, since I had to inform the public that my pupil had a magic stone that was quite rare for our lands. However, I had no other choice. I did not want to follow the High Priest anywhere. Of course, hanging a canopy of silence in the middle of the imperial palace was not the most reasonable action, but it was the lesser of two evils.

"You wanted to talk, Your Holiness?"

"Alone, without any unnecessary witnesses," the High Priest quickly pulled himself together.

"Count Sarento is connected to me by an unbreakable bond, Father Urg. He is not just any student — he is my confirmed pupil."

"With full access to all his parameters?" The High Priest knew how to play it close to the chest, but this news had definitely thrown him off balance.

"Absolute," I confirmed. "My pupil must know everything that I know. Such are the rules of apprenticeship. Although what is the point of me explaining to you what a confirmed pupil is? I am sure that the High Priest of the Fortress knows this very well himself. I suggest we put aside the question of why this happened and return to the topic that interests you. So what did you call me for, High Priest?"

"How is Alia? How is the child?" Father Urg clearly did not want to ask this, but the presence of Kimal Sarento had ruined all his plans.

"She's fine, thank the Light. We managed to eliminate the consequences of Elor's attack. Now nothing threatens the lives of either Alia or our child."

"May the Light be kind to them," nodded Father Urg. "That's all I wanted to know, Maximilian. It was not worth informing the public about the abilities of your pupil. The *Canopy of Silence* stone is extremely rare and is subject to mandatory registration. I am sure that Kimal Sarento, as a former chancellor, knows about such trifles, and in the register of rare stones there is a corresponding entry about the withdrawal of the stone from the imperial reserves."

"Such a record for this stone cannot exist," I responded calmly to the veiled accusation. "Kimal Sarento received this stone directly from me. I was lucky enough to obtain it during the destruction of the Fog of Pharapho in the ruins belonging to the Bartolomeo Clan. By decree of His Imperial Majesty, the magic stones obtained by me during the campaigns are the property of the autonomous city of Hearth. Including the *Canopy of Silence* that I gave to my pupil. My stones have nothing to do with the values of the Zarak Empire. May the Light protect you, High Priest! As the servants of the Light like to say, sooner or later everyone will be rewarded according to their deeds. Pupil, you can remove the canopy."

"What are you implying?" Metal flashed in Father Urg's voice. We returned to the hum of the main hall of the imperial palace, where an active discussion of what had been heard and seen was underway. The pupil, the canopy of silence, the angry High Priest. Enough scandal to keep them talking for at least a month!

"Hearth never hints. Hearth acts. The Nocturnal Guild, who thought themselves untouchable, is a witness to that. I recommended that they leave my city, they decided that the law does not apply to them. That they are above the law. They started killing my couriers. Harming my people. I had to intervene and explain that this should not be done. Explain clearly. If even one more hair falls from the heads of my people and the Nocturnal

Guild is involved, I will continue my cleansing campaign. Only this time I will not limit myself to one lair. The Zarak Empire will be completely cleansed of the shadowy plague."

"I don't really understand why you're telling me this," the coldness in the High Priest's voice could freeze you on the spot.

"It just happened to come up, Your Holiness. All the best!"

Turning around, I headed for the exit. Kimal Sarento walked alongside me, paying a few last compliments to the ladies on the way out. I could never reach such heights of self-control. Count Sarento didn't allow himself to exhale when we made it into the carriage, and even then only after he had hung the canopy of silence. The coachman also had eyes and ears.

"What can I say — we're walking a fine line. The emperor could well have given the order to take me into custody. Apparently, Zurgan the First proved too impressionable and did not think about the consequences of my freedom. Like everyone else, he did not believe that I would risk refusing to protect the academy. Now, I was certain that a whole team of investigators was compiling a list of all my sins. Collecting evidence, witnesses. If they put their finger on me, then they would do it in such a way that I would never squirm free again. They were waiting for us at the exit, but did not dare touch us. The information that I had a mentor came just in time. However, I had no illusions — the secret chancellery will definitely invite us to visit them. Both me and you. They probably have questions about the events at the Nocturnal Guild base."

"I don't think anyone will touch us before the tournament, so we have three days. We need to figure out how to escape from the capital immediately after the awards ceremony, preferably without a fight. Of course, I never liked Slovan Usminsky, but he does his job. We shouldn't kill him for that. Is there a tournament schedule?"

"There were very few participants — only thirty-two people. Or rather, thirty-one — I've been crossed out. A pupil cannot participate in the same tournament as his mentor. The brackets will be formed later, but it seems to me that the main participants will be separated. You will only meet Counts Shub and Vyazemsky in the final and semi-final, no earlier. As for Count Kuzminsky, I would suggest meeting him in advance to discuss the possibility of..."

What possibility Kimal Sarento was going to discuss with the old scholar remained a mystery, because at that moment the carriage was thrown asunder. The doors were torn off, the roof was torn into pieces, the top splintered and merged with the bottom. I flew back, knocking the walls of the carriage with my back. The canopy of silence was somewhere with Kimal Sarento. Hysterical screams of passers-by were heard. Screams of pain. Incoherent squeals and wheezing. I was flung into the air, spinning several times before being smeared against the wall of a nearby house.

Golden Dome of Protection absorbed the blow and the mithril armor coped with the aftershock, so I slid to the ground relatively alive and well. Stunned by what was happening, of course, but nothing more. There was no trace left of the carriage. It was scattered around the area in small smoldering pieces. The horses...I felt sorry for them. Nothing could help the animals. They had been obliterated. The coachman was gone. Either he had been flung out like me, or he had already left the carriage before the attack.

An inconspicuous-looking guy leapt over to my side.

"The Nocturnal Guild never forgives!"

With these words, he thrust something sharp and shiny at me. Sparks flashed, and the knife (he had attacked me with a simple knife!) was thrown aside.

"What the..." the man blurted out. *Analyze* revealed a set of beguiling magic stones. The level thirteen *Phantom* alone was worth something, so without further ado I plunged my hand into his chest to seize my loot. The knife fell from his hands and easily sank into the pavement stones up to the hilt. Vyrma?!

My shield sparked once again as several fireballs flew in my direction, as well as a couple of crossbow bolts. They were shooting from somewhere above. Only at the last moment did I notice a shadow flashing on the roof of the neighboring building. The assassins moved deftly and in perfect synch. As I was looking up at the roofs, a second blow came from the side. Several lightning bolts flew out of the windows of the nearby house, powerlessly skirting my dome. Crossbow bolts ricocheted with a screech and flew back. The sound of shattered glass, and perhaps even a wheeze — but at that moment the rooftop assassins drew my attention once more. They stuck their heads out from behind cover to attack me, but this was the last thing they ever did. Chain lightning passed along the roof of the building, turning everyone who was there, either purposefully or by accident, into ash. Kimal Sarento had finally joined the battle. Soon, I saw where the man himself stood. He had been thrown to the opposite side of the street. He walked forward without even thinking to look around. What was the point if he knew they weren't going to kill him?

"That's what I was saying! Something always happens to you!" Judging by Sarento's face, he was experiencing unspeakable happiness. It seemed like he was about to jump for joy.

"It's not exactly a reason to rejoice," I said. I had no desire to pursue the murderers hiding on the first floor. If I understood correctly, they were already gone without a trace.

"You just don't understand the beauty of what's transpiring!" Kimal Sarento grinned, coming closer. "This is the first attack by a Nocturnal Guild member on a high-ranking aristocrat's carriage in...I can't even remember how long. The two parties always found ways to come to an agreement. Just not in this case."

"Vyrma," I said, indicating the knife that was still stuck in the stone. "They most likely shot me with vyrma too. The assassins were thoroughly prepared. The one who tried to gut me like a pig had a level thirteen *Phantom.*"

"However, your shield worked, even without your armor," Kimal Sarento chuckled. "Someday my mysterious mentor will condescend to show me his current magical field. How he managed to block vyrma. It will be very useful knowledge to have."

"Not much has changed compared to the field drawn in our shared notebook," I said, nodding at the fake artifact. "Except I've leveled everything up. A lot. And added a couple of support stones. Let's pay a visit to the assassins again, this time together. Apparently, they didn't listen to the voice of reason the first time. There was still a lot of interesting stuff left in their treasury. The gold, in any case, should be repossessed."

"I don't think we'll find anything or anyone in the residence anymore," Kimal Sarento said. "If I were one of the three, I would have moved operations entirely a long time ago."

"We can't leave this attack unpunished!"

"Note, my beleaguered mentor, that I didn't say a word about us not doing anything. To begin with, I suggest we wait for the valiant guards and write an official complaint that the city is not providing protection to the noble lord and his pupil. That innocent people have suffered. As for you, my ardent mentor, it wouldn't hurt to walk around the area and treat all the victims. It would be much more useful than all this senseless shaking your fist in the air and calling for justice. We will demand it later and in another place. Let's start with the townspeople."

I had to admit, he was right. With everything that was going on, I forgot that we weren't the only ones who had suffered from the attack. Some of the passers-by and townspeople were in poor shape — torn-off limbs wouldn't just regrow themselves. If not for my help, these poor people would have died on the spot from something as simple as blood loss. Forgetting the regalia, I ran from one victim to another, using two, and sometimes three *Heals*. There were people scattered everywhere. I found several victims on the adjoining street. The terrified, crippled victims were trying to crawl away from the crazed assassins.

By the time the guards arrived, everything was over. Aside from the horses and the missing coachman, whom I never found, there had been no casualties. The guards barely managed to squeeze through the crowd and surround us. Crowd? Yes, crowd — as soon as the residents of the nearby houses realized what was going on, they poured out into the street, showing me cuts, scars, missing fingers and even limbs. At first, I found it amusing — it didn't take much mana to help, but with each passing minute, there were more and more people. People who had received their dose of treatment ran to other streets, screaming at the top of their lungs: "Healing! Free healing from

Archduke Valevsky!" I wanted to put an end to this all, but a warning gesture from Kimal Sarento kept me in place. Treat. Restore. Help. Doing for free what costs tens, hundreds, or even thousands of gold in the ordinary world. People who regained their sight cried. Those who grew an arm or a leg jumped and even danced for joy. It was as if I found myself inside a crazy human anthill that chanted incessantly: "Valevsky! Archduke Valevsky!"

When the guards arrived, the townspeople neary tore them apart with their bare hands, but after a few painful jabs the particularly zealous individuals calmed down.

"Follow us," the city guard said. The crowd tagged along behind. Not everyone had received their share of the treatment yet. All the guards' attempts to pacify the crowd were futile. When it came to their health, people became truly insane. But I couldn't heal anymore — several times I'd had to use the skill on myself to hide my nosebleed. Unlike my pupil, I had a limit to the use of high-level magical abilities. Constant practice was needed, and if I understood correctly, Kimal Sarento had given me that today.

The people stopped abruptly as soon as they realized where they were taking us. Not to the city administrative building, where the mayor and the chief of the guard sat. We were taken to a small dark building, standing alone in the center of a small square. The Turb branch of the secret chancellery. A place where no one with even a modicum of intelligence wanted to go. A place from which many never returned.

"Gentlemen, please follow me," one of the interrogators said as they met us at the front door. His face seemed familiar to me. Evidently, we had crossed paths before. *Analyze* showed that he was light. We spiraled down several underground levels, winding our way through the tangled corridors and moving in the direction of the flow. All the feigned complexity was for nought — the most zoomed in scale of the map showed where we were, as well as what houses and streets we were passing. Finally, we reached a large estate. I did not know who it belonged to, but that was unimportant. What was important was that in the room where we were taken was Slovan Ousmine, a colonel in the secret chancellery of His Imperial Majesty.

"Archduke Maximilian Valevsky and his pupil, Count Kimal Sarento," Slovan said slowly, as if tasting each word. "The capital is in turmoil over your sudden decision to leave the post of chancellor, Count Sarento."

"Just going into retirement, Colonel, that's all it is." Kimal Sarento smiled.

"So it is," nodded Slovan. "But only those who have earned it deserve to retire. Those who faithfully serve their empire. Who support it in all things. Which, as we have learned, cannot be said about you, Count Sarento. Some very sensitive details of certain cases have surfaced. Trade with the dark ones, transferring unregistered elixirs, magic stones and, what struck me most, providing the dark ones with devices for processing resources from the rift. You know what punishment is customary for such a thing, right?"

"If memory doesn't deceive me, a reduction in height of precisely one head length," Kimal Sarento answered willingly. "Anyone who risks such things will sooner or later make a mistake. How fortunate that during the time when I was the chancellor of the magical academy, such cases were not registered. Or does the secret chancellery have other information? Witnesses? Evidence? Or at least denunciations, if it comes to that. Is it so bad that a colonel of the secret chancellery of His Imperial Majesty is trying to intimidate us? Slovan, let's get straight to the point. We were attacked, and if you haven't noticed, we are the victims. You could even say that we are in shock. I personally am not interested in hearing about whatever strange cases have surfaced. Do you really think so poorly of me that you think I didn't clean up after myself? Everything you could dig up, Slovan, is tied to His Imperial Majesty. I don't think that Zurgan the First would share his secrets. Even with your secret chancellery. What do you need and what are you willing to offer for it?"

"A proposal?" The colonel frowned. "Count Sarento, I don't think you're in a position to demand anything."

"I don't want to upset you, Slovan, but that's exactly the situation we're in. You need something from us. Otherwise, there wouldn't be this whole circus with the attack on the carriage."

"Circus?" I said. "It wasn't the Nocturnal Guild that attacked us?"

"If you're talking about the ones that attacked you, then yes, it was the Nocturnal Guild. But even the most hardened scumbags will have enough sense not to ignore the agreement between the secret chancellery and the Nocturnal Guild. Yes, Slovan, I know about your agreements. The day belongs to you, the night belongs to them. And those who violate this rule are severely punished. And by their own kind. All of these attacks must be arranged. Like the one that just happened. I have too high an opinion of the secret chancellery of His Imperial Majesty to believe that two groups of low-level assassins were able to ambush us without hindrance, and even drive their carriage to the emperor's palace. You knew what would happen, but you did not interfere. You wanted to watch. To make sure that the Nocturnal Guild could not do anything to me or my silent mentor. So I will ask again, Slovan, what do you need and what are you ready to offer for it?"

"Marisa Shor," he replied reluctantly.

"Zurgan's daughter?" Kimal Sarento frowned. "Why is she here?"

"Two days ago, she was kidnapped from the palace. The kidnappers made a demand: the emperor must declare war on Hearth and wipe it off the face of the earth."

"Are you sure it was kidnappers? Maybe the girl ran away on her own."

"As a confirmation of the seriousness of their intentions, the kidnappers sent Marisa's right hand. Her hand, Kimal! The girl is only thirteen years old!"

"Who?" From the way my pupil's eyes narrowed, it was clear that there would be no talk of payment. "Slovan, two days have passed. You should have at least gotten a name!"

"That's the thing, we have no idea!" the colonel nearly screamed, admitting his own helplessness. "The first letter we received from the kidnappers had a deadline: until the tournament. If the emperor does not agree to the demands, he will receive both of the girl's legs. There are three days left, but we have not a single lead."

"Therefore, you decided to recruit us."

"Him." Slovan nodded in my direction. "There are rumors in the empire that Archduke Valveksy is capable of solving problems that no one else can handle. That trouble sticks to him. The emperor will not agree to the kidnappers' demands, even if his daughter is taken apart piece by piece. It is a matter of honor. We are digging for information, scouring the earth, but to no avail. That is why we staged today's performance. You could have been followed, and if we had decided to invite you to a conversation, the girl would have been killed immediately. We need information, but everyone who could have given it to us is dead."

From the look Slovan cast at me, I knew what sources he was talking about. The Nocturnal Guild assassins were known not only as liquidation specialists, but also as skillful reconnaissance agents.

"If we get Marisa back, I need free access to all the rifts and ruins of the Zarak Empire," I said after a pause. "Archduke Valevsky and his entourage will have the right to move freely throughout the Zarak Empire. Without the need to receive permissions from the dukes of the regions along our path."

Slovan glanced at Kimal Sarento, but he made no move to limit me.

"Alright."

"Then one more thing. I would like to determine how much authority we are being given. We will find Marisa. What should we do with her kidnappers? Store them and wait for the secret chancellery to arrive? What if the kidnapper is, say, Count Vyazemsky? Should I also wait for you then? Or can we resolve the issue on our own?"

"Count Vyazemsky was vetted first. As was Count Shub. All those who organized the riots in the capital with the aim of discrediting Hearth were checked first and foremost."

"So you were aware of what was going on?" Kimal Sarento grinned. Slovan looked askance at my pupil and nodded.

"We knew. We received the order: do not interfere. Watch what happens, but do not interfere. This business is between Count Vyazemsky and Archduke Valevsky. As for your question: Marisa must return home alive and well. With all her limbs. Everything else is at your discretion. For the sake of protocol: the secret chancellery has never involved Archduke Valevsky or his pupil in any sort of agreement. The only requirement is that if one of the parties can obtain any information, it must be shared with the other. There is no and can be no individual work done in this matter. Sergeant, show the guests to the carriage. You will be taken to the hotel. Three days, gentlemen. You have only three days."

Chapter 15

"WHAT ARE YOU PLOTTING?" Kimal Sarento was silent the whole time we were returning to the hotel. There were no new attacks, but that didn't mean we weren't being followed. Only after we found ourselves in a two-room suite and hung the canopy of silence did we continue our conversation.

"Are you familiar with the term *Fog Stalker*?" I asked point-blank.

"Only about the fragments. According to the notebook, you received these fragments from each destroyed Pharapho soldier and sergeant. The fragments create a certain key. That's all the information I have."

"The Fog Stalker is a being connected to Pharapho. It seems to want to destroy him, but I don't have any precise data on this. And it doesn't really matter. What's important is that it gives answers. The key leads to an arena where you can fight forty waves of beasts. The higher the level of the wave, the more difficult it is to destroy, the more serious the question you can ask and receive a reply. Last time I was in the arena, I only managed to get through twenty waves. But that was enough to get an answer to the question of how to remove the Light from my eyes. If we need an urgent answer to the question of where Marisa is, there's no better place. We don't have time to look for witnesses or ask beggars. I'm sure the secret office has already done it."

"Can you only receive answers to questions in the arena?" asked Kimal Sarento.

"Items, artifacts, answers. Everything that exists in this world. Except maybe the question about *Tainted Blood.* I assume the Fog Stalker won't answer that one."

Judging by the way Kimal Sarento frowned, the phrase was unfamiliar to him.

"I get the feeling you have something to tell me, my secret-loving mentor. Perhaps it's time for us to integrate our notebooks in both directions?"

"It's time." I adjusted a few settings, allowing the data to synchronize between the two artifacts. The records that had suddenly appeared in my book when I took on my pupil were enough to fill several lifetimes. People, their habits, weak points, descriptions of some events — after one-way integration, a huge pile of information fell on me. Structured, carefully organized, but still a truly gigantic sum. But the transfer of information was carried out in one direction. Mine. And the time had come to make a decision. Could I trust Kimal Sarento or not? My pupil had opened his life up to me. Parameters, information, a list of all the contracts and agreements he had signed with anyone. There was so much incriminating evidence in the records that Kimal Sarento could have been executed thirty times, no less. Moreover, confirmed incriminating evidence, with reference to witnesses. My pupil actually was actively leaking mechanisms and elixirs to the dark ones, and also shamelessly used his position as chancellor to create an ideal set of magic stones for himself. A perfect set of eight-sided gems. But I didn't care much about what he had done previously. The important thing was what he was doing now.

"The Abyss? Thirteen powers?" Kimal Sarento frowned, somehow immediately weeding out important information from the wealth of data that had suddenly filled the pages of his notebook. Or maybe there hadn't been that many updates on his side. What could I know that the chancellor of the magic academy, in all his eighty-five years, didn't?

"Eleven, now. We've driven two from our world. In all fairness, we should get rid of the rest as well. The ancients made a mistake by bringing Chaos into our world."

"Light, Skron, and Chaos are all primary tier entities, correct? Pharapho and the Abyss are the secondary. So, there should be six forces left in the third. Mechanoids, undergrounders, ghosts. That's from what you know. At one time, I happened to overhear something about waterfolk and troggs. Two more. What's the sixth?"

"I don't think this is the most urgent matter at the moment. The price for information about the princess' whereabouts shouldn't be too exorbitant. We have the chance to ask another question. Any suggestions? I don't even have a question, rather a demand — we must update Hearth's security system so that a pillar of light appears above the heads of dark humans as well. I believe we'll have to pass at least ten waves."

"I'm sorry to upset you, but I have the feeling that such an opportunity exists now. Only the dark ones won't turn it on, because it's not profitable for them. Now they are the sole administrators of this system. They can make any changes to the security policy, add any restrictions that are of interest to them first and foremost, and not to you or the city. They control your city, not you. Think about it: why did a division into light and dark suddenly appear within this integral security system? Because the mechanoids made a defense system specifically for the Temple of Skron? It even sounds strange. Did the dark ones never have internal conflicts? Did the clans that installed such a system only worry about light humans showing up, and not fellow tribesmen from other clans? No, my slow-witted mentor, there is no point in asking about what is already clear. Until you have the sole right to manage your system, you will not be able to control the dark ones with its help. And I'm afraid you will never have this as long as the system installed by the Temple of Skron remains in place."

"I need something else," I said heavily. Kimal Sarento knew how to press on a sore spot. I knew myself that my security system was far from perfect.

"Something else that's entirely independent from anyone else. Plus someone who can install it. Or detailed instructions written for simple-minded creatures. Because I, for one, can't do that. Trusting the dark ones is stupid, but trusting them to protect your city is even more stupid. Perhaps it was right once, but times, as you can see, are changing. Ask Fog Stalker about that. And, if possible, find out the exact list of forces remaining in this world. I have a feeling that this information could be useful to us. I have no idea how, but it might. I think this will be more than enough to start with. How many keys do you have left?"

"Four, besides this one." I embodied a Fog Stalker key. "I urgently need access to ruins with fog to replenish my stock of fragments. And I need to test my theory about the mithril."

"I'll think about what can be done. If possible, try to clarify about the dictionary of symbolic magic and remote communication through mithril armor. In general, it would be good to get a full list of all the available properties of Pharapho's flesh."

"I can only pass twenty waves. When Pharapho himself appears among the beasts, it becomes difficult. I don't think we'll be able to get through enough waves to answer all these questions."

"Understood. You have the resources to upgrade your stones to level thirty, right? Do it right now. You need to be maximally prepared before you go to the arena. And here, take these."

Kimal Sarento handed me several vials. I had never encountered such elixirs in my life.

"You could say they're a type of enhancement. Provides a temporary thirty percent boost to all five main parameters. Lasts for ten minutes. I repeat: you need to use your entire arsenal to get results. Including such a seemingly small thing as this. Use it only in the arena, starting from the tenth wave. And one more thing. I understand that you are a wise and adequate man, but do not dare to ask questions to which you already know the answers. If you ask a question as banal as 'Who kidnapped Marisa Shor,' then you will get a similar answer: 'Some grey human' — just a random name. So do not strain yourself. Your question should imply a full answer. We are interested in the customer, not the ones who performed the act. Even asking for her current location could be a trap, as she could be moved elsewhere. An answer that the princess was in the middle of the road leading somewhere ten minutes ago will not give anything. But I'm saying this just in case. For now, I have to read what valuable things you have discovered during the month that we haven't had integrated notebooks."

I nodded and activated the key. Sometimes Kimal Sarento acted like a mother hen, worrying about every little thing. I understood that I was only eighteen, that I could occasionally do stupid things, be unable to control my emotions, but in the last six months I'd been forced to mature by at least twenty years. I didn't think many of my peers would have managed to survive the chaotic events that I'd been put through. That was why it was so irritating to realize that I was still perceived as a fool. Infuriating.

The space spun, and I found myself in a huge arena. Nothing had changed since the last time. The Fog Stalker started in on his spiel about who he was, what he was doing here, and what his purpose was, but I didn't listen.

"I need the name of the customer who ordered that Marisa Shor be kidnapped and her hand to be cut off. The answer must be as complete as possible. Wave!"

At the same time as I said these words, I activated *Healing Aura*. Unlike in reality, in the Fog Arena, healing dealt damage to surrounding creatures much more effectively than *Dark Spike*. For some reason, the copies that formed around me could not stand such light magic. The first wave. The second. The third. The Fog Stalker was silent after each call, indicating that there were too few creatures killed for me to get an answer to my question. On the tenth wave, I began to worry. On the twelfth, I began to suspect that the Fog Stalker would never answer me. On the sixteenth, my heart began to beat faster, anticipating trouble. Big trouble. When the nineteenth wave ended and I still did not receive an answer to my question, a suspicion arose that the ghost-like four-armed creature that hung in the air simply did not know the correct answer, which is why it was silent. I was tempted to ask, but I was afraid that this would count as my question and I'd have to start all over. Okay, I'd try one more. Starting from the twentieth wave, among the creatures that appear, there will be a creature called Pharapho. A shapeless mass the size of an elephant, resembling everything and nothing at once. Last time I managed to destroy it with the help of *Heal*, but then the level of my stones was incomparable with what it is now. It should help, especially since Pharapho would not appear on the twenty-first wave. It only appeared every other wave until the thirtieth. Okay, I'd have to endure. I needed an answer!

"Wave!"

The simulacrum of Pharapho died suspiciously quickly. I was expecting a long and harrowing fight, but it was all over in a few moments. Five casts of *Heal*, and the huge mass of flesh dissipated into the air. The voice of the Fog Stalker rang out:

"You have passed twenty waves!"

It fell silent, as it had twenty times before, but after some time it finally said:

"The question has been asked, it's time to receive your response. The customer who ordered Marisa Shor's kidnapping is the padishah of the Shurgan Empire, Bayazid the Third. At the moment, Marisa Shor is unconscious in the palace of the padishah Bayazid the Third, in the main building, on the second basement floor, in the third chamber to the left of the stairs. The captive was delivered there using a portal opened by converts. The Temple of Skron brought gifts to Skron, and he closed the information on the current position of Marisa Shor up to and including the nineteenth wave. Above that, Skron has no right to interfere with the arena's actions."

"Is the Temple of Skron also involved in the princess' kidnapping?"

"She was kidnapped by a dark one. The one who walks in shadows, called Two. The Temple of Skron believes that Archduke Valevsky must be punished for not informing them about the infected rifts. That they no longer need to be closed. That he tried to bargain and profit from the dark. The Temple of Skron wanted to punish through the light so that during the attack of the army of the Zarak Empire on Hearth, they could lend Archduke Valevsky their hand and extort as many essences out of him as possible. They are of interest to the Temple of Skron. They know about the existence of the Abyss. They want to reach it and arrange a meeting. This is the full answer that you have earned in twenty waves. Do you wish to continue?"

"Yes. Wave!"

The news that the dark ones were involved in the princess' kidnapping threw me off balance a bit. I had just begun to think that Hearth was lucky to have partners willing to develop the city, but in fact it turned out that no one was going to develop anything. The dark ones were playing their own game and only doing what was beneficial to them. Those misty bastards. I was so angry that I passed level twenty-one without any problems. Since there was no simulacrum of Pharpho, all the common beasts died instantly from *Healing Aura*. I didn't even have to chase after them across the entire arena. I just stood in the center and waited for the monsters to run into the range of my aura.

"You have passed twenty-one waves! What reward would you like to receive? Material or immaterial?"

"I need detailed information on how to increase the effective range of my auras, as well as the ability to change the radius from a meter to the maximum allowed value. If any items or ingredients are required for this, I need them as well."

"The question and the requirements are clear, but in order to receive an answer, you will have to go through several additional waves, up to and including the twenty-fifth. Only then will you get a full response. Are you prepared for this?"

"Yes. Wave!"

Kimal Sarento was right, of course, when he said that the safety of Hearth should be the main goal of my trip to the Fog Stalker arena. But without properly functioning auras, it was becoming difficult for me to fight opponents. One-on-one combat was always welcome. But as soon as two or even three creatures appeared in different spots, my thirteen-meter radius of action quietly wept over its bitter fate. The battle with the lithoids and offworlders had clearly demonstrated this. My strength was too limited. If Kimal Sarento was able to pierce the mithril armor, then three or four high-level mages, even with level twenty stones, could do it too. Conclusion: I needed to increase my aura to such an extent that the attackers could never reach me.

"Wave!"

The twenty-fourth was a bit more challenging. The Pharapho copy had grown considerably in size. It began to occupy almost a tenth of the entire arena, and it was becoming increasingly difficult to dodge the attacks of the tentacles that whipped around with frightening speed. I leapt around like an antelope, never forgetting to send a dose of *Heal* the monster's way every time I could. Once, however, I could not dodge the attack. *Golden Dome of Protection* handled it well, but could not completely dissipate the momentum. I was carried to the edge of the arena, and only the statue I grabbed onto prevented me from plunging into nothingness. Because beyond the flat circle there was nothing but a terrible fog. However, I was able to *Heal* this copy of Pharapho significantly quickly. My pumped-up magic stone showed its true worth. The twenty-fifth level, where the main fog monster was not present, did not cause any problems, and as soon as the bar above the fog monster's head was completely filled and the creatures stopped appearing, the owner of the arena said:

"You have passed twenty-five waves. The question has been asked, it's time to receive your response."

Three shimmering objects appeared in the air in front of me.

"It is impossible to increase the effect of an aura using standard methods. The development model does not have a single key parameter that allows you to increase the aura without losing power. You need to use another mechanism. Your development model does not have a free slot for integration, so the first item you get is called a nest crystal. It is obtained from the Pharapho majors and allows you to turn any cell of the development model into a socket to place a crystal. Take it."

One of the three items started to flicker faster than the others. I extended my hand, and a development model appeared in front of me. The Fog Stalker not only provided me with items, but also acted as an altar. The development model had many passage parameters that I had to activate to get to the points I needed, so I used the development crystal on one of them without further ado. The *Ability Damage Increase* stat was reduced by a few percent, but for me it was a minor change — I rarely used *Dark Spike* anyway.

"The next step is to insert the aura variator into the development model. Take it."

The second object began to blink actively, but this time I had questions:

"The aura variator? Even my limited knowledge of mechanics is enough to know that a transmission is designed to transmit torque. How are auras and circular motion related?"

"What is an aura?" answered the Fog Stalker. "Why does it have such a parameter as a radius? The answer is simple. An aura is a circular movement of directed particles in three-dimensional space. The stronger the aura, the denser the directed flow and the more powerful the aura used.

"So the variator is already an innate part of the magic stones?

"Not the variator. There is another mechanism in operation there, based on the formation of static spheres. The aura variator takes control of the auras and allows changing the power ratio within a certain range, transmitting the changed values back to the sphere formation mechanism. Integrate this item."

The aura variator assumed its spot in the development model, but I didn't notice any particular change.

"The final step will be upgrading the mithril armor and integrating the aura variator control system into it. Take it."

And finally, the third object that was hanging before my eyes began to flicker. It was installed in my hip area, and a field with a slider that could be changed appeared on the status bar. Next to it was a numerical designation, apparently, the radius. I activated *Healing Aura*, and an icon of my ability appeared next to the slider. By default, the effective radius was thirteen meters, but by changing the slider, I understood the principle behind the way it worked. The effective radius could change from a meter at the low end of the spectrum to a hundred meters max. A hundred-meter radius! This was sheer madness! Especially considering the fact that the amount of mana it required did not change!

"Are you aware of the problem with Hearth's security system?" I asked once I'd played enough with the new device.

"Is that a question?"

"Not entirely. I want to estimate how many waves I need to go through to solve the issue of the dark ones having unauthorized access to my city. Right now I don't know how to solve it. Either upgrade the current system by taking control, or install a new one from scratch. That's why I asked, to estimate the number of waves needed for this question."

"At the moment, the full-fledged basic mechanoid security system installed in Hearth is only configured for light humans. In order to activate it on dark ones, as well as creatures without any affiliation, it is necessary to update the settings. This can only be done by the system administrator, who is currently One of the Temple of Skron. If you wish to receive a self-sufficient independent security system, as well as instructions for its installation, you need to pass three waves. Your current level is quite sufficient for you to receive what you need."

"Basic system? So there are more advanced options?"

"There are. Some allow you not only to identify, but also to block uninvited guests. The other is capable of providing full protection for the city. Not only at the level of identifying individuals, but also from a massive attack from outside."

"How much?" I asked, gulping. Hearth had a system that could protect against catapult attacks. It had supposedly already been installed by the Temple of Skron, but I no longer had any faith in them. I was sure that at the most unexpected moment, this system would simply break or malfunction. If I survived, the dark ones would apologize and even pay compensation so that they could set me up more gracefully next time.

"Five waves. Twenty-six through thirty."

"Will I be able to install it myself?"

"Humans are incapable of such a thing. In order to ensure that the security system is functioning properly, a mechanoid will have to come to Hearth. It will become the heart of the system. Its devotion to the city will be absolute."

"So the Temple of Skron also has its own mechanoid?"

"One mechanoid — one system. Regardless of the system. There are many mechanoids hidden in the Temple of Skron. You've exhausted your remaining points for completing the wave, human. If you wish to receive answers to your other questions, you'll have to complete another wave. The higher the level, the more points you'll get to ask questions."

"Wave!" I said. My insides sank — the battle with the Pharapho copy on the twenty-fourth wave was still fresh in my memory. Nevertheless, I had nowhere to retreat. I couldn't simply accept the basic system, which was incapable of protecting my city. If I was going to take the risk anyway, I might as well get as much as I could!

Wave!

"Judging by your appearance, my dumbfounded mentor, your meeting with the Fog Stalker was a success." Kimal Sarento had settled into a comfortable chair and was still studying his notebook. I didn't even have to say anything. The information about my visit to the arena automatically flowed into my artifact, and from there, through integration, to Kimal Sarento. He chuckled meaningfully several times, studying the new entries.

"Thirty-one waves? How did you do it?"

"A miracle," I answered honestly. My body was trembling all over and I couldn't do anything about it. The thirty-second wave showed that it was too early for me to take on anything serious. If it weren't for the key phrase that allowed me to escape right during the fight, the copy of Pharapho would have smashed me into a pancake. The creature that had begun to occupy almost a quarter of the arena was unkillable. A huge piece of flesh, completely oblivious to my defenses and inert to healing magic. Destroying a creature of this level was beyond my strength. At least, my current strength.

"Was it worth it?" Kimal Sarento returned to the last entry that had appeared. *Tainted Blood.* Surprisingly, the Fog Stalker didn't play hard to get and calmly replied that I could get the answers I sought.

But in order to find out what *Tainted Blood* was — find out, not even obtain! — I needed to pass four more waves. Waves thirty-one through thirty-four. I broke down on thirty-two. It was useless to go any further with the set of magic stones that I had. A significant boost was required. Up to level forty, no less.

There was no point in even going to the Pharapho Arena before that. Maybe I should throw Kimal Sarento in there? With his lightning, he could do a lot...

"It was definitely worth it," I replied.

The Fog Stalker's answer was still ringing in my head. It turned out that if I came to him with a question about *Tainted Blood,* I'd have to pass through thirty-three waves just to get an answer. Because the power gained from the thirty-fourth was equal to the sum of the first thirty! It was scary to even imagine what kind of creatures spawned there.

And this is far from the full power of Pharapho. Apparently, it wouldn't be long before we drove out the remaining forces from our planet.

"The Temple of Skron has been informed of your achievement," said Kimal Sarento, just in case. "They know that Archduke Maximilian Valevsky has passed thirty-one waves in the Fog Stalker Arena. I believe that the temple servants will have something to say about this. The only question is how they will react, and do they know that we are also looking for Marisa Shor?”

As if confirming Kimal Sarento's words, Eleanore's anxious voice appeared in his head:

“Max, we have…We have a guest.”

Chapter 16

ACCORDING TO THE IMAGE that had appeared in our shared notebook, the mechanoid in Hearth was a mixture of metal, wire, tubes of various diameters and lengths, and glass. In some ways, it resembled a chimera of a meter-tall hairless hedgehog and a snail. Our guest moved on four legs, had a convex body, an elongated muzzle, and several eye antennas. If the multitude of glass shards mounted on pins and moving in all different directions could, in fact, be considered eyes. The mechanoid did not communicate, remaining frozen near the portal, but the fact that this creature used the common portal network spoke volumes. At the very least, the mechanoids were somehow connected to it. The minotaurs did not show a hint of surprise at the appearance of the unusual guest and stood calmly, waiting for the city leaders to come see their new toy.

Alia tried to be as accurate as possible when adding the creature's description to the notebook so that I could evaluate my new acquisition. I had to explain to the shocked ladies, who had already decided that they should attack the unknown piece of iron, what it was and what it was doing in Hearth. And, most importantly, I had to tell them to provide security for the mechanoid. Because the dark ones would certainly do everything they could to get rid of the competitor. What would they gain from an independent Hearth? Finally, construction began anew in my city again. As soon as Eleanore, who was granted full administrative power over the system, installed our new guest in the network, and after immediately being given the maximum level of access, the mechanoid began to create. It could not speak, but it could form projections with lists of resource requirements. And they weren't the most common items. Mined from rifts level thirty and below. The fact that we happened to have them in Hearth was more a coincidence than the norm. Apparently, the clever mechanism had checked all the supplies and, like any other living creature, decided to work with the best of them. No one could blame it for this — if I had been forced to choose between a reliable security system and a cheaper one that was a little thrifty, I'd, of course, prefer the former. Eleanore provided the mechanoid with access to the treasury, and soon a countdown popped up. It would take twenty-four hours to create and install the new system. Moreover, this system would cover the entire city. What had taken the servants of the Temple of Skron a week, one mechanoid was prepared to install in a day! The first thing the new security administrator did was block portal access, so that not a single random servant of the Temple of Skron would come to visit us until the work was completed. Alia and Naira could deal with those who were already living in Hearth. The mithril-armor-clad women had pledged to protect our guest from any misfortune.

"So, Padishah Bayazid the Third." Kimal Sarento was clearly not too pleased about this news. For a while he sat and twisted a letter-opening knife in his hands. There was no point in saying anything — we did not have a portal. The usual route from the capital of the Zarak Empire to the palace of the padishah was about a week and a half. Five days, if we hurried. If we hurried a lot, running to the limit of our strength and constantly healing ourselves, it would still take nearly three. Horses couldn't keep up with such a pace. Only humans could.

"Somehow, information about the emperor's actions must reach the padishah's palace. And if everything goes badly, we'll receive her legs in response. That is, there will definitely be a portal. The only question is, where exactly will the portal appear and how will we reach it?"

"It's not that simple, my clever mentor. Information can reach the padishah through the Temple of Skron. They will also ensure the transportation of individual body parts. There is a dark coven operating in the capital — a gathering of humans who have sold their souls to Skron. And quite by chance, I have a complete list of all these madmen."

"Where did you get that?" I asked.

"When Magister Elor opened the Wave under the academy, he attempted to destroy me. He was actively assisted in this by the capital coven. When we met after my rehabilitation, Magister Elor admitted that the attempt had failed and, as an apology, provided me with a list of all these men. He took three with him — those who had invented the armored krona. The rest are still running around the capital and wreaking havoc. It's good I didn't have the time to destroy them earlier. The dark ones would have just sent new people, and I'd have no leads on where to find them."

"I don't understand how information about the dark capital coven is relevant to us."

"It is directly relevant to us, my blind mentor. Directly. Information needs to be conveyed to the Temple of Skron somehow. That's what the coven is for — its leader has a remote connection with someone from the Temple of Skron. Now imagine a situation where the leader of the coven informs his masters that the army of the Zarak Empire has set out for Hearth, and you, as its leader, have been charged with terrible crimes. The dark ones will want to check this. How? The portal to Hearth is closed. The transport hub near the capital was destroyed. And the leader of the coven suddenly stopped responding to messages. How will the dark ones check that everything is going according to their scheme? It's impossible to remotely order a convert to open a portal. It's also impossible to simply open a portal to the capital. What will they do then? The only possible option is to send an observer to the capital using another transport hub. For example, the one located near the palace of Padishah Bayazid the Third, to kill two birds with one stone. I have no doubt that the node is not only nearby, but on the very palace grounds. This is the moment, my frowning mentor. This is the moment we have been waiting for."

"Those who enter the coven are not converts," I began to reason out loud. "If they are captured, Skron will not take control. These 'madmen,' as you called them, can be interrogated."

"And we can make them do our bidding — convey the required information to their new masters. Our High Priest has many men at his disposal who know how to make someone hurt, but I would prefer to use the services of the Evil Engineer. He knows exactly how to do it."

"Have you ever had to use him before?"

"Naturally. So, we inform the secret chancellery about who the kidnapper is. This is a must — we will need cover. We inform the High Priest and hand over the entire coven to him. After we talk to the head and make him send the message we need to the Temple of Skron. If we get a list of converts, even if it is incomplete, it will be ideal — the fewer opportunities there are in the capital to open a portal, the more effective our plan will be. You, my nimble mentor, will have to demonstrate all the miracles of endurance and get to the palace of the padishah in a few days. I'm afraid to even think what will become of you in this time, but we have no other choice."

"There's just one thing I don't understand: how will I get to the tournament?"

"You won't. That's why we leak information to the secret chancellery. They will have to provide cover. The official story is this: you looked at the list of participants and realized that messing around with such small fry was beneath you. Instead, you sent your pupil to the tournament in your stead, and you yourself returned to Hearth. Which would fit in well with the legend that the Zarak Empire has declared war on your city. I will perform at the tournament and, if the Light is favorable to me, I will win, meeting Count Vyazemsky along the way. Ideally, Count Shub as well, but I don't want to kill him. He could prove useful."

"But not Count Vyazemsky?"

"No, he definitely needs to be eliminated. Or his son, if he is listed as a participant. I still haven't ascertained who is taking part in the tournament. There are no details listed. In any case, if I finish off George. his father will have no choice but to try to take revenge on me."

"I wouldn't want to kill George," I frowned. "He seemed like a totally decent guy to me."

"My humane mentor, in the matter of protecting the city there is no and cannot be any 'wants or 'don't wants.' There is only one word: 'must.' The entire clan is responsible for the decisions made by its head. If the eldest count imagined himself to be the center of the universe, then his son thinks the same way. We must cut them both down mercilessly, otherwise we will have no end to our woes in the future. That is why the Duke of Odoevsky wanted to destroy your entire line, including the women — so that there would be no one left who could take revenge. Count Fardi did not succeed, and where is he now? In the dungeons of the Citadel! Do you want to go there too? You should stop seeing the good and kind in people, my naive mentor. It's either them or us. There is no third option. This world does not want to see Hearth flourish. In any case, this will not concern you. Your task is to get to the palace of the padishah in a few days. Need I explain what my omnipotent mentor is supposed to do there?"

"Save Marisa Shor, find the waypoint, swaddle the padishah and invite the Citadel representatives," I answered, grinning. "Any direct aggression will lead to bigger problems. The Shurgan Empire will consider that a violation of its borders and will want to punish Hearth. But if I, as a Hunter of Darkness, find a waypoint on the territory of the padishah's palace, Bayazid the Third will not be able to prove to the Citadel that he supposedly knew nothing and didn't suspect anything of the sort."

"Your conversations with more intelligent people have clearly rubbed off on you." Kimal Sarento could not help but praise himself. "Everything is correct, except for one clarification, the treasury of Bayazid the Third. No one knows where it is, but everyone knows that it contains items unique to our world. Maps, artifacts, resources, products of the ancients. Perhaps there will be something valuable among this collection. Something that can shed light on symbolic magic. When will you be able to visit the fog arena again?"

"With a key, in a month," I answered, checking the timer. The last time I had been transported to the arena was from using nine hundred cutting stones, so I hadn't been given this rollback time. Apparently, even in its worst nightmares, the Fog Stalker could not imagine that someone in our world would be able to use such a number of rare stones.

"That's bad," Kimal Sarento pressed his lips together. "That means the issue with the dictionary must be resolved independently. As well as with the remote connection. I will continue to research the subject. It must be in the mithril armor. It simply must be!"

* * *

Kimal Sarento worked late into the night. He sent messengers, warned some people about something or other, and constantly received memos confirming tasks had been fulfilled. My pupil never even retired to his room, instead staying downstairs on the first floor of the hotel. The flow of couriers was staggering. Watching the spider spread its webs throughout the capital was a thrilling experience. My student did not ignore the slightest detail — who went where, who met with whom, who and at what time they should strike. Kimal Sarento managed the flow of couriers and the important figures behind them with the grace of the conductor of a huge imperial orchestra. Soon the Evil Engineer arrived. The dark one, who had turned gray, now had a pair of deep, blue eyes. This completely changed his countenance, especially considering the inky black darkness that had resided in his eyes before. My former mentor did not say anything to me — everything had been said before. Except he did shake my hand.

"Let's go," said Kimal Sarento as soon as darkness descended on Turb. An open carriage was already waiting for us at the entrance to the inn. Or rather, a cart, which was not exactly appropriate for high-born gentlemen to travel in. The Evil Engineer changed out the coachman and cast us a pointed look, indicating that moving around the poorer areas in such extravagant garments was not wise. But he remained silent, allowing Kimal Sarento to solve this problem on his own. He did, in the blink of an eye wrapping himself in the clothes of the Nocturnal Guild. Even his face was covered with a bandage. My mithril armor went to work, forming a similar suit for me. The next time the Evil Engineer turned in our direction and saw our new suits, there was a single surprised snort. That was all he allowed himself in terms of emotions.

"Today, the dark coven is going to rally all its forces to solve an important issue: finding a new place to live," Kimal Sarento explained as we entered a darkened area of the city. Only a few lanterns on the cart dispersed the evening gloom. "The mayor suddenly decided to clear the street where several members of the capital's dark coven live. Don't even ask me how much it cost me. As a result, Skron's followers are now urgently running to their secret lair to moan and groan and think about how to solve this problem. After all, everyone needs a roof over their heads."

"Security?" asked the Evil Engineer, not letting go of the reins and not even turning in our direction.

"They'll have sent the guards away. And there's no real security there. It's a dark coven. Their best form of security is the secret nature of their meeting place. These aren't warriors or mages. As it turns out, they're completely ordinary people who aren't getting any attention. Teachers, minor officials, even a couple of merchants. Not a single aristocrat. That's why the housing issue has everyone so excited. Stop near that house and we'll walk. It's not far. Turn off the lights."

The street was plunged into darkness. There was no light in any of the windows. A feeling of recognition washed over me. I had run along a similar street when chasing that convert. Kimal Sarento moved quickly and silently, with the grace of a cat. I followed him like a hippopotamus in a china shop. Despite all my supposedly good training and agility, I kept stepping on pebbles that clattered under my feet. The Evil Engineer remained next to the cart — we'd summon him later.

The house we approached was no different from the neighboring ones. Just as dark, small and gloomy. Only two lifeless bodies by the door showed that we were moving in the right direction. *Analyze* reported that the dead were converts who had not yet begun their song to Skron. I could not resist and drove my glove into both of their chests, tearing out fragments of *Mentor*. War is war, but this stone was a priority, and I was not going to just pass one by.

"Basement. Twelve people," the shadow next to us whispered. As always, I no longer had the *Invisibility Identifier*, so I did not see our accomplice. And the voice was unfamiliar to me. Apparently, Kimal Sarento had employed all his secret groups for this operation.

"We are ready," another whisper was heard. I recognized it — the girl who was unable to die from the poison. Or rather, whom I did not allow to die. It turns out that Kimal Sarento had led his protégé out of the lair of the Nocturnal Guild before I arrived there. That was good. I would not have wanted to slaughter her with the rest.

"Forward!" Kimal Sarento commanded and was the first to rush down the stairs. Two shadows darted after him, but I had to linger — another convert was lying near the stairs. Another fragment of *Mentor*. Another small step toward increasing my *Devour* to the fourth level.

By the time I descended the stairs, it was all over. Twelve people were lying on the floor, and their hands and feet were being actively tied. It was easy to identify the head honcho, as he was the only one present wearing a headdress. But Kimal Sarento's people did not limit themselves to just binding their limbs. They poured tranquilizers down the captives' throats and carefully watched to make sure that at least half of the bottle was drunk. That was ten to twelve hours of deep and healthy sleep. But these people would wake up not in a warm bed, but in the dungeons of the Fortress. Not every deep sleep leaves you feeling refreshed.

"This is a mage," I said, nodding at the leader as I checked him with *Analyze*. As Sarento had said, there were no converts among the coven members. Only true dark ones who had decided to dedicate their lives to serving Skron.

"Very good," Kimal Sarento grinned and gave the order. Soon the Evil Engineer appeared, laying out a large torture kit in front of the dark human, who had turned white with fear. His serene demeanor revealed that this was a commonplace thing for him. He had performed these duties more than once, or even twice. His movements were too precise and dexterous.

"The situation is as follows," the Evil Engineer said in a low, somewhat metallic voice, addressing his victim. "There is a task, and you must complete it. Now you can nod and agree to everything, but we will have no faith in what you are saying. You will do what is required of you only when I decide that you are ready. Max, make sure he does not die. And do not turn away. You must see how the Church of the Light conducts its interrogations and breaks people down."

What transpired over the next two hours could only be described as complete insanity. The Evil Engineer had cut the head of the dark coven into pieces without even thinking of asking him any questions. He simply hacked away. He simply caused pain. He simply enjoyed the man's maddened shrieks. It was hard to watch, but I was forbidden from turning away. These people had known what they were getting into. They had built the Wave within the academy. They had prepared the armored krona and unleashed it on the streets of the city. They were ready for their Skron to take charge, and now the Evil Engineer was giving the head of the coven such a chance. The chance to transform for their god.

But I had been tasked with preventing this. *Heal* returned the head of the coven to an ideal state, and the Evil Engineer started again. The man did not hold out for long — after about five minutes he was screaming at the top of his lungs, showering us with curses. He tried to bargain. Tried to find out our demands. Listed all the converts that he or his closest associates had turned. Begged us to stop. Begged us to kill him. Begged us to at least explain what we needed. Because we were silent and simply inflicted pain, without asking about anything. The Evil Engineer knew how to break a man down with razor-sharp precision.

"Your hands will be unbound now," Kimal Sarento said in a saccharine voice, leaning over the sobbing dark one. Two hours of senseless torture had brought the man to a state of complete prostration. Three times over he almost went to meet his maker, unable to bear the pain, but I was on guard and did not allow him to slip away. Finally, the Evil Engineer gave a signal and my pupil stepped forward.

"You must contact the Temple of Skron and inform them that the Zarak Empire has sent its forces to Hearth. The emperor has declared that Archduke Valevsky is an undesirable person in the empire and must be destroyed. Repeat it back."

The dark one gazed up at Kimal Sarento through eyes glazed with madness. There was no sense left in that horror-filled stare. The Evil Engineer stood next to Sarento, and the head of the dark coven jerked as if struck by a whip. A second later, he was already muttering what was required of him. Word for word.

"Less emotion. Slower," Kimal Sarento demanded. The man complied, never taking his eyes off the Evil Engineer. When the coven leader had fulfilled this task, the Evil Engineer took a few steps back. Hope appeared in the man's face. Hope that his pain was over.

"Do not let me down, otherwise he will return and the pain will continue," said Kimal Sarento in the same unctuous voice, cutting his bonds. I had to pour *Heal* into him to restore normal blood circulation. "Just do all that is asked of you. Make it so that there is no more pain. Go!"

The leader put his hand to his chest and repeated everything that Kimal Sarento ordered him. A moment later, he looked up at him.

"They ask me, where did you get this information? They are the ones asking, not me!"

"The emperor's order was announced in the central square, and then posted in all the taverns."

"Where is Archduke Valevsky?" The head of the coven again broadcast the question.

"He escaped to Hearth. I saw a detachment go through the gates in pursuit. The capital is restless. There are raids."

"Lay low. It won't last long. It will all be over soon. You are doing the right thing!"

"Drink," Kimal Sarento said gently, offering the head of the coven a sleeping potion. He didn't even argue and drank the potion to the last drop. The body went limp, and Kimal Sarento was given a list of the converts that had flooded the capital. He took a pencil and scribbled something on a piece of paper and handed the sheet to me.

"The list is incomplete, it requires clarification and significant additions. I have circled the most important names. These are counts, fairly highborn people. We need to verify. I don't rely on the Fortress — they will not interfere in Count Vyazemsky's affairs. They will destroy the lesser men, of course, but they will not touch these three. Will you do it?"

"Check, and if they are converts, destroy them?"

"Yes," he replied simply. "The most desirable scenario is making them fall into a trance. So that no one has any doubt that these are converts. This is important. I did not think that the dark infection had penetrated so high. It must be rooted out. And mercilessly. Go now. In half an hour, the secret police and the servants of the Light will arrive here. If they catch you here, unnecessary questions will begin, and then there will be no result. For everyone else, Archduke Valevsky returned to Hearth. I wrote down the addresses of the estates, these people should be at home at night, take the Evil Engineer. He has nothing more to do here either."

"Don't be late." I shook his hand, and the Evil Engineer and I ran out of the house. Three red dots were already marked on the virtual map. It was as if fate was mocking us — they all lay on one straight line leading to Al-Khorezm, the capital of the Shurghan Empire. The estate of Padishah Bayazid the Third was close.

"We'll need to figure out how to bypass the guards," the Evil Engineer was thinking in terms of mere mortals. I had long since abandoned that perspective. After my magic field increased in size to six cells, I never got around to upgrading it. Even now, instead of rearranging the magic stones, I just stuck a few trophy ones in there. It took time to make the right structure. I sincerely believed that after the lithoids I would have the time, but apparently this was my fate, running between empires like an archduke with his head cut off. I once thought that the true calling of a leader was to find people capable of completing tasks and delegating them correctly. It seems that I wasn't fit to be a leader, because I couldn't even imagine a person capable of doing what Kimal Sarento demanded. Vetting three counts was a trifle. But getting to Al-Khorezm in three days...that was a feat worthy of a crazy person. There was only one such person in the world. Me.

"There won't be any problems with the guards. I have *Phantom* and *Silent Step*. Let's go. The sooner we start, the sooner we'll understand whether the head of the capital coven lied to us or whether there was some truth in his words. Three convert counts. This isn't even a challenge to the lands of the Light — this is an outright spit in the face from the Temple of Skron. This will not be forgiven. I won't forgive it."

Chapter 17

PEOPLE SHIED AWAY and watched my back for a long time, unable to comprehend how I could run with such speed and not fall to the ground, exhausted. I ran so fast that sometimes I only touched the ground with my toes to propel myself forward again. *Heal* enveloped my body every ten seconds, allowing me to get rid of my fatigue and somehow restore my tense muscles. Al-Khorezm was waiting for me.

There were three corpses behind me. I killed the converts without pity or doubt. Good family men, loving husbands and fathers, three high-born counts, they had nevertheless sold their souls to Skron. Why? What reason? What did he promise them that they did not have initially? Eternal life? The possibility of reincarnation? I was not interested in asking. I made my way to the bedroom, confirmed with *Analyze* that there was a convert lying in front of me, pulled him off the bed and, holding his mouth, activated the dark aura at its smallest radius. The eyes of the convert immediately darkened as Skron took control of the body in an attempt to open a portal and let the minotaurs in so that they could deal with the villains who dared to destroy the property of the dark god. Everything else was a matter of seconds — the katara sliced from below into the jaw and skewered the head through and through. The body would fall to the floor, and I would retreat into the shadows, allowing the dumbfounded wives or mistresses of the traitors to scream at the top of their lungs. According to *Analyze* only the old counts were converts. They hadn't dragged their loved ones into this business. That was good — I didn't want to kill women as well.

Phantom proved a truly fascinating stone. If activated in a place with a lot of light and no place to hide, the space in front of your eyes instantly began to swim. It felt like you were looking at the world through distorted, cloudy glass or a layer of rippled water. But as soon as you retreated into the shadows, all these distortions disappeared — outlines became sharp, space ceased to be deformed. Moreover, I gained a hypersensitivity: I heard, saw, and felt everything more acutely. The darker the place I hid, the more omnipotent I felt.

I took my first break twenty hours later, when it started getting dark again. My body said it needed rest and no *Heal* would help. According to the map, by this point I had managed to do the impossible — cover almost half the distance. I reached the nearest large village and found a tavern there, then ordered food. During my run, I discovered a significant downside to my crazy waste of energy — I was ravenous. Seeing the gold, the innkeeper rolled out the red carpet. Meat, flatbread, cheese, beer — they laid out enough for five men. Someone even laughed, saying that the courier couldn't eat that much. Naive peasants! The food fell into my mouth as if into a bottomless pit. I don't think the first serving even hit my stomach, as it dissolved in my mouth. Silence hung in the tavern. People were shocked at how quickly I managed to absorb food. Only after I leaned back in my chair, wiped my hands and burped contentedly did they begin to murmur, which grew into a standing ovation. Apparently, there was a real shortage of entertainment in this village, if the meal of a random passerby was causing such a stir.

"I need the best room in this stinking shithole!" The doors of the tavern almost flew off their hinges as several people burst in. Four steel-clad guards accompanied a well-groomed man who looked at the assembled group with undisguised contempt. My mithril armor had been transformed into a courier's travel suit, so the guest's gaze hovered over me for only a few moments. I had to make an effort to look away. My heart began to beat wildly. This was no coincidence! It is simply impossible! But *Analyze* showed that my suspicions were correct — the same bastard who had so rapturously read out the death sentence for my family was here! The one who managed to survive my shot from *Dark Spike* — he was saved by an amulet. The one who was in third place on my list of people to be eliminated. Right after the Duke of Odoevsky and his daughter, who had lost her human form.

Should I attack right away? Killing this man would pose no issues. But how would I explain later why Archduke Valevsky suddenly killed Count Fardi's assistant? This would be an open confrontation with the Zarak Empire, for which my city was not yet prepared. Once I saved the emperor's daughter, this could be hushed up, but certainly not now. So, I needed to find another way to rid this world of the bastard before me. Servants appeared and began to drag things into the room he had rented. Unlike most of the highborn, Tari, if I remembered the name of this bastard correctly, preferred to spend the night in taverns, and not in the middle of an open field. Soon the fop left, too disgusted to eat in the same room as the simple peasants. Having paid, I went outside and exposed my face to the cool night air. A fine, irksome drizzle fell from the sky. Autumn was making a strong entrance.

"Hey, brother, can you bring me something warm? I'll pay well," a hoarse voice said. Next to the tavern stood a covered carriage, evidently the one Tari had arrived in. The horses had been taken to rest, but no one had released the guard. So the coachman had to guard this man's goods so that the locals wouldn't steal anything important. Deciding that I wouldn't lose anything from being kind, I went for a mug of warm soup and returned, taking a large flatbread as well.

"Oh, wonderful!" The coachman relished the smell of fresh bread. "Where are you headed?"

"To Turb. I'm delivering a letter. And where are you going? I see you have strict rules. How will you work tomorrow if you don't sleep all night?"

"My partner will relieve me at three in the morning, I'll get some sleep then," said the coachman with his mouth full. "We're going to Al-Khorezm. To rescue our master. The clergy have nabbed him, so we're taking the nobleman there so that he can give evidence. Have you ever heard of such a thing? A Duke of the Zarak Empire held captive in the citadel!

"Wow!" I even widened my eyes in faux-surprise. "So, your master is a duke, you say? Why are you staying in such a sty?"

"We were in a hurry," the coachman softened noticeably as the conversation went on. "The nobleman was in a hurry. He says that he is the only one who has some proof that the owner is innocent. Some papers. So we had to drive through several towns, although the hotels there are not comparable to the ones here. And you don't need to guard the carriage there. But no — we must hurry! We have been on the road for almost four days now. All the way from Odoevsk."

Figuring that a courier running around the empire must know the capital of the region, I didn't ask where this Odoevsk was. The map told me how

I had managed to avoid crossing paths with the carriage earlier — they had been moving along a different road. The fact that we stopped in the same place was a coincidence. Lucky for some, not so lucky for others.

"So, you didn't stop in the capital?" I asked just in case.

"No, we moved along the eastern highway. Sometimes we drove along such wild paths that even foxes are afraid to shit there. It's good that the nobleman thought to bring security. One time some bandits tried to lift stuff off of us. Brainless scumbags."

"Bandits? Don't you have a mage? They never attack mages."

"A mage?" the coachman grinned. "Well, Mr. Tari is a mage. But he had no time for bandits. He was suffering from stomach pains at the time. So the guards had to root the scum out of the forests themselves. We even made a stop so they could hang everyone from the trees. They will know better than to attack the Duke of Odoevsky's people."

"That's for sure. I'd like to find myself some guards like that," I said, nodding knowingly.

"Are you attacked often?" asked the coachman. People tried not to kill couriers. Except for those who belonged to Hearth. Even the most crazy bandits would only rob them, steal their transportation and message and then let the courier go. Because a living courier was an investment in the future. He would certainly travel this way again.

"It happens," I sighed heavily. "It's part of the job. Risky. And who doesn't take risks these days? Look, my horse was taken, now I have to walk. Okay, I'll go, I need to get some sleep. I still have three days to run to the capital."

"Go on then. Thank you for your help. The nights are already so cold. If this winter is like the last, things will get dire."

The coachman stayed to guard his goods, and I pretended to go about my business, but as soon as I was immersed in darkness, I activated *Phantom*. I had no intention of neglecting such a gift from fate. Especially after I learned that there was some evidence that would allow the Duke of Odoevsky to avoid the punishment he deserves. What could it be? Papers? Witness testimony? Something else? This point must be clarified. Count Fardi must not leave the Citadel. Ever.

Tari made such a ruckus that everyone in the inn knew his room number. I crept up to the tavern windows and looked inside. Two guards were having dinner, which meant two were upstairs, guarding their master's peace. Since this group had been on the road for four days, it meant that the men were exhausted and unlikely to perform their duties well. Who would want to watch the windows on the second floor? Especially in such a backwood where you couldn't find a representative of the Nocturnal Guild during the day, even with a lit torch.

Finding the right window was easy. Tari was sitting in the room, drinking heavily, occasionally snacking on meat. There were no guards in his room, as they were guarding the door. The window was closed, but I didn't see a problem with that. I just had to wait until that bastard turned off the light. I didn't want to make any extra noise. Everything had to happen as quietly and calmly as possible. Revenge, as my pupil liked to say, was a dish best served ice cold.

The long journey had taken its toll on Tari, too. After finishing his meal and taking a bath (I supposed I could use a wash too), the man extinguished the lamp and lay down on the bed without even drawing the curtain. It was unlikely that this man suffered from insomnia, so I waited another fifteen minutes, then carefully pulled the window open. The vyrma katars did real miracles with the fastenings, cutting them without a single sound. True, there was a hitch: I had nowhere to throw the window without causing unnecessary noise. I had to twist and pull it into the room with me.

Tari, as I expected, was fast asleep. The chests that the servants had dragged in were next to the bed. In the dim light of the stars, you could see that they were open. Lighting the lamp would be dangerous. The guards who were on duty at the door would sense something was wrong. I had to act in the dark. Tari first. I went up to the bed and leaned over the man. Over the past seven months, this face had become even more rounded. Apparently, a well-fed life and lack of training had taken their toll. The rage that seemed to have died out began to boil in my chest. I wanted to strangle the bastard. Wake him up so that he could spend his last minutes in full awareness of the nightmare he had gotten himself into. So that he would understand who would kill him and for what. I wanted many things, but emotions are not the most reliable companion.

I took the ordinary knife from the table, the one Tari used to cut his own meat, and with a sharp movement plunged it into the man's heart. Everything had to look like a Nocturnal Guild attack. Let the High Priest figure out later why such a thing was done without his orders. I had done it — I personally finished off the bastard who took part in the execution of my family. The fact that I didn't say any good one liner or stare into the man's eyes while the light left them...well, I wasn't a sadist. This certainly wouldn't bring me pleasure. Especially after watching the Evil Engineer at work for two hours. That just wasn't my thing. Amazingly, I didn't feel any emotion. No inspiration, no boost of strength, no joy from what had just happened. Just the feeling of dirty and unpleasant work. My old family can't be brought back, and reveling in death was a one-way street. I hoped that I had many years of a cloudless life ahead of me, and to exchange it for the pathos of slaughtering everyone who was guilty of the death of my relatives...this man had to be killed; it was a fact. But his death was not worth dwelling on, and this was also a fact. I did not intend to slide down the slippery slope of destroying everything that bore the Fardi name. I only had two targets left, and I was placing my hopes on the Citadel doing all the work for me.

But for that to happen, I needed those documents. Trying not to make any noise, I searched the corpse. Who knew, maybe he kept them on his person, in bed. Nothing. I found nothing in the clothes either, although I felt them quite carefully for various secret pockets. I poured the gold out of the pouch and put it in mine, and I did not touch the rings or other jewelry that Tari wore. Nor his stones — the dead man had a standard third-level *Fireball* with two facets. Insane wealth for any commoner, which Tari was, but trifles for any self-respecting mage. Would the Nocturnal Guild take such a thing? Never in their lives!

In the boxes strewn all over the room, I managed to find several dozen documents and a couple of books. Considering how carefully everything was packed, this was probably the very evidence I was looking for. Throwing everything into my immaterial backpack, I decided to sort it out later. Including a small, locked box. I was unable to find anything else of value. I wasn't going to pay attention to the rags stuffed in the other boxes, was I? The thought occurred to me to check the carriage, but I dismissed it. Tari wouldn't leave anything valuable there overnight. There were scum and hooligans all around!

I deactivated *Phantom* only when I got out onto the street and walked a few houses away from the tavern. The fatigue that had forced me to pause in this village was no longer there. Apparently, the heavy dinner had taken its toll. I wanted to sleep, but I had no right to allow myself such weakness. The village was simple, without a palisade. Of course, there were some guards on duty at the entrance, but they were there more for show than for control. They were physically unable to check everyone who arrived in the village. Having made a small detour through the vegetable gardens, I escaped to freedom, returned back to the road and, checking the map, jogged forward. Only after moving a sufficient distance from the village and taking out the Gourfan Clan crystal, which illuminated the space for me, I rushed forward with doubled strength. Not maximum speed, but close to it. The crystal, which I placed on my head, turned night into day around me and helped me maneuver. It, like my auras, had a new mechanism of increasing and decreasing the radius, so I could create for myself both a small patch of light and a bright sun, guaranteed to illuminate the space for a hundred meters. Having such good tools made the journey much more pleasant. It made no difference whether it was during the day or in the pitch-black night. The only thing that prevented me from going all out was the rain, which had gone from a fine drizzle to a pretty decent downpour. The road became soggy and I had to leap over the deep puddles that began to form. Running in these conditions was difficult even for me.

Kilometers flowed under my feet one after another, but suddenly the realization came that my body could go no further. *Heal,* constant food intake in gigantic quantities, and even a two-hour rest was no help. In two days I'd run almost six hundred kilometers and had approached the limit of my capabilities. Al-Khorezm was a stone's throw away, just a hundred kilometers, but I had no idea where to find the strength for the final spurt. Especially considering the fact that another night awaited me. I desperately wanted to sleep. My muscles ached even after all my recovery attempts. My breathing was disrupted by the slightest tension. My body had reached the edge of its limits and was giving me a warning: one more sprint and it would crumble into tiny pieces, which I would then have to collect from all across the Shurghan Empire.

Sleep the night through to reach the target in the morning? This would be the third day after the ultimatum given to Zurgan the First. How much time would it take for the dark ones to get their bearings and carry out their threat? Alia, who was in contact with Father Nor, had given me concentrated information. Mass raids were taking place in Turb. Experienced investigators of the Fortress, having received living representatives of the coven, went into full swing. They managed to extract from the people who sold their souls to Skron all the names that were connected with the dark ones. Converts, dark humans, secret shelters, even those who simply sympathized and turned a blind eye to what was happening — the list of names was huge. The clergy worked without rest, and the Fortress did not cease to put out black smoke for even a minute. In just two days, more than a hundred converts were burned. The servants of the Light had never had such a catch in the entire history of confrontations with the dark ones. But the Fortress was not limited to just the capital. The head of the capital coven told about other covens located in the regions. Not as numerous in membership as the central one, but also existing and doing their dirty work. More names, secret hideouts, sympathizers. The way the dark infection had spread across the Zarak Empire was truly frightening. There were so many dark ones that they could at any moment come into open confrontation with the church and, if they were helped by the Temple of Skron, they would cause significant damage to the light ones. How the servants of the Light had allowed such an outrage remained a mystery. An investigation was required within the church itself. How many of the highest hierarchs of the Fortress were dark or sympathizers? No less than in the Citadel, I was sure!

"Thirty gold pieces!" I showed the next coachman a bag of gold. My courier's clothes were a thing of the past. Now I looked like a young, crazy aristocrat who threw money around left and right to make an impression. One who would make a night-time visit to Al-Khorezm.

"I cannot, Your Radiance! There are bandits there!" the cabby almost wrung his hands. For a common man, thirty gold pieces were a pretty good supplement to his salary. Consider it two months of work!

"I am a mage!" I stuck out my chest proudly. "If those masochists attack me, they'll be dead where they stand! Fifty gold, Skron take you! Another twenty if we arrive in Al-Khorezm before sunrise. This is my final offer!"

"Seventy gold pieces?" the cabby swallowed. The way his eyes darted around made me question who these bandits actually were. They had already looked me over several times, trying to find the sword typical of highborn people, but there was none. Not even a knife on my belt, something no one left the house without these days. I looked like a spoiled rich boy who had lost touch with the real world, looking for adventure that would bite him in the ass.

"And not a gold piece less!" I said pompously, which attracted additional attention from random passersby.

"Alright, Your Radiance, I'll take you to Al-Khorezm!" said the driver. Judging by the way his eyes were sparkling, in his mind he had already robbed and killed me three times, taking all my belongings. But I wasn't going to get angry. I needed a cart, and I couldn't buy one now. The only way left was this rather bold plan.

We set off twenty minutes later. During this time, the waiters filled the cart with food. I needed to recuperate, and, as it turned out, food was the best way to cope with the loss of energy. The driver did not object. On the contrary, he was pleased that he was carrying a lot of free and, most importantly, good food and drink to his accomplices.

After sitting back leisurely on the wide seat, I gestured that I was ready to set off and bit into a meat pie. Despite another hearty dinner, I was incredibly hungry. The sun had already disappeared behind the horizon, and the dark of night was gradually taking over. The measured rocking and the fatigue accumulated over two days took their toll. As if in spite of all my precaution, I simply passed out, allowing the driver to do his thing without constant supervision.

I was jolted awake by screams of pain. The cart was stopped in the middle of the forest, and my driver was screaming and writhing on the ground, clutching his stomach. The dim lantern barely dispersed the night gloom, but I couldn't help but notice the homemade crossbow. It was lying next to the screaming driver. Despite the situation, sleep left me reluctantly. For some time, I looked indifferently at the suffering of the driver, and there was not a single thought in my head. Then something began to move in my brain, and I activated *Heal*, pulling the murderer from the clutches of death. The crossbow bolt had ricocheted off the *Golden Dome of Protection* and crashed into the stomach of my would-be assassin. It didn't even reach the mithril armor. But the fact that the guy tried to kill me himself, and did not bring me to his accomplices, had given him a chance to survive. I loved desperate people.

"Have you calmed down?" I asked and yawned widely. The driver stopped yelling and lay on the ground, waiting for the magic strike. He shrank and cowered, preparing to meet his ancestors. Not today.

"Get up, I said! It's still eighty kilometers to Al-Khorezm! And you don't have much time left to get an extra twenty gold pieces. Look at him — instead of driving the horses, he's rolling on the ground and screaming with joy that he agreed to carry such a high-ranking gentleman as me. Get up, take the reins and go! Or should I take different persuasive measures?"

"N-no, Your Radiance." The driver rose to his feet and almost fell over again. His right leg was strangely swollen. I frowned, not understanding what was going on, but then the cabbie pulled a wooden block out of his pants. Judging by the shape, it was a prosthesis. Rolling up his pants, the murderer stared at his leg as if he was seeing it for the first time in his life.

"Have you seen enough? Or should I take the leg back?" I asked, guessing what had happened. *Heal* had not only saved the murderer from the crossbow bolt, but also returned his limb. Judging by his reaction, it had been lost quite a long time ago.

"No, you don't need to take anything!" His voice showed genuine emotion. Almost for the first time in our short acquaintance.

"Al-Khorezm is there, we are here," I reminded him. "We should be there by sunrise. Got it, or do I need to repeat myself?"

"We'll make it there, Your Radiance!" He assured me ardently and jumped to his feet, jumping up and down several times on the one I had returned. "We will eat as we please!"

"I hope no one will disturb my sleep again. Because there will be no healing magic next time."

I closed my eyes and fell asleep again, as if everything that had just happened was a minor misunderstanding. When I opened my eyes the next time, the sun had just risen over the horizon.

"Al-Khorezm, Your Radiance! We made it!"

Chapter 18

"WELCOME TO THE DIAMOND GOOSE HOTEL, sir! Do you have any special requests?" The receptionist was smiling and polite. Which was no coincidence — my appearance literally screamed that I had money and was ready to spend it. In fact, I didn't have all that much gold, but still enough to secure a room in the best hotel in the capital of the Shurghan Empire and have a good time for a few days, without denying myself anything. Last time, when I arrived in Al-Khorezm, there was no time for hotels.

"I need a room worthy of such a majestic hotel," I answered and placed several tall towers of gold coins stacked on top of each other on the table in front of the administrator. "The room must be registered to Count Nameless."

"Welcome to our hotel, Count Nameless." He

didn't even bat an eyelid in befuddlement at my fictitious name. All the stacks of gold disappeared, and a massive key appeared in their place. "Sixth floor. You can use the elevator. Do you have any belongings?"

"Unfortunately, all my things are gone," I sighed. "I need the contact information of a good store where I can dress in accordance with the level of your establishment, as well as the contacts of a person who is developing a chain of hotels. In my humble opinion, the Diamond Goose would do very well in one particularly interesting and unique city in the Zarak Empire."

"Does Count Nameless have any connection to this unique city?"

"Count Nameless will tell the person in charge about it," I answered. "We will be meeting today, sometime before the evening. One more thing — tomorrow morning a guest may appear in my room. I would not like for her presence to be registered. No one should know that she is even in my room."

A few more stacks of gold appeared on the table.

"We have no need to register our clients' guests." The speed with which the gold disappeared was astonishing. And the receptionist acted as if nothing had happened.

"Right now I need a set of fresh clothes, a hairdresser and a few pretty girls to help me rub my back. And serve breakfast in my room, I don't want to go down to the restaurant. Wine. The best Shurgan has to offer. Two bottles. I think that's all for now. Will that be enough to satisfy my requirements? I don't want to write a check. And don't forget the address of a store where I can buy clothes."

Another stack of gold appeared on the table. The administrator thought for a few moments, as if making an internal assessment, after which the stack disappeared from the table again.

"Of course, Count Nameless, that is sufficient," the man nodded. "You will be shown to your room. Enjoy your time at the Diamond Goose Hotel. We hope our service will meet all your expectations."

The porter approached me. Not seeing any suitcases, he glanced at the receptionist, who made a few barely noticeable short gestures. This language was unfamiliar to me, but the result was achieved: I was escorted to the elevator, taken up to the sixth floor and the massive door was opened.

"If you need anything, ring the bell," the porter bowed. Judging by the fact that he did not leave, he wanted to receive some kind of reward for his work. Although there was no work as such. However, I did not break character, and I placed three gold coins in his palm.

"I need the latest important news from the capital in a condensed form on one sheet of paper. A list of all upcoming high society events. A way to get an invitation to them."

"I'm afraid that in order to do that, the count

will have to provide his name," he said, bowing again.

"I will provide it if I see something that catches my fancy." I did not succumb to the provocation. "I will say right away, events at the level of barons and viscounts interest me little. Counts, dukes, padishahs, the emperor. And not all counts are worth my time. Far from all of them."

"I'll pass your request on to the receptionist," the porter did nothing but bow. "That is out of my personal domain. Your bedsheets will be delivered to you in a few minutes."

The porter left me alone, and I could finally breathe a sigh of relief. Tarra Loyd, when she was still a simple magister and not a chancellor, had taught me an interesting way to get lost in an unfamiliar city. In the most visible place. In the most expensive hotel. In the most expensive room. Forming the most unusual requests. Tonight I was going to visit the palace of Padishah Bayazid III, and by that time I needed to make sure that I had showed the public that I had come to the capital to burn money and communicate with the coordinator of the Goose hotel chain. They used to have a branch in Hearth, but after reconstruction it had to be torn down. And its was only at level "red," not even "silver," like in Turb. And now, when I visited a "diamond" level room, it became clear that I needed one in my own city. I knew that the coordinator, like the owner of the network, lived in Al-Khorezm, so killing two birds with one stone would be ideal. Getting Marisa out, and negotiating with the hotels. If I managed to go to some event today or tomorrow, that would be great. Of course, I couldn't stand the pomp and circumstance, but these things were useful for character building.

Soon I had everything I needed in my room. Clothes, a hairdresser who turned my tangles into something acceptable, and two beautiful girls who started helping me wash myself without asking any questions. Before that, of course, I had to do something quite frightening — take off my mithril armor. There was no cleaning system in it, so the stench brought tears to my eyes. I needed to make it a rule to take off my armor and clean it at least once every two or three days. The girls did their best. Not only did they clean my body, which also smelled like a cesspool, but they dealt with my armor, removing any unpleasant odors from it. And there were no questions about where they came from. The servants at the Diamond Goose were well trained and, when I allowed myself to let my hands go, squeezing the soft spots of the beauties rubbing my back, they skillfully nipped a potential conflict in the bud. If a gentleman wanted sex, he could order the best courtesans of love that the capital had to offer. The hotel staff was not intended for such purposes.

My old clothes were thrown out. They weren't just worn out, they were so deeply imbued with sweat that no alchemy could remove the persistent smell. Having sent the girls to work again, handing each of them five gold pieces, I put on the clothes I had bought and, barely suppressing my trembling, began to pull on my mithril armor. Lately, I had become so accustomed to its protection that I felt naked without it. Even the *Golden Dome of Protection* hadn't given me such security. In order not to arouse suspicion, I gave the armor the shape of the clothes that had just been brought to me. I would definitely need to go to the store and try on several dozen different styles. Not to buy them, although I would have to buy one set so as not to arouse suspicion. I need to update the list of potential disguises for my mithril armor so as not to invoke the ridicule of those around me. The clothes should be beautiful, expensive and immediately show that their owner has authority. It pissed me off, of course, but many people first judged you by your clothes and only then looked at your regalia. And as an archduke, I had to maintain my reputation...How much easier it was in the rifts! The riftbeasts didn't care how I looked. They only wanted to swallow me whole.

Soon there was food, wine, and, what pleased me most, several sheets of paper briefly listing everything that was happening in the capital. Who was feuding with whom, whose estate had flooded, who had fallen out of favor with the emperor, who the padishahs were friends with, what was happening in the Citadel. This information cost me another ten gold pieces, but it was worth it. These were potential topics for conversation.

Having opened the map, I began to examine the palace of Padishah Bayazid the Third from all angles, thinking about the approaches. I had no doubt that the richest man in the world, as Kimal Sarento called him, had taken care of protection from all sorts of invisibles. Perhaps the palace would have a defense system on the level that the dark ones had installed in Hearth. Of course, I was told that there were only three or four of them in the whole world, but I had no more faith in the Temple of Skron. I had to assume the worst-case scenario — that I would have to fight my way through, and a huge pillar of light would rise above my head.

I immediately identified the point where the transport hub might be located: in the inner courtyard of the palace. There was plenty of space there, there were convenient entrances and, most importantly, if the map was to be believed, a lot of empty space, for some strange reason not built up or occupied by various gazebos. This area was not visible from the main building, where guests were usually allowed, there were probably still tall and thick evergreen spruces growing there, blocking the view of random witnesses who decided to stroll through the inner park. Plus some walls covering the portal arch. It was in Hearth that it was on public display. Here, in Al-Khorezm, right next to the Citadel, this was unacceptable. All that was left was a small matter: somehow warn the Citadel and get its representatives at the right time for me. A courier? Perhaps, but how could I make the Citadel believe this courier and not burn him at the stake for slandering Padishah Bayazid the Third himself? If, for example, someone came to me and said that Eleanore was trading resources from the treasury on the side, would I listen to such a person? I didn't think so. Although I would check, of course. Later. When my emotions had subsided. But they definitely wouldn't listen to the courier. So it must be someone the Citadel would trust. But who?

Help came from an unexpected source. Alia couldn't help. The High Priest had no remote connection to the Citadel. All communications were conducted through couriers. Eleanore also chuckled meaningfully and offered options, one better than the other, but then my manager had an idea. Magister Meram! The old man had been sitting in his workshop the whole time, trying to figure out the basics of the *Author* skill, but his old connections were still there! As were the remote connection symbols. Most of them, of course, were dark, but there was also one symbol that connected the former runescribe with a representative of the Citadel. This was done in case the Church of the Light urgently needed Magister Meram. They would definitely listen to the old man!

There was a knock at the door. I had no servants, so I had to open it myself. A respectable man stood on the threshold. *Analyze* showed that although he was a mage, he was a rather mediocre one. And the man did not have many enhancements of any kind. Nevertheless, he exuded the aura of a leader. He knew how to give orders and enjoyed doing it.

"It has reached me that Count Nameless

wished to meet with someone authorized to negotiate the opening of hotels. Shah Rashid Al-Abdullah at your service."

"Please, come in," I said, standing to the side. The man's name was familiar to me. Eleanore had done her best to gather information for me on the Goose chain. Shah Rashid Al-Abdullah was one of the top ten people with decision-making power. He was not at the very top, of course, but I did not expect Padishah Amir the Seventh would personally honor me with his presence.

"I don't have much time, so I'd prefer to get straight to the point of our meeting," said the guest. "Count Nameless? Or should I still call you Archduke Maximilian Valevsky?"

"Perhaps here, behind closed doors, it would be prudent to use the second," I answered, not at all surprised that I had been exposed. "Well, let's get straight to the point. After the unpleasant events with the Wave in Hearth, we had to completely rebuild. The old buildings were torn down, including the Red Goose. Now that the city is under construction, I would like to bring back the magnificent franchise. And I'll need a whole flock of geese. Starting from some more modest options for simple visiting townsfolk, all the way up to the diamond level, like this wonderful establishment. Although perhaps silver will suffice. And we'll need two of those, to ensure there's enough space for everyone."

"Who is paying for the construction? Three hotels is a pretty decent investment. Especially in the upper and middle price ranges."

"You provide the permits, Hearth will take care of the construction and implementation. Any details about profit distribution and cash flow can be resolved with my city manager directly on site. She has been warned and is waiting for an authorized representative of the Goose in Hearth. And you can select the best locations while you're there. For now, we're only agreeing on intent."

"What about the employees? We have strict standards for our employees.'

"Hiring can be done on your side, with one caveat: all employees will have to pass a check through our internal security system."

"What does it consist of?" Shah Rashid frowned.

"A test of their good intentions. So that we know those working in the hotel are truly hotel employees, and not spies from all manner of interested parties. And one more thing. Hearth is a location legally authorized to deal with dark ones, so the hotel staff should be able to handle this calmly. There should be no conflicts on religious grounds."

"When are you ready to start construction?"

"Yesterday. Hearth has a pressing need for elite accommodations, so I am ready to invest. I am going to make my city a pearl not only of the Zarak Empire, but of all the Light lands. And yes, I understand perfectly well that I have just significantly reduced the profit percentage of Hearth. This demonstrates my interest in the project and that it will take off, and not end up in some dusty folder on a distant shelf."

"We will certainly take advantage of this during our negotiations with the manager of Hearth," nodded Shah Rashid. "However, hospitality does not allow me to take advantage of such an obvious gift from the guest without thanking him in return. Therefore, people will only discover the fact that Archduke Valevsky has arrived in Al-Khorezm tomorrow. Today, you will remain Count Nameless."

"But they will definitely find out?" I grinned.

"Trading information is an integral part of our business, Archduke. Especially such important news. Here is an example of the information our people collect: you asked for the reception places of the high society of Al-Khorezm. Today, Padishah Bayazid the Third is holding a closed party in his palace. Strictly invitation only."

"And Shah Rashid Al-Abdullah can help me acquire such an invitation?"

"The Diamond Goose can do a lot for its guests. Including this. But Count Nameless will never make it into the palace of Padishah Bayazid the Third, even if he has all the invitations in this world."

"The invitation must be for Archduke Maximilian Valevsky," I replied. The entire road to Al-Khorezm had been one coincidence after the other, so I wasn't even surprised when I learned that Padishah Bayazid the Third was holding a reception at the very moment I arrived in the capital. In fact, there was an explanation for this coincidence, and I didn't like it. Today marked the third day since the Zarak Empire had been given the ultimatum, and the Padishah was celebrating his victory. He had clearly fulfilled everything that the servants of the Temple of Skron demanded of him.

"In that case, I won't keep you any longer. The invitation will be delivered to you before you leave. Right now, a carriage is waiting for you at the entrance. It will take you to the store, where you can choose suitable clothes for today's reception. A negotiation delegation will be sent to Hearth tomorrow. We need time to agree on our terms and choose a representative."

The store left an indelible impression. Apparently, the salesperson assigned to help create my "look" had been off his game when picking out my sets of clothes. Bright, colorful, provocative. Some even had feathers embedded in them. To my puzzled question "What *is* this?" I received the answer that it was "the pinnacle of modern style!" Only the best of the best could afford to wear this, and my title perfectly suited this gaudy nightmare.

I had to ask for a different salesperson and explain that I needed outfits for receptions, not for performing on stage or trying to hide among peacocks. Things went more smoothly after that, and soon my mithril armor had four suits for all occasions in its memory. As I had feared, I still had to buy one, so as not to arouse suspicion. This luxury cost me three thousand gold, so I had to write out a check. The elongated faces of the salespeople will remain in my memory for the rest of my days, and only the first one, who had offered me peacock outfits, snorted contemptuously. The Zarak Empire was clearly backward in terms of modern trends. And these archdukes simply did not understand the charm of vivid fabrics.

Back at the hotel, I finally got a little free time. First, I took out all the loot I had gotten from Tari. The box, the books, and the papers. I decided to start with the books. The way they were carefully packed spoke of their value, but the reality was not as exciting as I had imagined. Two identical gifted editions of a collection of poems, depicted in bright colors and made with an eye for art. Mediocre poetry, in my opinion. I leafed through each page, hoping to find some secret message, but there was none. Pure greed prevented me from slicing through the covers — these would look lovely on the shelves of my still modest library. After all, shouldn't Hearth be the home to my personal library as well? And Alia and Naira would like the poems. Saccharine, maudlin. Everything that young girls love.

Returning the volumes to my immaterial backpack, I began to examine the box. It was closed with some kind of intricate lock. I didn't have the key, so I had to resort to my tried and true method of slicing through the lid with vyrma. Seeing the contents, I suddenly regretted that Tari had left this world so peacefully. The box was brimming with small green crystals. I hadn't thought to look at his body count, since I hadn't even considered he might be sitting on oblivion crystals. The fact that he hadn't turned into a dried-up mummy indicated that somewhere on his body was the symbol *Firth*, and in order for Tari to be able to calmly consume this garbage for a year, twelve people had to be killed. Condemned soldiers, peasants, random townsfolk — it didn't matter. The point was that the Duke of Odoevsky's assistant had sacrificed twelve people to Magister Meram to satisfy his desires. And the old man, who was currently sitting in my city, had accepted this sacrifice. What had the servants of the Temple of Skron said? Twelve thousand confirmed lives? And how many unconfirmed? If the old man failed with *Author*, would he go mad? Would he start attacking people, causing mischief, wreaking havoc? And did I need the trouble? The idea of leaving Meram alive didn't seem so good to me anymore.

Carefully pouring all the contents into a bag, I hid it in my immaterial bag. I had nowhere to burn it right now, and pouring it into the sewer would poison the river. I'd go back to Hearth and destroy this infection at the training grounds. It had no place in this world.

I was in a rather gloomy mood by the time I started in on the documents. That was the only thing that stopped me from smashing apart the room, destroying the furniture and breaking all the windows. The Duke of Odoevsky was playing his own game. He no longer had any invisible spies at his disposal, but he always carefully recorded all the orders he received from his "master" verbatim, and also tried to get them in writing. From the same "master" who had ordered the duke to work with the Elor. Who ordered the cleansing of the province where three rifts were discovered. The one who now sat on the throne of the Zarak Empire.

My family had not died because the Duke of Odoevsky was a capricious eccentric who had decided to demonstrate his power. They were murdered because Zurgan Shor wanted to get his hands on the resources contained in three four-level rifts while bypassing the Fortress' authority. And Kimal Sarento had known this? Most certainly — he had been watching Zurgan Shor. Opening the notebook, I began to carefully study everything concerning the current emperor. There was a lot of information, but it was presented in a strange and compressed form. Apparently, Sarento only cared about the bare facts, no details. I flipped through several pages that described the sins of this "master" in trading equipment with Elor and finally came across an order to clear the lands of the Barons Valevsky. More precisely, Zurgan Shor had no idea who even lived in this territory. He knew there were three rifts there, and he ordered his loyal dog, Count Fardi, to clear the area and provide him with the necessary legal cover. A court order, the signature of Devalon the Sixth, and the removal of my family from the register of aristocrats. All this was provided by Zurgan Shor, and not the ordinary Count Fardi.

On impulse, I opened the information on Kimal Sarento and stared at the handwritten text: *"My curious mentor, there are things I would like to keep only in my memory. Everything that concerns me personally, what I have had to face in my life and what I have gone through is mine. You can add whatever you want about me. It is even interesting how people see me from the outside. But what Kimal Sarento did in his youth, it is better for you not to know. No one needs to know. (Edits made by Kimal Sarento.)*

There was no anger. Just disappointment. Yet another one. Transparency breeds transparency, eh? But I had to be the one to open up first, otherwise others wouldn't even try? Did I really expect anything different from Kimal Sarento? He only acted to ensure his own needs, nothing more. The only reason he became my pupil in the first place was to use me as a shield from the Orthodox.

How long I sat there staring out the window, I couldn't say. I was overcome with disappointment in humanity, multiplied by the understanding that I was taking revenge on the wrong person. What was the point of destroying the Duke of Odoevsky and his people if they were only performing their duties? What was the point if the mastermind who destroyed my family was sitting somewhere else, and here I was tripping over my own feet to save his daughter?

There was a knock on the door, and without waiting for an answer, the maid looked into the room:

"Sir, your carriage is here. Here is your invitation and...Oh, you're not ready yet?!"

"I'll be down in five minutes," I answered, returning to reality. Taking the invitation, I sent away the maid who wanted to help me get dressed, after which I stuffed the clothes into an immaterial backpack and gave my mithril armor the appropriate look. The decision about what to do came quickly — Count Fardi would live. I would not leave him in the Citadel. I had no idea what I would do with him later, but I was not going to allow the clergy to do to the Duke of Odoevsky everything that the Evil Engineer had showed me. As for the true hand behind the murder of my family, I thought that Zurgan the First had occupied the throne of the Zarak Empire for too long. It was time to return the true heir!

Chapter 19

"ARCHDUKE MAXIMILIAN VALEVSKY, Zarak Empire!"

The buzz in the hall died down as soon as I entered. A lot of people had gathered to visit Padishah Bayazid the Third. The huge room was filled almost to capacity. Running *Analyze* over those closest to me, I couldn't help but grin. Three of those standing near me were converts. The rest were hidden by the crowd, but I had no doubt — here, among the upper class of the Shurghan Empire, were plenty of people who had sold their souls to Skron. The Citadel was completely failing in its duties.

Padishah Bayazid the Third was still absent and his throne was empty. Evidently, he'd appear later, after all the guests had arrived. This was only to my advantage. I had no desire to go through the crowd and bow to this man. I was much more interested in the tables bursting with all sorts of snacks and sweets. Without stopping to use *Analyze* for a second, I reached my target and with no unnecessary embarrassment began to try everything in reach. The private chefs of the richest man in the world had pulled out all the stops for this feast. Everything was spectacular!

"You should leave this house, Valevsky!" A stranger said as he approached me. The fact that my title was brazenly ignored indicated a direct challenge. If I didn't react somehow, I'd never be taken seriously. Putting down another serving of divine hors d'oeuvres, I turned to the impudent fellow. A light human, according to *Analyze.* The man turned out to be quite remarkable in terms of magic stones, amplifiers and amulets. They hung around his neck like festoons from a may pole. The magic stones, however, were what immediately attracted my attention. Not every dark one had level twenty-five stones, but here *Fireball* and *Ice Spike* had reached quite significant values. The support stones were no worse — almost all of them were level twenty or above. If I were to put him up against Count Vyazemsky, the latter would pale in comparison. The man standing before me was one of the strongest mages among all the light ones. Behind him stood a posse of ten people. And all of them, as if handpicked, possessed remarkable magic stones, all level twenty. Not bad! Apparently, trade with the dark ones in the Shurghan Empire was in full swing. And trade in rather serious matters. The kind brought to the Zarak Empire only on the most special occasions.

Despite the large number of people in the hall, the area around us cleared out. Before letting me into the palace, the servants carefully checked every fold of my clothes, looking for secret knives or anything that could harm other guests. They even put special steel bracelets on me that blocked magic. On my wrists, legs and even neck. All to guarantee the safety of the padishah. I did not object — the bracelets didn't work on me, and all the guests had similar adornments. Or rather, I had thought that everyone had them. The group of mages who brazenly prevented me from enjoying the snack table did not have bracelets. That said, I saw the swords and knives swinging from their belts. Considering that the symbol of Padishah Bayazid the Third was not on these people's clothes, they could be considered servants or personal guards. So that meant someone in the padishah's palace was allowed to carry weapons? An interesting observation.

"I see that the great Padishah Bayazid the Third gives his jesters a long leash. Including permitting them to ignore the titles of guests. Apparently, I still have a lot to learn about the Shurghan Empire, since such things are allowed here. I apologize, gentlemen, but I must recommend that you find another subject for your jokes. As you can see, I am eating."

I couldn't just pretend I hadn't noticed the insult. But in any palace there was a separate category of people whose insults could not be taken seriously. Jesters. Buffoons. The "blessed." There were no such people in Hearth — I never understood the charm of laughing at those with disabilities, but Zurgan the First had a couple of such disadvantaged souls. I'd seen them at one of the receptions.

"You called me a buffoon?" By how his countenance darkened, this was not the reaction he had expected from me. "Duel! Now!"

"So then issue a challenge according to the rules," I still had to look up from my meal. "Name, regalia, title, conditions of the duel. What, are you so low on the hierarchy? Or don't they teach jesters such things? My advice to you is to go and read how to properly challenge a person of a higher class to a duel, rehearse it with your comrades and come back. I'll wait for you here. I'm curious to see how far the jesters of the great padishah will go."

Whispers began to spread around the hall. Apparently, the person who wanted to throw me out of this event was quite famous among the local aristocracy. He had been clumsy, of course. It was immediately obvious that he had not prepared in advance, he had to improvise. Had Padishah Bayazid the Third actually condescended to throw me out of the event? Or was this someone else's initiative?

The enemy pulled himself together. Apparently, it wasn't every day that he encountered such indifference. I didn't care. My armor couldn't be penetrated by a level fifty *Lightning Strike*. Could a level twenty-five *Fireball* really do anything? I didn't think so.

"Archduke Valevsky! I, Emir Jafar, consider your behavior unworthy of high society and challenge you to a duel! Only your death can wash away all the shame that you brought to this lovely event! I am ready to fight you with weapons or magic. I will kill you in any way. I leave the choice of place and time to you!"

"Why go anywhere? There's a nice courtyard here, I suggest we move there and settle everything right away. But I have a counter-condition. I see that you, Emir Jafar, have a whole crowd of hangers-on. They stand there, puffing out their cheeks, listening to your every word. I want to fight them all at once. There are eleven of you, and I am alone. We need to somehow even the odds, right? Do you want to fight to the death? No problem. Let it be to the death. And one more thing. Your bodies will belong to me. I am not going to give them to your families to bury with honor and send them to the Light. I will feed you to riftbeasts, so that even after death you will have no peace. Are these conditions acceptable to you, Emir Jafar? You and your little posse?"

The way the emir's cheek twitched spoke volumes — I had managed to hook him. And judging by his reaction, quite hard. A buzz went around the hall. My proposal was clearly out of line with what ordinary people were used to. Some even called me crazy, so I decided to add a little wood to the fire. If I was going to pretend to be crazy, I might as well be committed.

"Is there anyone else here who wants to express their dissatisfaction with me? Who disagrees with my right to be at this event? If there are any, join in. Eleven, thirty, forty — I don't care how many of you I kill. If there are none, I suggest everyone shut up. I will take any word against me spoken to anyone who does not wish to fight me as a personal insult, and that person will be killed on the spot without any duel. You have my word!"

"How dare you say such a thing?!" Outrage immediately flared up in the hall. The young and zealous men, as I expected, were the first to be outraged by my words. "I, Bey Ali-Hasan, will stand next to my brothers to personally spit on your dismembered body!"

"Any other takers?" I looked at the assembled mob. "Who else wants to teach the presumptuous Archduke of the Zarak Empire a lesson? Or are there those in the Shurghan Empire who are not ashamed to stick their heads up their asses, just so that no one touches them?"

The number of participants increased. By the time we entered the courtyard, there were already thirty-seven people standing up against me. Among them were converts — five of them immediately sided with Emir Jafar, demonstrating their loyalty. The padishah's servants tried to keep us from going into the courtyard, but I managed to wind up the assembled people so much that they wouldn't accept anything else. Only my death could wash away the shame I had brought upon their heads, and those who wanted to prevent this would be killed on the spot. In any case, the two servants were in a tough spot.

When I went out into the courtyard, a satisfied grin appeared on my face. The performance, which I had not started but which I had managed to seize control of, had been a great success. There was a fenced-in area in the courtyard. The fence was high and solid, and it was impossible to see what was behind it. Of course, I could have been mistaken, and there was some kind of construction site hidden behind this barrier. But one small circumstance confirmed all my suspicions — next to the gates, which were also high, solid and opaque, there were two guards in combat gear with the symbols of Padishah Bayazid the Third on their chests. For any ordinary citizen there was nothing reprehensible in this, but not for me. Both guards were dark. And non converts at that! For only dark humans were allowed to guard the portal arch of the transport hub.

Turning to the crowd, I couldn't help but grin. The entire hall had followed us. Everyone wanted to watch the unprecedented spectacle of thirty-seven to one. Some even started betting on how many seconds I'd be able to hold out. Because I still had no weapon, and no one was going to remove the magic-blocking bracelets. Since I didn't include such a thing in the terms of the fight, it meant I knew what I was getting into. No one was going to meet me halfway. Honor and dignity? Clearly no one had heard of such concepts in this place.

"What's going on here?" a menacing voice rang out. A moment later, the crowd became even denser. The Padishah's guards ran up, surrounding the assembled group. A gloomy man of about fifty stood between me and Emir Jafar. The warrior had clearly been through more than one battle — he had earned the network of scars across his face. The only sad thing was that the brave warrior turned out to be a convert. As were all the guards who had run into the courtyard with him. How many of them? About fifty? How many dark ones were there in the Padishah's service, and why was the Citadel so careless? Such a hotbed of darkness has sprung up right next to the clergy, and yet they were busy catching all sorts of Count Fardi-types in the Zarak Empire! Where was the logic?

"Duel!" someone shouted from the back rows.

"And who is fighting whom?" the squad leader frowned. He also did not understand why there were so many people inside the circle formed by the spectators.

"Archduke Valevsky against all these gentle-men," I replied. "Thirty-seven pieces in total, if my count is correct."

"Since when is the highest aristocracy meas-ured in pieces?" the squad leader frowned even more. What was happening clearly did not fit the status quo.

"Since the gentlemen decided to express their disagreement with me. Do you have any com-plaints about what is about to happen here?"

"A duel in magic-blocking bracelets? Without weapons?"

"I need to give my opponents at least some sort of chance," I answered with a Sarento-esque smile. It wasn't quite as effective as his was, but I had to start learning some time, right? I had already put all the pieces in place and now all I could do was enjoy the match. I needed to make sure that the survivors had a firm understanding that it was better to leave Archduke Valevsky alone. Fighting him meant certain death.

"You should move the duel to another location," the commander of the guards said after a pause, for some reason addressing me. "This place is not suitable for a fight." "We will decide for ourselves which place is suitable for us," my opponent answered with undisguised anger. "This man dared to tarnish the honor of all those present, such a thing can only be washed away with bloodshed. Immediately!"

"And yet I must insist that you move to another place. An order from the great Padishah Bayazid the Third!"

From the way Emir Jafar was thinking, he was ready to run away, which I absolutely could not allow. Since there was not enough wood on the fire, I needed to stoke the flames so high that it would flare up across the entire empire!

"If Emir Jafar wishes, he can leave this place. Personally, I don't give a damn about the orders of the great Padishah Bayazid the Third and his watchdog. Honor is more important. I, Archduke

Valevsky, confirm that I am ready to fight here and now with thirty-seven corpses who for some strange reason continue to call themselves people. And if these corpses are so weak-willed that they are ready to shamefully flee the battlefield, then I do not intend to meet them next time. Because I do not intend to fight against yard dogs with their tails between their legs. The only fate for such a wretched creature is to be beaten with sticks!"

"Fight!" Instead of an answer, Emir Jafar shouted and my mithril armor shook. *Fireball, Spike, Lightning Strike, Earthen Spike.* Eleven high-level abilities fell on my shield, attempting to sweep me away and turn me into a pancake. It was unpleasant to realize, but I had been right: the *Integrity* bar appeared. It was not decreasing at the same speed as during the battle with Kimal Sarento, but it was still decreasing! Which meant that my armor was not a panacea for all problems. If thirty or forty people with pumped up stones gathered, it would give me problems.

But not today. The Fog Stalker said that Marisa Shor was on the minus second floor of the main building. And unconscious. So, the dark aura would not affect her. No consciousness — no influence. If so, then nothing held me back anymore. I was tired of playing the role of an obedient boy, capable only of conquering the next rift. Meet the new Maximilian Valveksy — mean, nasty and monstrously effective.

Dialing my aura up to forty meters to be sure to take the entire courtyard and not to touch the palace entirely, I activated the tenth-level ousel. I didn't go any higher, as I wasn't sure that those who didn't sell their souls to Skron would be able to survive. In fact, even ten was too high, but I couldn't take too much of a risk. I'd only turn the aura on for a few seconds. No more — I wasn't going to chase converts all over the palace. First, I needed to deprive them of control so that Skron could intercept their consciousness, then make them start summoning the portal. For the latter, I needed to remove the aura — under its influence, the creatures wouldn't sing their dark song. They would try to escape, and I had no right to allow them to do that. Converts had no place in this world. The freaks wanted eternal life? What a pity they weren't warned about the small detail that they could lose control of their body as Skron took over.

The courtyard of the grand padishah's palace was echoing with the dark murmur. The people affected by the level ten aura were just beginning to stir, coming to their senses, so I wouldn't have to pay attention to them for a while. It was much more important to cut the song short and prevent portals from appearing here. For who knew who the Temple of Skron would send? They might even use Karina Fardi. I wasn't ready to fight her yet. To do that, I needed to somehow learn how to block the dark influence of a level one-hundred rift. Where could I find one?

The steel hoops that held my arms, legs, and even my neck fell to the ground. Vyrma was stronger. Of course, I could still use magic with these adornments around my arms, but I'd inevitably experience a kickback that would turn me into a vegetable. For today, that was unacceptable. *Dash* carried me from one group of converts to another, where I quickly cut off their dark song. At some point, I even had to reactivate the aura to force the converts to stop — I simply did not have time to deal with everyone in a minute. There were too many people who had sold their souls to Skron. This trick had to be repeated three times before the last dark song was cut off. Having turned on the aura once more, checking that none of those gathered suddenly jumped up and began to call the portal, I went to the gate in front of the permanent waypoint. Both guards were lying on the ground, showing no signs of life. It was hard to show any vital signs when your head and chest had exploded. The dark ones didn't have the key skill *Adapt,* so the tenth level of the rift had been fatal for them. I broke the gate down with a kick and nodded with satisfaction — the portal arch opened in front of me.

"Alia, hand Meram over to the Citadel — in the palace of Padishah Bayazid III there is a waypoint to the dark lands, as well as at least a hundred converts. Some of the converts have been eliminated, the waypoint has been cleared, now it needs to be destroyed. Let them send investigators here. There are still many converts left."

"Got it, we'll do it now..."

I did not break the portal arch — in that case,

the padishah could later claim that he simply wanted to make a beautiful sculpture for himself. As long as the portal worked, Bayazid the Third would have no way to avoid punishment. But I began to wonder about another question. No matter how I looked at it, I had been challenged to a duel, and thirty-seven, or rather, thirty-two people were still awaiting their fate. I was not going to forgive or pardon anyone. I wasn't the one who had challenged someone to a duel, I had not united in a crowd to kill the archduke, I did not keep silent about the fact that I had no weapon or that I could not use magic. The creatures that opposed me were not worthy of living. They were bereft of honor, therefore they must perish without it.

I didn't switch off my aura. With the calmness of an executioner, I walked from one opponent to another and pulled out their magic stones. Unfortunately, only ten of Emir Jafar's henchmen had reached level twenty, the rest were much less prepared. The maximum these lackeys could afford was level seven. But I wasn't going to leave a single stone behind. All of it could prove useful.

It so happened that I left Emir Jafar for last. My opponent was clearly struggling with the dark influence — he was wheezing, his eyes rolling back in his head as he tried to turn over and rise to his feet. It was obvious that this man had visited the rifts. Perhaps he had even reached level five. After spending a couple of seconds watching Jafar's attempts to come to his senses, I leaned over to remove the magic stones and end this man's life, when Alia's voice appeared in my head. A tense voice.

"Max, stop! The Citadel orders you to immediately leave the palace of the Padishah Bayazid the Third and wait for its representatives at the entrance. The waypoint in the palace of the Padishah was agreed upon by the Pope himself! The clergy use it to communicate with the Temple of Skron. Therefore, Padishah Bayazid the Third was forgiven many things, including the fact that there were converts in his palace. If you do not obey, the Citadel will declare you an enemy of the light world. Max, this is...This is betrayal! The Church is working directly and openly with the dark ones!"

"Or not the Church, but the one with whom Meram cooperated. Who was he talking to?" I asked angrily.

"The head of the Citadel supply service," Alia answered after a pause.

"Did Meram extend this man's life? What symbols did he install on him?"

"Life extension, rejuvenation, *Firth*."

"I see." Rage welled up in my chest even more. *Firth*, huh? The head of the Citadel supply service is sitting on oblivion crystals? If so, there is no point in expecting help from the clergy now. My mistake. I should have first found out who Meram had connections to before relying on this contact.

"Max, get out of there," Alia pleaded. "If the clergy come to the palace and find you there...Hearth is not yet ready for war."

"It will never be ready," I answered. "But war

never asks nicely. No, Alia. I am not going to leave. I am not going to run around, glancing around in fear, terrified to anger the great Citadel. Maybe not all of them, but some of them have sold out to the dark ones. Let's see how the Inquisitor reacts to this. Blockade the city. Take the clergy of Hearth into custody — I don't need any surprises. Who knows how the servants of the Light can communicate?"

"What are you going to do?"

"What I do better than anyone in the world. Sew chaos!"

Removing my hand from the communication symbol, I looked at the wheezing Emir Jafar. His stones were still of interest to me, but I no longer had the desire to kill. I had found an opponent more serious than some lowly fighter. Having removed the dark aura, I went towards the portal arch. First, I needed to destroy the transport hub so that unexpected guests would not show up here, and then...

I couldn't figure out what would happen next. And would there even be a "next?" When I entered the gate, the ripples on the shimmering veil of the portal were dying down. On the platform next to the portal stood two minotaurs, as well as one extremely unwelcome guest in these parts.

"Archduke Maximilian Valevsky, what an unexpected meeting. The Temple of Skron has long since begun to notice that if something does not go according to plan, the Archduke of Hearth is most likely involved."

"I can't say I'm glad to see Seven in the lands of the light," I said, preparing to turn on the dark aura. But I was in no hurry. First, I wanted to find out what the temple servant was doing here.

"Many in the Temple of Skron are against working with Hearth. I, Six, Five, and even Two are against having anything to do with your city. We don't like unpredictability. But One is stubborn. No one understands why, but he sees in you what the others don't. If it weren't for One, Archduke Valevsky would have ceased to exist several months ago. You were given a chance to prove your usefulness, but you didn't seize it. Instead of engaging in trade, you blocked the portal to Hearth, and also destroyed the guardians of this portal point. Which is a key node of the transport network. In accordance with the protocols, I have every authority to eliminate any threat to the portal, even if it is someone who, for some reason, One is protecting. I can't say that I'm sorry, Archduke Valevsky. I have anticipated this moment for a long time. Karina Fardi is right — the dark ones must remember that this world belongs to them.

The mist surrounding Seven suddenly flew off in all directions, revealing a naked, anthropomorphic, genderless creature made from a single piece of metal. I pulled the level twenty-five ousel to my belt and, reducing the radius to ten meters, I activated the dark aura and *Dash*ed towards my opponent. What was the point of speaking when everything had already been said?

The blow that flew into my chest tore *Golden*

Dome of Protection to shreds and threw me far to the side. The gate I crashed into stood firm, but the people who were within the radius of my aura all died. I knew this for sure. Jumping to my feet, I was about to run toward Seven again, when I noticed something strange — a new detail appeared on the shoulder of the servant of the Temple of Skron. It looked like six hollow tubes that were filled with cigar-like objects. I took a step towards Seven and the oblong objects activated, flying out of the tubes. They left a trail of smoke behind them and moved monstrously fast. The thought came to me to move to the side, but the objects reacted and changed trajectories. The *Golden Dome of Protection* returned to its place and, absorbing these cigars, once again flew apart into small pieces. The blast threw me aside, and before I crashed into the barrier, I managed to remove the dark aura. An unpleasant metallic laugh rang out:

"Darkness will not help you, Archduke Valevsky. Vyrma will not help you. Mithril will not help you. Nothing in this world will help you. You are powerless against the true power of the Temple of Skron. And so you will die now."

Chapter 20

DASH CARRIED ME TO THE SIDE, away from the strange flying cigars. They adjusted their trajectory again and new ones joined them, but I didn't hesitate a moment. As soon as the nimble smoking cylinders approached me, I *Dash*ed to the side to dodge them. In fact, I found myself repeating the same motion over and over again, jumping along the perimeter of the fence to avoid attacks. The mithril and vyrma were truly powerless against the highest hierarchs of Skron. I managed to get close to the creature, but it did me little good — the glove powerlessly hit the chest and flew off. As did the blade, which almost broke. With a blow of his hand, Seven threw me to the side and launched another volley of homing cigars. I had to run, often at top speed. This mechanical creature must believe that its weapon can harm me. That it was the master of the situation. Why? Because I was still waiting to hear something specific. Something that could shed light on the events happening in the world. On the plans of the Temple of Skron. Surely the villains must enjoy their position? Killing the enemy not only physically, but also morally? Of course they must! That was why I was running around the perimeter like crazy, in no hurry to leave the danger zone. The temple servant must believe that I was losing!

Why was I so sure of myself? The answer was simple — the twelve explosions that the mithril armor absorbed only dropped the armor's *Integrity* by two percent. Even the mages I had to kill were more dangerous than this strange weapon. Some kind of homing arrow with a *Fireball* effect. It looked scary, but in fact, it was nothing serious. Finally, a satisfied metallic voice was heard:

"It's no use, Archduke! Give it up and submit to fate! Your time has come, as it has for all of the lands of the light! Soon, very soon, the Temple of Skron will launch its offensive. Karina Fardi has begun to understand the essence of her gift. She can control the vessel for up to five seconds. With her in total control, without giving herself to Skron for fifteen minutes! In no time at all, she'll extend this by several orders of magnitude. The vessel will become invulnerable and invincible! She will crush the light ones under her foot like rotten wood."

"You are creating a monster!" I shouted, continuing to sprint madly around the arena.

"The Temple of Skron is creating a higher being! A new force capable of taking the place vacated by the offworlders and the lithoids. The Temple of Skron is bringing imbalance to the world order. The balance of the system has been shaken. There must always be thirteen forces in our world in order to keep it from falling apart. The Temple of Skron is ready to provide a replacement! Karina Fardi will be the first power, and One will become the second. They will gain more power than the humans or mechanoids ever had! A couple more years and the process will be irreversible. But you will not live to see it. Your time has come! Stop running and take the blow of fate on your chest!"

"Gladly!" I muttered under my breath and used *Dash* once again. Only this time not along the perimeter, but directly at Seven. He swung his arm to throw me aside and a new portion of smoking cigars flew straight from his chest, but I was faster. Just a split second, but faster! It was not for nothing that Meram demanded that I strengthen my body — with my previous one I would never have withstood such a heavy blow. Ducking under Seven's arm and somehow miraculously avoiding the six cigars, I sharply turned around and clung to his back.

"Say hello to Skron, freak!" I managed when all the cigars I had released so far finally found their target. But Seven's body was between me and the flying *Fireballs*, and he didn't have time to get out of the way. The explosion was so huge that the temple servant couldn't stay in place and flew to the side. I was blinded for a moment. I even had to use *Heal* to restore my damaged eyes. The *Integrity* bar of the mithril armor decreased by almost a third. There were too many flying cigars. If they had all crashed into me instead of Seven, they could have done much more damage.

Looking around, I found myself on the edge of a huge pit. The fence and gate hiding the portal arch no longer existed. Nor did the arch. The groans of the wounded were heard all around — it turns out that not all the people escaped from the courtyard. For which they had paid dearly. All the highest society of the Shurghan Empire had gathered for the event of Padishah Bayazid the Third, meaning that Hearth had just brought a whole heap of trouble on its shoulders. But it still did not compare to the doom Seven had foretold. In two years, they planned to wipe the light ones off the face of the planet. And I was one of the mechanisms they had used to achieve this grandiose goal.

"Valevsky!" Emir Jafar's voice was filled with pain and suffering. However, there was also anger, multiplied by the desire to finish what he had started. Turning around, I saw the mage. He was lying not far from the place where the fence once stood. Thus, he had been hit a lot harder than the others. Considering that in this world, only a very limited number of healers could restore limbs, Emir Jafar would have to spend some time legless and with only one arm. Or would he? I thought for a second, then used *Heal.* Emir Jafar had played his part perfectly. Thanks to him, I'd made it to the courtyard, seen the courtyard, and destroyed a bunch of converts. The fact that in doing so, with a high degree of probability, I had picked a fight with the entire Shurghan Empire, the Citadel and the dark ones — these were trifles that the Emir could not influence in any way. This was my luck. Once again.

I found Seven not far from the portal. More precisely, I found what was left of the Seven near what was left of the portal. On the ground lay what looked like a broken doll that had been thoroughly worked over by a bad child armed with a sharp knife. Its chest was completely busted open, revealing its strange metal innards. It had no limbs — they'd been torn off. Its head was still barely in place, hanging from the neck by several wires. Amazingly, the temple servant was still alive. In any case, the mechanisms inside his body were still working. Realizing that it likely wouldn't work, I nevertheless bent down and activated the mithril glove again, aiming at the mechanisms.

Supreme Mechanoid Core obtained.

Devour went completely bonkers. It was as if the magic stone was trying to make up for all the times that there had been no loot to extract. The lithoids, the Fog Stalker Arena copies, the fight with Seven. Now, as my hand entered the inner cavity of the temple servant, the insatiable stone sucked up absolutely everything. And this was not an understatement. It took not only the mechanical guts of the mechanoid, but even its hull. My inventory recognized it as a "Kevlar alloy," inert to almost any type of damage. It could not be destroyed by magic, vyrma or mithril, in particular. There were a lot of parts, but, to my disappointment, the vast majority of them were single units. If something could be created from this, it would only be suitable for one person. Me, of course.

Once again examining the spot where Seven had lay, I placed my hand on my thigh.

"Eleanore, how is our mechanical guest treating you?"

"It's fantastic! Max, it's simply fantastic! I wasn't going to tell you, I thought I'd keep it a surprise for when you come home, but since you're asking — Hearth is now secure and protected from any uninvited guests of any kind — dark, light, minotaurs or other entities. They've all got a pillar of light! And they're not just highlighted, they're blocked from acting until vetted by someone with a certain level of access. Two Nameless, six *Phantom*s, and two dozen dark ones — that has been our catch over the past day. We identified them all! One Nameless was able to escape, Naira was able to finish off the second. A promising girl. They did not spare the invisible spies either. They all worked for the dark clans. Including the Bartolomeo Clan. Naira wanted to go home to deal with the chief personally, but we have not yet activated the portal."

"Don't do that just yet. The Temple of Skron has declared war on Hearth. I just had to destroy the Seven. The temple servants are mechanoids. As is the Temple itself. One *is* the entire dark pyramid, not some being living within its walls. That was why I was concerned about our guest. I don't fully know where its loyalties lie."

"From what I see," Eleanore said, any enthusiasm in her voice replaced by her usual severity, "our guy is completely subordinate to Hearth. He gave me and you access not only to the city management system, but also to his security system. That is, we can disable or destroy the defender at any time if we consider his actions dangerous to the city. I figured out the settings a little — the mechanoid cannot change or delete these settings without confirmation from one of us. So from this side, we are protected. But I will still observe what he does. Right now he is running along the wall, setting up additional protection. How did we get wrapped up in a war with the Temple of Skron?"

"They have been planning to kick us to the curb from the start. At least, numbers Two through Seven. They were operating purely on the orders of One, A.K.A the dark pyramid. Okay, I'll go save the princess and get out of the palace. I'll tell you the details when I get home."

"Valevsky!" Emir Jafar's voice grew stronger. The pain and suffering were gone, but the anger and hatred were still there. Strangely, no fireballs flew my way. In theory, the enemy should have finished the duel, but he hesitated.

"Jafar!" I returned the courtesy. If he ignored my title, then I wasn't going to observe etiquette either. The Emir had already risen to his feet, but remained in place. Two dead converts lay next to him. Their eyes, filled with darkness, left no other interpretation — the men had sold their souls to Skron. Rising to my feet, I brushed myself off in a businesslike manner, as if it made a difference, and went back to the main building. My path passed next to Jafar, and when I came closer to him, he blocked my way.

"Valevsky, we're not finished here!"

"Everything I wanted to say and do to you, I have already said and done. You are dead, Jafar. In about a minute you should have bled out, and not a single healer in this world, not a single elixir or amulet that hangs around your neck could have prevented it. The fact that I cured you, returned your limbs and blood, can be called the whim of a young up-and-comer from the Zarak Empire. I wanted it that way. Prepare, grow stronger, and I will gladly face you again. For now, you are no opponent of mine. My enemies, as you can see, are lying next to you. And here, in the palace of the great Padishah Bayazid the Third, who ordered you to toss me out, there is an insane number of these creatures. Turn around. All the guards. Twenty-seven highborn. How many servants, I don't even want to think about. Now this is a goal worthy of my attention. Fussing with you, of course, is interesting, but nothing more. You are a light one. What is the point of killing you?"

"So the whole spectacle was just for that? So that all the converts would gather in one place?"

"All of them? You're getting ahead of yourself, Jafar. Not all the converts on the palace grounds are here. But I have no desire to catch them. This is the Citadel's business. And I did not come here to hunt the dark ones. My sights are set elsewhere."

"Do you wish to kill the padishah?" Jafar could barely restrain himself from attacking me.

"There's not much else to do. Your beloved padishah has kidnapped and is holding my emperor's daughter captive and unconscious. Oh, don't make a face as if you didn't know that. Yes, here, in the basement of the main building, is the princess of the Zarak Empire. And she is not there of her own free will. Moreover, one of the girl's fingers has already been cut off so that her father would be more accommodating. Today they promised to cut off her legs if he does not do what the great padishah Bayazid the Third wants. Yes, I have a claim on your padishah, but I am not going to kill him. Not today."

"What you are saying is nonsense! The Great Padishah would never get involved with blackmail!" Jafar declared. "I am going with you! No one is allowed to defame the honor of the Great Padishah. I want to see for myself that what you are saying is nonsense. I want to look you in the eye when you realize how deeply mistaken you were about this great man."

"You know what, let's go!" I agreed, also barely holding back my anger. The fanatical devotion to the padishah was starting to piss me off, to be honest. Jafar looked like a capable enough guy, and it was unlikely that some random crazed townsperson would be able to pump their stones up to such high levels, but he lacked common sense. And I, too, wanted to look into the man's eyes as he learned the truth about his great master.

Surprisingly, Jafar did not argue. He obediently followed me and did not even interfere when I killed another convert. There were many servants running around the palace, as well as guards, and it so happened that almost all of them sold their souls to Skron. Only a few turned out to be light, all the rest lost control and gave themselves over to the power of their dark master. I wasn't showing any mercy. Evidently, Eleanore's hatred had passed on to me. I had no quarrel with the dark, gray, and even the supreme converts — they did not choose their fate. They were born that way, or, in the case of the supreme converts, they were forcibly made that way in childhood. But the simple converts I treated differently. They had consciously betrayed everything they were taught. That the Light was more important than Skron. Therefore, I walked around with a two-meter level ten dark aura and, as soon as people fell inside, I ended their lives.

I never found a way to the lower level, so I had to make one. In the main hall, I cut a large hole in the floor and jumped down. No one could stop me. Jafar followed me, casting a pointed look at the vyrma blade that seemed to have shot directly out of my bare hand. But he remained silent. There were even more converts on the first basement level than on the top. Moreover, there were even dark ones — something like a transit base was organized here. It seemed like a palace, but far removed from human eyes. I spared no one, never inquiring about the purpose of the dark ones' visit to our lands. At one point, I even had to switch from the level ten ousel to the level fifteen. Some of the dark humans proved immune to darkness of this level. Low-level magic stones began to accumulate in my inventory, which caused another meaningful chuckle from Jafar. I had no visible backpack, and it was physically impossible to stuff the loot I extracted from the dead into my pockets. But the stones had disappeared somewhere, they didn't fall to the floor, and this puzzled my temporary companion. But I wasn't stopping to explain and continued with my bloody harvest.

The passage to the lower floor was hidden behind closed doors and a closet. In fact, if I had not interrogated one of the servants, I would never have found it and would have had to try my luck, cutting holes in various places and hoping that it would lead me to the right point. The second basement level of the palace of Padishah Bayazid the Third was quite small. Just a few corridors with cells for prisoners and a torture chamber. Nothing extra. The executioners, surprisingly, turned out to be light ones, but they went along with the converts. I understood that people of this profession were necessary in this world, but they must either work for me or not at all. I couldn't leave something so valuable to the padishah. Let him find new specialists.

The door that the Fog Stalker had shown me was locked. It was clear that no one in their right mind had thought that I had come here not for the dark ones, but for the princess. Having turned off the aura so as not to accidentally kill Marisa, I chopped off the locks with my blade and opened the door. She was lying on a wooden bench. Until now, I had never seen Marisa Shor in reality, not even in paintings, but the striking resemblance to her father left no other opinion. This was the princess. The only difference was that Marisa was a petite and not so homely girl, completely different in build from her corpulent emperor father.

She was unconscious. There were several elixirs on the table next to the shop. Jafar opened the cap of one of them, sniffed it and said sullenly, abruptly closing the bottle:

"A sleeping potion based on oblivion crystals. She won't survive for long."

"We'll see about that," I answered, activating *Heal.* If my magic could restore people's limbs, couldn't it cure them of the green drug running through the princess' veins?

I saw a result only after the sixth time I cast the spell. The girl groaned. Deciding that I was moving in the right direction, I continued to pour magic into the princess in such huge quantities that it could resurrect the dead! After the twentieth spell, the girl arched, then bent sharply, as if from a spasm in her stomach, and vomited something bright green.

"Who are you?" Jafar whispered for the first time in all this time, when Marisa Shor opened her eyes. Clear, full of consciousness, and not the foggy haze of a narcotic dope. Judging by the way she began to frown, not understanding where she was, she did not remember the events of the last few days.

"Marisa Shor?" I asked, just in case? The girl nodded, showing that half the job was done. The girl had been found. The only thing left was to somehow get her out of the palace.

"Princess, let me introduce you to Emir Jafar. Emir Jafar, this is Marisa Shor, Princess of the Zarak Empire."

"You are Archduke Valevsky, right?" she asked. Her voice was astonishingly low, completely unbefitting of such a small girl. "Are we in Hearth?"

"Madam, you are in Al-Khorezm," Jafar answered.

"Princess, I'll be brief: you were kidnapped four days ago and drugged the entire time. As I now understand, no one was planning to bring you back alive. But these are all minor details, now the main thing is getting out of here."

"Is the army already at the capital?" The girl's eyes became two slits.

"There is no army and there won't be. Only a small circle of people knows that you were kidnapped. The emperor was given fairly clear instructions, any failure to follow which would result in one thing: your death. Can you walk? We need to get out of this Light-foresaken place."

"Looking like this?" Only now did I notice that she was wearing a simple, floor-length nightgown, so thin the fabric was nearly transparent, and nothing else. She had a point — any stray arrow would be the princess' last. I examined the rest of my resources. I had dumped most of them into Hearth's treasury, but I still had some left. Including such important armor materials as riftbeast essences. Realizing that no one would ever be able to give me back all the resources I'd have to use now, I nevertheless began creating the armor. I couldn't leave the girl without protection.

"Put this on. It should be enough."

Jafar chuckled meaningfully again as I began to manifest the green-glowing golden armor one by one. The *Thunderer* set, although it looked impressive, was useless against a serious opponent. Alia was proof of this. However, against simple magic or physical attacks, this armor would be perfectly effective. I didn't think even Jafar could break through it on the first try.

"Yes, that's much better!" A thick bolt of lightning flashed in the princess' hands. Even with rather mediocre magic stones for her role, the girl could do a lot with her suit.

"Let's go! We need to get out of here before Padishah Bayazid the Third realizes the real reason why I came here."

Escaping from the palace took great efforts. The padishah's guard met us on the first basement level and we had to resort to Emir Jafar's help to break through the dense barrier. I couldn't use the dark aura because of the princess and the emir, so I had to act the old-fashioned way, but when I carelessly walked out from behind the corner and received three dozen crossbow bolts at point-blank range, which managed not only to sweep away my *Golden Dome of Protection* but also to reduce the *Integrity* of my mithril armor by one percent, I knew they weren't playing around. Pharapho's flesh proved susceptible not only to magic, but also to banal physics. A hundred shooters with crossbows would turn me into a hedgehog in a matter of minutes! Quite an unpleasant discovery.

Nevertheless, we broke through. With a fight, using *Dark Spike, Fireball,* and lightning from the *Thunderer* set, but we broke through! In the main hall, I went up at first, forcing the princess and Jafar to hide. There were many guards here too, but I could work without having to worry about the others. Switching on my dark aura, I began to run from one convert to another, cutting off their dark song. There were so many of them that it felt like everyone in the palace had sold their souls to Skron.

But this small tussle in the palace was nothing compared to what awaited us at the exit. We ran out of the main gate and stopped abruptly as we saw two people standing at the front doors. The Citadel had come to the palace of Padishah Bayazid III to protect the dark ones!

"Archduke Maximilian Valevsky, you are under arrest!" A stocky little man in a blue cassock of a supplyman stepped forward. Next to him stood the commander, who was holding a sword blazing with fire. The Citadel's warrior was ready for battle.

"I order you to slowly lower your head to the ground and put your arms out at your sides. Only then will you be seen by an impartial church court. Otherwise, you will be destroyed on the spot!"

"How dare you, you creature corrupted by darkness, talk to me about an impartial court?" The man's words had pushed the limits of my patience. I was ready for anything: a battle against the converted, against the Temple of Skron, against the entire Shurghan Empire in the end. But that I would be threatened by someone who identifies as a "modernized human" — this was more than I could tolerate.

"Exactly the proof I need," the blue-robed cleric grinned evilly. "Even without the dark inquisition, it is clear that this man sold his soul to Skron. Both he and his city, which let the dark ones in. They must all be cleansed. Commander, do your job. Archduke Valevsky does not deserve the right to appear before the Pope."

"It's not up to you to decide," I said angrily, frowning at the approaching commander. The Citadel warrior was in no hurry. We both understood that I had nothing that could hold him back for even a few seconds. I couldn't run away, I couldn't fly away — it was all useless. So why run in vain when he could calmly walk up to me and bludgeon me with the sword from above? This wasn't a security guard's dagger, which the mithril glove could handle. Mithril was useless against the true fire of the Light. Vyrma was useless. If Kimal Sarento were in my place, he could still compete with the commander in terms of strength, but I was not my pupil. Against this man, I was weaker. Therefore, fully understanding that every second counted, I turned to the sky:

"Chaos, I know you hear me. You can't help but hear me. You are always following in my footsteps. I need an Inquisitor to cleanse the Church of the Light from Skron's influence. I am ready to pay any price you name that does not contradict the Light. It is time to stop running from responsibility and take it into your own hands."

The princess and Jafar retreated, leaving me alone with the commander. The guards who ran out of the palace fell to the ground dead. The commander destroyed ordinary converts ones with his aura alone. The warrior approached me, standing a mere arm's length away, but I did not flinch. I did not try to escape. Now or never. The decision was made, there was no turning back. The fiery sword soared into the air and began its descent, threatening to cleave me in twain, but bright sparks flashed, and the sword was thrown aside. A new dome appeared around me, protecting me from the commander's blow.

"Keep going!" the blue-robed cleric shouted when he saw that instead of a second blow the commander suddenly knelt. Not to me — to the creature that came out of the portal next to me. Chaos had heard me and sent its reflection. The Inquisitor had come to decide destinies. The *Golden Dome of Protection* stone left my magical field literally an instant before the Inquisitor spoke:

"Your call is heard, banisher of darkness. The price is set, but will be announced later."

'Modernized," I pointed at the white-faced cleric. The Inquisitor was at the supply man's side in an instant, and he collapsed to the ground, convulsing.

"Modernized," the higher power of Light confirmed. Leaving the cleric lying on the ground, the Inquisitor slowly approached me. The commander stood there, kneeling, and continued to act like a statue, pretending that he had nothing to do with it. But, as I already said, my patience had long since crossed a line, so it was stupid to hold back. If I had to pay, then I wouldn't be the only one paying.

"Inquisitor, how can the Church of the Light be trusted if among its highest hierarchs there are those who have sold themselves to Skron? How can the Church of the Light be trusted if its commanders are ready to blindly follow any order of the dark ones, without asking questions? How can the church be trusted if its High Priests are the coordinators of the Nocturnal Guild of Assassins? How can the Church of the Light be trusted if it has forgotten what it was created for? It has forgotten its main mission: resisting Skron. Turn your gaze to this palace. How many converts will you find here? I have destroyed several hundred! How many are left? And this is only a few dozen kilometers from the Citadel! Was the Wave not enough for the Church of the Light? Do they need something more powerful? But the dark ones already have it — Karina Fardi, Skron's vessel, can already channel Skron's full power and remain in control for five seconds! In two years, she will learn one hundred percent control, and what will happen to the Light lands then? What is the Church of the Light doing to get rid of this scourge? They are trying to destroy me! The only person who is truly fighting Skron!"

"Your words have been heard, banisher of darkness, and will be passed on to the Pope," the Inquisitor replied. "As for the commander's attack, you were granted protection from accusations of darkness, but Skron burned it away. Are you ready to accept the Light once more? It will be the best defense against accusations of aiding Skron. Not absolute, but sufficient."

"Last time, you didn't ask."

"Last time, the circumstances were different. They have changed now. You have changed. The world has changed. Everything changes, Archduke Valevsky."

"If I receive this piece of Light, will it somehow affect my ability to receive *Tainted Blood*?" I asked bluntly.

"He who carries pure Light within himself can never receive *Tainted Blood*," the Inquisitor answered after a pause. But the look he gave me said a lot. This Chaos reflection was clearly wondering how I knew about this ability.

"In that case, I will refuse. I need to arrange a meeting with someone who can give me *Tainted Blood.*"

Only then did I realize that the sounds of the surrounding world had disappeared. The Inquisitor had thrown up a canopy of silence, making our conversation private.

"You will receive it, Archduke Valevsky. Even faster than you wish. Return to Hearth. The Citadel will resolve the conflict with the padishah and the deceased high aristocrats of the Shurghan Empire. There will be no claims against your city. You will receive all the compensation due for this conflict. The Citadel will determine what this entails a little later."

"Conflict? The Padishah kidnapped the princess of the Zarak Empire! This is not a conflict — this is a declaration of war!"

"The Light world is not ready for war now, Archduke Valevsky. You know the reason for this. Karina Fardi is gaining strength, and something must be done about it. Chaos has no right to interfere — the goal declared by the Temple of Skron is to completely restore the balance. But we can read between the lines. The destruction of the light ones will entail the destruction of the Light. A first-order entity. This cannot be allowed. Restoring the balance after this will be impossible. Therefore, there will be no war. Not now. Not between empires, not within."

"And that is why you want to break the balance even more." I was beginning to guess what the Inquisitor was getting at.

"To restore balance," he corrected me. "Eight forces in the third orbit provided stability. Now there are six. This introduces an imbalance. The Temple of Skron wants to fill the forces with two new participants, but we propose something different. The system will become stable again if there are only four forces in the third orbit. In this case, Chaos will have the right to interfere, if someone wishes to upset the balance. But for this, the waterfolk and undergrounders must leave this world. Within the next three months. This is the price of my services."

End of Book Eight

Want to be the first to know about our latest LitRPG, sci fi and fantasy titles from your favorite authors?

Subscribe to our **New Releases** newsletter:
http://eepurl.com/b7niIL

Thank you for reading *Condemned!*

If you like what you've read, check out other sci-fi, fantasy and A LitRPG series published by Magic Dome Books:

NEW RELEASES!

The Hunter's Code
A Portal Progression Fantasy Series
by Oleg Sapphire & Yuri Vinokuroff

Kill to Live
A LitRPG Progression Fantasy Adventure Series
by George Bor & Yuri Vinokuroff

The One Who Changes the Future
A Dystopian Portal Progression Fantasy Series
by Boris Romanovsky

The Selected
A LitRPG Action Adventure Series Kindle Edition
by Vasily Mahanenko & Yuri Vinokuroff

How I Built a Magic Empire
A Portal Progression Fantasy Series
by Konstantin Zubov

The Afflicted
A LitRPG Apocalypse Adventure Series
by Konstantin Zubov

An Ideal World for a Sociopath
A LitRPG Apocalypse Adventure Series
by Oleg Sapphire

The Healer's Way
A Portal Progression Fantasy Series
by Oleg Sapphire & Alexey Kovtunov

Kill or Die
A LitRPG Series
by Alex Toxic

The Last Portal Jumper
A LitRPG Progression Fantasy Series
by Konstantin Zubov

The Dark Healer
A Historical Progression Fantasy Series
by Alex Toxic & Nadya Lee

The Strongest Student
A Portal Progression Action Fantasy Series
by Andrei Tkachev

A Shelter in Spacetime
A LitRPG Apocalypse Series
by Dmitry Dornichev

The Coming of God of Death
A Portal Progression Fantasy Series
by Dmitry Dornichev

The Village
A LitRPG Progression Fantasy Series
by Dmitry Dornichev & Alexey Kovtunov

Law of the Jungle
A Wuxia Progression Fantasy Adventure Series
by Vasily Mahanenko

Living Ice
A Portal Progression Fantasy Series
by Dmitry Sheleg

Ghost in the System
An Apocalypse LitRPG Series
by Alexey Kovtunov

Crossroads of Oblivion
A Portal Progression Fantasy Adventure Series
by Dem Mikhailov

More books and series are coming out soon!

In order to have new books of the series translated faster, we need your help and support! Please consider leaving a review or spread the word by recommending *Condemned* to your friends and posting the link on social media. The more people buy the book, the sooner we'll be able to make new translations available.

Thank you!

Till next time!

www.ingramcontent.com/pod-product-compliance
Lightning Source LLC
LaVergne TN
LVHW020725200726
843506LV00009B/619